T0078014

ENCOUNTER *with* Obsession

DONALD E. NADEAU

authorHOUSE®

AuthorHouse™
1663 Liberty Drive
Bloomington, IN 47403
www.authorhouse.com
Phone: 833-262-8899

Published by AuthorHouse 06/06/2022

ISBN: 978-1-6655-5552-4 (sc)
ISBN: 978-1-6655-5600-2 (e)

Library of Congress Control Number: 2022905630

CONTENTS

CHAPTER ONE

Pete Masters is a man without a life. At least one that he feels has any worthwhile substance or validation. This is and has been his reality for longer than he cares to remember.

How and why this emptiness became his fate, haunts and torments him, at times unmercifully. Lately, this undeniable conclusion has become increasingly distressing. At 57, and with some debilitating physical infirmities, longevity and vitality have become diminishing resources.

As a boy in the 1950's, Pete once scored 140 on an IQ test, and subsequently did 'skip' the fifth grade. Today, he probably would have been described as "gifted." His intellect has never been a problem; the same cannot be said for his emotional make-up.

At long last, Pete has come to believe it really doesn't serve any useful purpose to try assigning blame for all of his failures as a human being. He had made his choices, and there were ample opportunities along the way.

Was being a SOBER alcoholic going to be the 'crowning' achievement of his entire life? Around Alcoholics Anonymous, he'd be chastised severely for being "ungrateful." There, extended sobriety is regarded as the ultimate gift, and how it most certainly is. Pete will never deny that, for he remembers well sick, desperate, and defeated he was, when he finally stopped trying to obliterate his frustrations with alcohol.

Undeniably, this did give him a second chance at some semblance of a meaningful existence; however, in the final analyses, it hasn't materialized. Instead, he finds himself sober, but despairingly 'incomplete.'

His nagging physical infirmities are unquestionably a major impediment to any substantial transformation, and they aren't about to disappear. Emphysema for a smoker, and a progressive degenerating cervical condition are challenges he deals with on a daily and sometimes

1

hourly basis. It is both depressing and discouraging when he can't breathe or move without exacerbating these ailments.

He subsists solely on Social Security Disability Insurance, and barely gets by on the $734.00 payment every month. For years now, Pete has wrestled with the social isolation that early in his sobriety, enticed him with its security and alluring comfort zone. As the months turned into years, he gradually and unwittingly became a prisoner of his own design. When sometimes recklessly attaching labels that best describe his status; "social misfit" and "arrested development" seem to fit most appropriately. It's the "why" that troubles him most.

Pete's emotional stability or lack of it, now have come to represent a much more acute and threatening dilemma. The battles waged within his fragile psyche are inescapably crippling and unforgiving. There are no 'victories,' only the most haunting, cowardly retreats to inevitable self-defeating compromises. Concessions he has made for so long to these unrelenting demons, now have whatever meager reserves of patience and tolerance he is still occasionally able to muster, wearing razor thin.

His escalating sense of desperation supplies all the adrenaline in his life. Unfortunately, it comes in the form of intensely conflicted emotional energy. Ultimately, this "tug of war" will prove to be the next, and perhaps his final battleground.

His most passionate focus or source of stimulation for the last year or so, has been Dr. Leslie Greer, a psychiatrist at the Tri-Cities Mental Health Center. For two years now, Pete has been in treatment there for chronic feelings of sadness, anxiety and episodes of panic. His regimen consists of two relatively new anti-depressant drugs that have stabilized him somewhat, while concurrently all but snuffing out his libido. Additionally, he belongs to a group that meets for ninety-minute sessions and medication monitoring, on the second and fourth Thursdays of every month.

Dr. Greer, along with a therapist (Wayne), lead and facilitate. The group of eight, through all their interaction and focus. Pete feels he thrives here, assuming a leadership role early on. He is virtually the only member who has yet to miss or arrive late for any scheduled session. This absenteeism and tardiness have been a major issue for Pete on many occasions. To him, in order for these groups to function effectively, each member that expects to be trusted, confided to, or fully acknowledged, must make consistent attendance and punctuality an investment priority.

Pete's reasons for being so reliable and even enthusiastic, are twofold. He believes that therapy, in whatever form, represents the only chance he will ever get to somewhat understand and maybe come to some kind of terms with, the personal demons that have succeeded in maintaining their stranglehold on him for much too long. His other motivation is much more powerful.

In fact, over the last few months it has intensified to what it undeniably has become: an all-consuming obsession. He is hopelessly in love with Dr. Leslie Greer, and would stop at nothing to be in the same room with her. She has become the reason he gets out of bed in the morning. His thoughts and visions are filled with images of her exquisitely dainty and petite presence. Her obvious youth, in reality probably mid-thirties and appearing even younger, combined with her energy, intellect and ability to articulate analytically, fill Pete with an ever-increasing sense of admiration and awe. He is nothing less than mesmerized.

To him, she moves so gracefully and effortlessly around that facility, exuding purpose and confidence. Pete cannot help himself from seeing her as the perfect solution to all that is painfully missing in his world.

Pete feels very strongly that he and Dr. Greer have shared an intense subliminal connection during their many months together in this group. He knows that psychiatrists rarely, if ever, divulge what their feelings might be with regard to most issues, and absolutely never on any personal level. It is part and parcel of 'objective' analyses. However, he and Dr. Greer had shared many very similar insights and affirmed each other's perceptions on way too many occasions, for it to be simply some manner of dynamic or clinical coincidence. This added fuel to Pete's assessment of what could possibly be wrong with being attracted to, and having these kinds of feelings for this fascinating, charismatic little dynamo?

Dr. Greer has even accepted gifts that Pete had mailed to her on two separate occasions. Neither was expensive; one a small brass dish he had painstakingly polished, and the other was a rather nice crystal flower vase that he had received from a mail order house as a bonus gift. Both were openly displayed for a long time, and may still be on the top of a bookcase in her office. After the second gift, she conveyed her appreciation along with the deflating and explicit instruction that she could not accept any more. At the time, Pete saw no alternative other than to reluctantly accept this reality.

There also have been many letters to her that she neither encouraged nor discouraged. In them, Pete made it quite clear just how much he admired and respected every aspect of her being.

In the beginning, she suggested that these letters could have some therapeutic value, and that perhaps they might be addressed or examined within the context of the group.

As the months passed and the letters took on a more personal and romantic flavor, the group became less and less of a desirable outlet for Pete to purge these feelings. He had sensed down deep in his heart, that to present or acknowledge them in group therapy would involve having to face certain truths and realities imperative to clinically productive doctor/patient relationships. Pete was not about to voluntarily subject himself to any such scrutiny. The fire was burning, and he wanted no part of anything that in all probability would be bound to extinguish it.

He had let Dr. Greer know in no uncertain terms how important she had become to him, how much he longed to be with her away from the clinical setting and just how uniquely suited he felt she was to meet all of his life-long needs. He had even gone so far as to 'offer' himself in any manner of trial relationship she might be inclined to engage in with him. He outlined one example in which he would take care of all her domestic needs: cooking, cleaning, laundry, shopping, whatever her needs might entail. Then at the end of each long day, he would be completely satisfied to support and pamper her every requirement. Pete couldn't understand how anyone could so readily, reject such an overture.

Intellectually, Pete knows that the chances of his romantic inclinations have of ever being realized, are slim and none. He is acutely aware of the uncompromising boundaries and guide lines that permeate her very existence in this doctor/patient relationship. Paradoxically, they are not designed to protect her from him; but to protect him from her.

These impediments or restrictions are so comprehensive, they apply long after treatment has been terminated, and there hasn't been any contact for decades. Until recently, a seven-year statutory limitation had been in place; however, now it is an indefinite period of time, or obviously till either one passes.

Pete's perception of Dr. Greer's character and professionalism dictate to him that she will adhere to this edict absolutely.

Unfortunately, in matters of the heart, Pete is not able to be nearly so objective and logical. For too long now, these amorous visions of togetherness have been the primary motivation of his day-to-day existence. He finds it relatively easy to dismiss complications that conflict with his ever-increasing desires. He now lives only to nurture these fantasies; they fuel the fire that has brought him back to life.

The ill-fated course of Pete's desperate yearning along with Dr. Greer's intuitive discretion have set each of them on a path that will result in a dramatic altering of their relationship, one that will compel Pete to seek a dangerous solution, and ultimately change both their lives forever.

CHAPTER TWO

Pete's feelings are dictating to him that he has reached a point of no return. He has become thoroughly and completely obsessed with this lady, and through pure happenstance, she is by definition, an untouchable. He can no longer be content with being just one of her patients or one of the "malingering" eight that sometimes make up the group every two weeks.

His frustrations and intensifying emotional needs are becoming more evident and visible at every session. It has become increasingly difficult for Pete to contain what he feels. His comments now, purposely veiled, and ostensibly directed at one of the group members who has presented an issue for discussion, are now more pointed and desperate in nature, and are directed explicitly at Dr. Greer. He voices his stinging disappointment with regard to the lack of time allotted him that he feels is necessary to properly address the complex, debilitating and lifelong issues he faces. This outpouring is at best, rooted in half-truths, for at the core of his motivation is the all consuming desire to spend more and more time with Leslie under the guise of virtually any setting he can manufacture.

Towards the end of their most recent group session, Pete had blurted out that he felt intensely the need to somehow 'empower' himself; "I'm sick and tired of feeling helpless, and seriously considering acquiring a gun that enables me to "take" what I need for a change." His closing declaration seemed to accentuate his resolve, "It's about time I execute the courage of my convictions, and stop settling for at best, very little, and most often, nothing at all."

This escalating and unyielding assertion most definitely succeeded in warranting Dr. Greer's undivided attention, at least for the moment. Her responses at the time, probably limited by time constraints were, "You're too smart to do something that foolhardy, and "Will you call before you do anything of an impulsive nature?" Pete answered affirmatively, and said little else, even though he did feel some strange sense of exhilaration from having brought into focus, the intensity of his frustration, while still managing to retain the integrity of the more sinister secrets he obsessively harbored.

Unbeknownst to Pete, in the ensuing couple of days, Dr. Greer had discussed this issue with Charles, her companion therapist from the group. Ordinarily, aside from his role in the group, his function is to collaterally see her patients individually as needed, and when medications are not the overriding issue. He had covertly (at least from Pete's perspective) already been apprised months earlier with regard to Pete's letters to her, and was keenly aware of the nature of their content. Pete had met with the two of them once before, maybe three months prior, for what they said was "to get a sense of what might be going on with him." At the time, Dr. Greer appeared to Pete to be just a teeny bit flattered, but never did deviate one iota from coldly clinical observations and suggestions.

This attention was seemingly focused on confirming that Pete's feet were still firmly planted on the ground, and he wasn't getting carried away with what she termed his "attachment" to her. Pete volunteered very little during that meeting, feeling he had all he could handle dealing solely with where their leads were taking him. He was a little intimidated by the tandem structure of that exchange, but never denied the depth of his feelings when the opportunity presented itself. Charles complimented his writing skills, saying they were beautifully crafted. That was the meeting of three months ago; there would soon be another.

Pete didn't receive many phone calls, meaningful ones, that is. His most frequent contact strange as it might be, was from his former mother-in-law, ten years removed. Her name is Madeline and she is 84 and lives alone in Lincoln, a town about seven miles northwest of Providence. She is no longer able to drive and has come to depend totally on Pete to take her on her 'errand run,' usually once a week. There have been occasions when he has made special trips to accommodate an urgent need, also.

He had lost touch with her after the divorce until about a year ago, when he was made aware of her predicament. He was happy to offer his assistance. It felt good that he was both needed and appreciated for such a simple humane gesture.

On this particular damp and cloudy Monday morning in June, Pete's· phone would ring for a more ominous reason. It was Charles, and he was calling to try and schedule an 'impromptu' appointment for Dr. Greer that would again be made up of the three of them. Pete had fervently hoped he could meet with her alone, but that wasn't going to happen. Did she need some manner of corroboration or protection for some reason, or was this simply an extension of the group, minus the other members? Pete had no way of knowing, and he gave Charles a "yes, of course", reply. The meeting would take place in less than two days, early on Wednesday morning.

The wheels of destiny were now in motion, and where they might lead, no one could know.

Pete had struck a nerve with the astute little shrink, and not the kind he had hoped to. She had seen and heard him voice his frustration and desperation, and now there was a possible firearm being introduced into the picture. She was keenly aware of what she termed "his attachment" to her, and she did not like much of what her perceptions and instincts were suggesting. She was more than concerned, and not just on a professional level.

Pete endured the next day and a half dealing mostly with nervous energy prompted by the anticipation of his upcoming encounter. That Wednesday morning, he arrived at the Center parking lot twenty minutes early. He sat in his car sipping his home-brewed coffee, smoking a cigarette, and gathering his thoughts before going up to his appointment. Foremost in his mind were not only what the exchange might involve, but also what if any decisions that might be arrived at which might have a direct impact on his immediate future. He always tried to consider all the possibilities, even if they weren't going to necessarily mesh with his plans.

Strangely, as if on cue, at approximately 8:20 a.m. a late model Audi IV passed in front of Pete's little Toyota and proceeded to park in a space at a right angle, up the hill about 50 feet from where he was sitting. He knows this car belongs to Dr. Greer. He even knows the registration plate by heart. He acquired this knowledge as a result of only part of some serious and methodical 'tracking' he had undertaken perhaps a month ago, just in case his amorous pursuits didn't progress in the direction he so desperately wanted them to.

As she bounced from the Audi and paused for a few seconds to gather her satchel, purse and what appeared to be a large iced coffee, Pete couldn't help but admire how she moved so briskly and elegantly. The air around her seemed to flow in unison with the energy, control and confidence she embodied.

After watching Leslie quickly disappear through the glass door entrance of the stucco four-story structure, Pete shifted his focus to another location that she no doubt approached in the very same manner. He had recently discovered that this was not the only setting she practiced her analytical/psychotropic craft. Only the location, the clientele and the fees were different.

Pete was ready to go in now. He felt somewhat prepared for whatever might transpire during this tete-a-tete. Up the elevator to the top floor, (the route was familiar to him, down the long hall to her office in the far western corner of the building. It is very spacious, maybe 20 x 25 feet, probably because she is the chief honcho on that floor. In contrast, the therapists like Charles had little cubicles with doors that three chairs made crowded.

The three of them sat down together. The chairs were placed strategically so that Pete would be facing the two of them in kind of a condensed semi-circle, no more than three or four feet between each of them. It was definitely designed to facilitate eye-to-eye contact, and body language as well.

The questions were pointed, the tone deadly serious immediately. No lighthearted banter to break the ice; not a good portent for what in fact would follow.

Dr. Greer began by letting Pete know in simple and direct terms, that the gun mention that he had introduced into the treatment equation needed addressing now. Pete had surmised as much; however, this is where the sameness in their thinking or agenda would cease. He had hoped and prayed that this development would help her recognize the depth and urgency of his needs and offer to treat him more frequently, more comprehensively, more anything, with the only exception being, no more drugs. He had made his feelings in this regard known to her, often. Instead, a much more ominous and less desired scenario began to unfold, one that was a bit more confrontational than he had expected. Confounding Pete even more was this intermittent mix of genuine concern for his well-being that was also being conveyed. He couldn't help but get the feeling that the dreaded "T" word was about to rear its ugly head.

TERMINATION was the one outcome that Pete had not been able to prepare himself for. He needed desperately to get closer to Dr. Greer and to have her evaporate from his life now would be nothing less than crushing and devastating. What was going to happen was all spelled out in detail and sequence.

Pete sat there virtually helpless and in shock. She had presented the overall case and recent developments to the Medical Director of the Center, who in effect is her supervisor, and had left the decision to him. The Director determined that Pete's emotional attachment to Dr. Greer and the potential introduction of a firearm into the situation made it virtually impossible for the two of them to continue in any type of productive therapeutic relationship. Pete would be transitioned to a satellite unit of the Center where he will be assigned a new doctor and therapist. In the interim, Pete can see Charles as needed to deal with this crushing reality. Any medication issues will also be filtered through him. Pete is given direct instructions to not, under any circumstances, initiate any manner of contact with Dr. Greer.

This is the bottom line, and it is the worst possible outcome. She had buffered her message nicely, at times injecting what felt to him like a genuine concern for his acute distress.

She even went so far as to impart that occasionally there are 'failures' in what they try to accomplish, due to the sheer numbers and profound complexities of some cases. She added that she regretted that she did not somehow sense earlier the intensity and urgency of his susceptibility.

As the session ended, Dr. Greer wished Pete the best of luck, turned away and left the room. She was literally and figuratively gone and seemingly lost to him forever. Or was she?

Pete left the Center for the fifteen-minute drive back to his apartment. His emotions were raw, his body felt numb. He now had to deal with unintentionally sabotaging the most cherished of all his needs, HER. He had reached out and revealed how desperate he felt, and it had blown up in his face. Once inside his apartment, his impulses were to curse and wail in frustration and to smash his fist into a wall in anger.

Turning on the TV and radio momentarily did little to soothe or distract Pete's overwhelming pain and frustration. He paced around his apartment smoking one cigarette after another, until eventually collapsing in a heap, sobbing.

He pleaded over and over, "how could this honest, wholesome and selfless love that he felt for this woman lead to such an agonizing and pathetic conclusion? So, what if she was his doctor: she is a human being that has to have basic needs and feelings, very much removed and distinctly latent, from the clinical shell she so efficiently operates within.

Pete was thoroughly convinced that not only would she be good for him, but he also has a lot to offer to her. He had concluded rightly or wrongly early on that she could not have gotten where she is at such a young, ripe age and had time for much in the way of substantive or intimate relationships. In fact, it was a huge factor in what attracted him to her. In many of his letters he had appealed shamelessly to her sense of female vanity, describing in detail how exquisitely dainty, pretty and radiant he felt she was. He asked himself, how she could be so coldly immune to all of these things: the letters, the compliments, the attention, the gifts. And in addition, on a purely professional level, hadn't he made an undeniable investment and been amenable to virtually any kind of treatment, except the drugs. Maybe that was it. She did write a lot of prescriptions for other members of the group, as though she had an antidote for every symptom one might represent to her. Pete had learned to be wary of this notion long ago, primarily through his experiences in that regard. He had learned the hard way that the vast majority of any mood altering drugs can be rife with undesired and complicating side effects and are only at best a partial element of what is necessary to effect any meaningful change.

That in no way was the overriding issue right now. What troubled him to no end was his inability to comprehend how striving to be so thoughtful, caring and selfless could be so stoically ignored, and ultimately place him in a position to be what felt like chastised and punished.

Pete was convinced that 'giving up' was not an option he could accept. He had invested too much of himself and waited much too long for something that felt this unique. His goal with heart and soul attached was to experience something extraordinary with Leslie Greer M.D. If that couldn't be realized through the most appropriate and conventional means, then he would have to do whatever was necessary to reach that end.

He would not regress to having absolutely nothing to look forward to, once again acquiescing to his fears and discounting his conviction that this objective was a once-in-a-lifetime opportunity, and worthy of desperately pursuing, for once in his pitiful life.

CHAPTER THREE

Pete had already taken a bold step in the direction his convictions were leading him. He hadn't been totally honest with Dr. Greer or anyone else, for that matter. He had felt in his gut for some time that his misguided and awkward attempts at romancing Leslie were doomed to failure, he just didn't know how or when. So, in his totally obsessive frame of mind, he had begun developing a contingency plan. He had already started in motion the purchase of the attention-getting gun he felt had so necessary to disclose in the group that fateful day. In fact, half of the eight-day waiting period required by law had already lapsed. The paperwork to the Providence police and Federal Bureau of Tobacco, Alcohol and Firearms was already being processed. Since Pete had no felony record, he didn't anticipate any problems. He would know for sure in a few days. He had already passed the mandatory handgun safety test that was made up of a lot of common-sense questions dealing with the handling, storage and transporting of such a weapon. Pete had never held a gun in his life prior to walking into this well-known gun shop located only about a mile from his apartment. The week before they had run a block ad in the local newspaper. For some reason, even though he had seen similar ads dozens of times before, it jumped out at him, and he couldn't wait to get over there. An added bonus was 25% off all second hand pistols.

Sick as this may be, when the clerk handed him the one that had caught his eye as being both small enough to easily conceal and powerful enough to exact some serious damage, a rush of adrenaline shot through Pete's body. At that moment, he knew there would be no turning back. He felt a tremendous sense of empowerment that would eventually enable him to make something happen that he didn't feel he could ever come close to experiencing without this pistol.

A very strange and scary dichotomy or paradox was taking shape now. On the one hand, he felt love, caring and admiration for this woman. He wanted to treat her only gently and tenderly, to comfort and support her, and share some of the beautiful moments only human beings are so uniquely capable of experiencing. On the other hand, he is seriously entertaining the idea of taking her by force and subjecting her to all the fears, restraints and indignities that will no doubt be thrust upon her. When the latter thoughts managed to infiltrate his consciousness, although it was difficult, he would have to dismiss or minimize them as best he could. He had to, for to acknowledge their truth meant putting a damper on the only worthwhile and sustainable enthusiasm he could muster and snuffing out his cherished fantasies completely. Pete that couldn't endure that reality.

His most palatable and reliable rationale would be grounded in the hypothesis that she is a psychiatrist, trained at resolving, or at the very least diffusing, threatening situations.

Most assuredly, she had to believe that Pete could never intentionally hurt her, at least not any more than is necessary to keep her from escaping or completely turning the tables on him. After all, what was at the core of the whole idea? She would be forced to need and rely on him for her most basic necessities, and he would be more than prepared to indulge them.

Pete's most fervent and perhaps bizarre hope was that after some time has passed and the threat of imminent danger was removed, they could lie down next to each other and at least begin to relate at some personal level. Maybe she was capable of feeling empathy for the acute sense of desperation that initiated such extreme measures in an attempt to gain some measure of relief.

Pete realized at some level that he was probably asking for way too much. Something very different and much less desirable was most likely nearer to the truth. He had thought this through with every conceivable scenario on many occasions, usually while lying in bed and trying to fall asleep. Leslie had recently been prominent in his dream state also, but usually they were hopelessly conflicted, and amazingly similar to his conscious ness. He knew that if he carried out this sick fucking plan, there could be only two final outcomes for him, and neither was independently attractive.

He could not envision himself rotting away in a federal or state penal institution, so that only left some form of suicide, either by his own hand, or orchestrated in a manner that prevailed upon law enforcement to fire at him while he pointed his weapon at them. Pete had not even the slightest inkling or desire to see Leslie injured in any way, shape or form.

Deep down, he felt her responses, attitude and inclination to cooperate or not, would dictate how much of this would all be played out. At least early on, and up to a point after that. She could be the obstinate, bitter, vindictive bitch that he had yet to encounter in any form, and ultimately not care one iota what happens to him as long as she gets away. Or a more workable scenario would be one in which she instinctively assumed the role of the professional, compassionate and understanding clinician that allowed her to feel a genuine and humane sense of concern and care for what Pete would undoubtedly endure or suffer as a result of this episode. Naturally, Pete could not help from putting most of his faith in the latter occurring.

In either case, Pete felt more than capable of dealing with any of these eventualities. To him, they were both a lot more enticing than facing another ten or fifteen years of emptiness and declining physical and spiritual health.

Pete had a lot of time on his hands. When he wasn't busy with some manner of domestic chore, there were a few hobbies he found some solace in dabbling with. They became vital to helping him maintain what little grip he tried to sustain on his sanity. He loved movies that he could rent and watch at home, keeping close track of new releases and weekly reviews. This enjoyment he would usually put off until 9:00 in the evening when he was just tired enough sit back and take it all in.

He also followed with interest all the major sports at the college and professional levels. This was an interest he began cultivating way back in his youth when he played them a lot and also had a seven-day-a-week paper route. He had always felt that charting the players and their daily statistical changes was instrumental in nurturing his fascination with numbers and how they worked. He taught himself how to figure batting averages so that he would have them before any other kid, and well before the newspaper hit the streets. It apparently helped him to skip the 5th grade because he was able to solve problems in his head that his classmates needed pencil and paper to work out. He also excelled at reading, spelling and formal handwriting which was a specific subject way back in the early fifties.

Lately, Pete has found himself becoming more and more disenchanted with the overpaid and pampered athletes, and what he felt was the diluting of competition through overexpansion. Another sore point was the major influx of foreign-born players into major league baseball. He had always viewed this particular sport as the quintessential American game.

He also had developed late in life an interest in refinishing older, small pieces of furniture such as chairs, desks, and later picture frames. He found it gratifying to slowly transform these worn and neglected articles into something fresh and rejuvenated. The woodworking was enjoyable, but the sanding dust made a mess of his apartment and exacerbated his breathing problems. Eventually, he ceased altogether due to accumulated clutter and shrinking living space.

Pete had never been a meticulous housekeeper by any stretch, and often, when he was busy with a project, he would only maintain what he felt essential, like dishes and trash.

Lately, he had been too depressed to be involved in much of anything. He had talked about this in group with Dr. Greer. She had offered those hobbies were fine, but they weren't people and could not fill a need at the level he was hurting. If she only knew how precise her opinion would prove to be, only her reference to "people" would be reduced to its singular sense.

One kind of fulfillment Pete took pride in was his ability to acquire high quality food and pay only minimal costs for it. He methodically scanned supermarket flyers and matched sale items to the manufacturer's coupons he cut out each and every week. He routinely visited two and often three different stores in order to realize maximum savings. He was convinced everything tastes better and is more enjoyable when it's a bargain.

Right now Pete had to contend with what his new reality had become, and it didn't have anything to do with hobbies or shopping. It had to do with him losing, at least for the time being, the one reason he had for feeling alive. The immediate impact had him reeling and if he did nothing more than try to accept it, he would experience an all-consuming feeling of having nothing to live for. He knew all too well how debilitating and despairing that can be. The world would become a dark and ugly place for him. He would feel shamefully defeated once again. He wanted no part of any of that.

What it boiled down to was choices of either nurturing an obsession, with an intricately woven and exciting plot attached to it, or hoping to survive another descent into the abyss of a major depression. He had already had his fill of the latter in the years before Dr. Greer. To Pete it was a "no-brainer."

His task now, was to slowly but surely immerse himself in all the details that would have to accompany his preparation. Equally important as the gun would be the most opportune time and place to 'grab' her. It would have to be somewhere that is not easily visible to the casual passerby or nearby residents. Pete could not afford to have someone dial 911 while this event was in progress. Having the police only a few minutes behind them would not be conducive to a clean getaway or any long-term possibilities with her, for that matter. He would need at least an hour to get out of Rhode Island and start heading west.

The timing ostensibly had a little more flexibility built into it. Thanks to a phone book listing that gave Pete an address, he was able to establish where she practiced part time on the other side of town, commonly referred to as the East Side. It was the most affluent part of the city, and Pete was quite familiar with the area, having taken his children to various doctors and dentists there when they were youngsters. In fact, he knew within small city block exactly where this listing for Dr. Greer's office would be.

In the morning, Pete couldn't wait to make the two-mile drive from the North End to where she just might be at that particular hour. After a couple of slow driveby's of the immediate area, he found a place to park, and made his way around the entire block on foot. He needed to be sure of the numbers on the specific buildings since there were multiple occupants in most, and some had more than one numbered designation. There were both large and small parking areas to investigate as well.

The large Victorian house that he was able to conclude she was leasing space in was on the corner of a main thoroughfare and had two entrances in the front, and one in the rear. There were parallel side streets that ran across the front and rear of the building. The parking lot that served these offices was in the rear and also might accommodate a small apartment complex on adjacent property, perhaps during the overnight hours.

Pete couldn't believe his good fortune. The first time over there, and there it sat - the ivory-colored Audi IV with the registration plate LG 658. He made a note of the day and time, Thursday, 10:50 am, the more he assessed the parking lot and the surrounding landscape, and the better it looked, especially visualizing it at night between 9:00 and 10:00. She had to have some evening hours; he had seen her at a lot of varying hours at the Center, but they were all during the day. He liked what he saw there, a smallish lot just sufficiently sunk back from the adjoining streets and hopefully not too well lit. He would confirm this illuminating detail soon enough.

The Center's parking lot was virtually out of the question. It had way too much activity and visibility and the escape routes were not what he would need. On top of that, they employed full-time security in and out of the building.

Ideally, there should be one more conceivable location - where she lay her head at night. Pete had struck out a little more than a week ago when he presented her plate number to the Registry of Motor Vehicles. He used the pretense that that he needed to contact the owner of this car because it had bumped his car slightly and innocently driven off. No sale. He was informed that due to the Privacy Act legislation passed and enacted in 1997, they could no longer give out such information. Pete had successfully tracked a guy who gave him a bad check in 1989, utilizing this government resource, but it wouldn't be available to him anymore. Leslie definitely did not have a listing for her private residence, which was apparently fairly common for physicians of any kind, he concluded.

Pete felt relatively good, although he didn't like sneaking around ·and acting very much like a stalker. He followed the news and read the papers. He had always felt that predators who engaged in this kind of pursuit had to be pretty sick and without much of a conscience. He could relate to part of that, but it didn't mean he found it wholesome or admirable.

What else was he to do? This petite little bundle of energy and magnetism had gotten under his skin and into his blood. He needed to hold her and kiss her and share something neither of them would ever forget.

The reality of it all was they were worlds apart. She was the accomplished professional with a purpose and a focus in her life. All the difficult, tedious work of medical school, internship and years of residency behind her, and now, her career and practice were probably close to where she'd hoped they'd be.

In contrast, Pete was in the twilight of his life, much of which had been wasted. He had no focus or purpose other than filling long days with forgettable experiences. He was still trying to find himself, and it seemed futile and too late for the most part. It didn't seem fair, especially to her. His desperate attempt to salvage his existence could very well ruin hers.

CHAPTER FOUR

For the time being, Pete would immerse himself in all that was necessary to realize his goal. He had to. There were many articles or situational tools that need to be acquired. He started the list: duct tape, some type of gag for the first hour or so, some toiletries for each of them, a blanket or two, a urinal that will minimize the stops for a few hundred miles, lots of coins for tolls and soft drink machines, some petite sweats and pullovers for her, a few sandwiches, and drinks in a cooler for the initial hours of their trek, and as much cash as he could come up with. There could be absolutely no use of credit cards, be it his or hers. Also, a length of flexible rope that might be easier to work with than tape.

Last, but certainly not least on the list, which was by no means complete yet, a package of ribbed and lubricated condoms, the coup de grace, if there was to be one.

Pete had pretty much already settled on a feasible escape route. It's one he had driven a lot when he went completely around the perimeter of the United States back in 1991. His plan was to go north and then west across Massachusetts on Interstate 90, continuing across upstate New York on the thruway, skirting upper Ohio and Indiana and around Chicago to Interstate 94. From there, Wisconsin, Minnesota and North Dakota would lie ahead. Lots of open road and small towns with decent lodging and not a lot of cops. Timewise, he felt he could drive the seven hundred miles to Cleveland in one stretch, and by the end of the second day they would be over a thousand miles from Providence, Rhode Island.

His hope is that by then, Leslie would have calmed down some, maybe to the extent that she was somewhat resigned to the fact that she wasn't going anywhere that he didn't want her to go for the time being. She might even be able to sit up front and engage in some manner of civilized discourse with him, even if it was in the form of frightened, desperate queries such as, "Where are we going," "Why are you doing this," or "What do you really expect to accomplish?" Pete could visualize this happening quite clearly, and his answers, for once in his life, will be short and direct. "You'll see where we are going," "Because I have to," and "A lot of that will depend on you."

He might even feel the need to ask her to drive at some point, and since he would be holding a loaded pistol when he wasn't behind the wheel, she wouldn't have many options open to her. As much as she might want to believe Pete is not capable of putting a .380 caliber bullet not only in her, but through her, one wouldn't think she could be too readily inclined to cultivate that risk.

Pete is very much intrigued by the possible dynamics that could come into play in such a perilous scenario. People seem to react or acquit themselves according to what they have got to lose or gain, but not everyone. He is quite certain Dr. Greer's advice to someone who might be in grave danger would be to give up everything but your life, much like women who have a choice in whether they will try to fight off a rapist or any armed assailant, and risk getting beaten to a pulp or worse. Conversely, the ones who passively submit may survive with most of themselves intact physically, but emotionally and spiritually, the wounds are just as severe.

What will this tiny but highly trained and intuitive psychiatrist instinctively draw upon? Will she mount an appeal to him while attempting to calmly understand his motivation with empathy as she tries desperately to sort out and neutralize the immediate crisis? Pete didn't think so. She would have absolutely no control in the early phases of this encounter, none. She would not be able to pee unless he allowed her that freedom. As for later, in their journey, even though she would try for all she is worth, it would be him that would always have the final say about everything that will happened. This will be the case right up until the moment she is either rescued or Pete's capricious sense of compassion weakened him enough to let her go.

Pete knew one ploy she was guaranteed to attempt to utilize and that was to remind him over and over of his sweetheart of a granddaughter, Hillary. Leslie is acutely aware through exchanges within the group context and his letters, just how much this little girl indeed means to him. This child who Pete has come to cherish has become a very positive and enriching component of his life ever since she was born on October 11, 1998. He has done everything in his power to nurture a meaningful bond with her, something he was largely incapable of doing with his own children so many years ago. Leslie has seen how he gushed with joy and amazement when he would relate to her and the group some of his more rewarding experiences with Hillary over the past two plus years. Like everything else in Pete's life, there were a few complications along the way. In his unbounded eagerness to spend time with this child, he had sometimes been inappropriately aggressive and inconsiderate with his son Davis, and Hillary's mother, who were divorced. This led to some hard feelings and estrangements that Pete had difficulty understanding, but all in all, it remained a huge plus for all of them to have this little girl in their lives.

There are not many relationships that Pete values as much as this one, and Leslie knows this. He has three adult children whom he loves very much, but they all have lives and children of their own. It was very hard for Pete to reconcile what he feels so strongly he has to do, with the painful losses he will no doubt suffer in this regard as a collateral but unavoidable consequence. It was not a reality he will allow himself to entertain at any length right now, if he could help it.

Pete didn't know a goddamned thing about Leslie, the sweet doctor's personal life. Is she married now, or had she ever been? There were no telltale rings at least that she wore to the Center. Did she have a lover, male or female? Has she ever been satisfactorily fucked, and if so, how long ago? What about siblings? She has a very sexy accent that Pete is pretty sure was not acquired anywhere in New England. If he had to guess, it would be mid-south in origin, one of the Carolinas or Virginias. There is definitely a distinctive 'twang' to her speech pattern. Pete had asked her once how she landed at the Center in Providence, and her reply was that she was doing some kind of work study in Boston, and came across this opportunity by chance, and followed up on it.

All of this seemed so mysterious and magnetic to him, he could barely stand it at times. He had sat across from this lady, studying her every move word and mannerism for over two years, and all he had ever discovered factually he could itemize on a tiny piece of paper. She said a lot, but it was all so objectively clinical and totally devoid of any hint of emotion.

What were her secrets, her passions and her weaknesses, and what manner of ruinous price was Pete prepared to pay to find out.

Pete decided he needed to step up the surveillance. He had discerned that so far, she arrived at the Center on Wednesday at 8:20 a.m. and Thursday at approximately 11:30 a.m.

The latter coincided with the sessions scheduled for Pete's former, but ongoing group twice a month, so that would appear to be solid. Her car, however, was at her East Side office in the morning of this past Thursday. What he really needed was knowledge of what evening hours she kept there, along with when she was finished with patients and, on average, how long she remained in the building after that. He also needed a fix on just how many cars are usually in that parking lot at that time. Is it lighted, and if so, how brightly? These factors would be the most critical element of Pete's plan and by far the most difficult to coordinate and feel comfortable with - precisely when and where to actually take possession of her.

He was awake and up early. It was Saturday, and the designated day for him to literally finalize ownership of his much-needed firearm. It could not be before the specified 1:00 p.m. according to the gun store salesman, so Pete has a few hours to kill. As he pondered the possibilities, he felt at least 80% sure there wouldn't be any kind of technicality that would in effect put the screws to him. His primary concern was that Leslie might have called the Providence police or the Attorney General's office to advise them that he is a patient of hers and in her professional opinion, he is not emotionally stable enough to be in possession of a firearm. That chances of that happening, were at best slim, but it wouldn't be the first time a shrink had resorted to similar prophylactic measures when dealing with perhaps, a homicidal or suicidal patient at imminent risk.

The paperwork that had been submitted to the ATF was borderline ludicrous. Their questions, such as, "Are you an illegal alien," Have you ever been committed to a mental institution," or "Are you now a fugitive," had Pete wondering if people who could truthfully answer YES to any of these questions, and actually did. He had never been arrested or convicted of any violent offenses or felonies for that matter, so the local police shouldn't return anything negative either. Leslie represented the only legitimate concern he had, but he also knew her 'modus operandi' well enough to know that doing things surreptitiously would be totally contrary to her style and everything Pete had come to respect and admire about her efforts. She was very articulate and up front with her thoughts and concerns when it came to patient issues.

His plan to kill the approximately four hours that were left after he finished breakfast was to first walk around a medium sized flea market he frequented up in Smithfield about eight or ten miles north. After that, he was thinking of taking What has to be considered another bold leap for him: checking out the local casino/dog track that is on the way back.

Although it was a five-minute ride from his apartment, he had never set foot in the place; he was afraid to. He had learned too much about addiction and his life-long vulnerabilities to take such a foolish risk.

At one time or another, Pete had found himself firmly in the clutches of most of the adrenaline rushing indulgences that one can so casually venture into. They all ended abominably.

Married at 17, and with two children by the time he was 20, Pete gradually made a habit of spending his lunch hour at the French Club in North Attleboro, Massachusetts, a bar within a stone's throw of Barber Electric, where he was employed as a fledgling machinist. He was underage but had an altered draft card that would enable him to drink his lunch and shoot pool just about every day. On paydays, he would be there until late into the night and usually lost money at either pool, gin rummy or poker. On many an occasion he would not make it home until the next morning with just pocket change left and very much hung over.

The guilt and shame were unbearable. In his naiveté, and unrelenting denial, he failed to see the self-destructive pattern and continued to bang his head against a wall for a long time. Soon, he was drinking earlier in the day and heavier to blot out his pain and degradation, and it wasn't long before he spiraled down to drinking and gambling virtually full-time, leaving the support and care of his family to little more than the chancy outcome of any particular horse race, or the desperate turn of a card.

Perhaps the perfect example of how addicted and irresponsible he could be was the fateful day he impulsively decided to quit the only job he had ever had, spanning 4½ years, with a simple phone call during one of his alcohol fueled lunch hours. He requested his pay which was in cash in the early 60's, so he could drink and gamble all afternoon instead of going back to work. The next morning, while in the haze of a major hangover, he phoned his boss and begged for his job back. The answer was a firm negative, for this had been the last straw. They had tolerated him coming back late from lunch and missing days, but that phone call was totally and finally unacceptable.

What followed for many years was a chronology of short term employment, welfare on and off, and overnight stays in jails and detoxes. He and his wife, had borrowed money from loan companies before he lost his machinists job, using his phony ID and putting up their furniture as collateral. With his gambling now a full-blown addiction, there was never enough money, often even for the basic necessities of his family.

In 1965, after having his paycheck 'attached' while working at a decent job in an ITT warehouse, Pete entered all his debtors into his petition for bankruptcy. Things did improve, but only short term. His alcoholism wouldn't reach the acute stages for another eight chaotic years.

Pete had learned some very painful lessons, and these realizations had come at tremendous costs. His ex-wife, Laurie, was a trooper in every sense and loved him unconditionally during those years. Looking back, she unwittingly played the part of an enabler; however, awareness of any such concept was at best minimal in those years, and they were both very young. She enjoyed a party and gambling to a degree also, but she was by no means an alcoholic or compulsive gambler. Pete was. As things progressively deteriorated and became more desperate, Laurie found steady work as a domestic on the East Side, and for years literally kept herself, Pete, and the children from ending up on the street.

So, with what Pete knew about gambling and his disastrous history in that regard, why was he planning this little excursion into that realm once again today? The answer was twofold. He was curious after being exposed to years of their shameless advertising, to see for himself exactly what was there, particularly with respect to blackjack and games of 21. He had been sharpening his skills with a hand-held version made by Radio Shack for months, with some measure of success, and he wanted to see if his strategies were compatible with what they were offering. It is probably the only card game that can be equalized somewhat by employing plus or minus betting formulas, relying heavily on the law of averages. He realized this logic also required considerable investment capital, and he had other plans for all of his cash right now. It was definitely a casual bit of curiosity that was attracting him, and nothing more.

Pete arrived there at approximately 11:30 a.m. and had to park a good 300 yards from the entrance. It was that busy.

Coincidentally, they featured greyhound dog racing as part of the attraction here; in fact, there were simulcasts of races run all over the country if one was so inclined. Once inside, Pete felt a sense of deja vu almost immediately. It had been many years since his last exposure to this much 'vice' all in one place, but it ·didn't feel that way: the distinct sound of coins clanking as they made their way into the bottomless pits of these gaming devices and the chatter along with the clouds of smoke hanging everywhere. People shuffling around thru the haze and maze clutching mixed drinks, on a seemingly endless search for the next receptacle designed exclusively to ultimately separate them from whatever cash they still had.

Throughout the whole cavernous operation, there had to be literally thousands of gamblers. Demographically, Pete would guess that at least 2/3 of them were over 55, if not bona fide senior citizens. It kind of validated a news article he had recently read that alluded to the ever-increasing numbers of this population that are experiencing serious gambling problems.

He wasn't interested in the dog racing, stayed far away from the bars, and made his way through three large rooms, all chuck full of computerized wagering machines. With the help of an attendant/security type guy, he was directed to the far corner of one last room, where he found a few rows of what are designated as "multi-action" Games. Within these, it is possible to pull up a variety of 'pay-as-you-go' wagering opportunities, including blackjack. After a brief examination, he inserted his first paper dollar, and lost it within five seconds. He tried again and this time won. As luck would have it, he would beat the damn thing for five straight hands and eight out of the next ten. He calculated that the cards were not going to 'run' like this for much longer, and by getting one blackjack and one stalemate, he had found out what he needed to know. They paid 3-2 for blackjack and a draw was a draw. He had seen enough, so he pushed the icon that would release his winning claim tag which he promptly brought to the cashier window and redeemed for $13.50. He enjoyed the little 'rush', didn't feel he was "hooked" again, and walked away, feeling he had much more important needs to tend to.

It was now 12:50 p.m. and time to imminently and hopefully finalize the acquisition of his much-needed firearm. It was only a ten-minute ride but seemed longer. Pete couldn't help feeling a little anguish, as a kind of 'pall' sneaked briefly into his psyche and dampened his spirits for the moment. It made him a bit uncomfortable and necessitated him once again questioning what kinds of forces were really percolating within him. He was leaving a gambling experience and, on his way, to take possession of a lethal weapon, which he planned to use as intimidation in the perpetration of an abduction of another human being.

Were these harbingers of his most recent descent towards another and more abhorrent form of depravity? What of all the therapy and insight he had gained, the newly experienced feelings of love for Hillary and yes, Leslie too? What about his unsolicited and continuous assistance to his ex-mother in-law? How could this dichotomy of change and commitment be reconciled with these latest urges toward almost certain self-destruction? How could all of this be somehow entwined in one man's chameleon-like perception of what he believed was wholesome, and worth nurturing, when contrasted with what he was he also hell-bent on recklessly pursuing, and that would ultimately destroy his life?

Pete had no easy answers, only this burning desire to bring himself and Leslie closer together. Acquiring a deadly weapon, he could only perceive now as one vitally important component of making that happen.

CHAPTER FIVE

Pete's apprehensions were short-lived as he entered S&N Antenna on Orms Street in Providence. It's a name they had retained over the years, even though they rarely, if ever, sell any TV antennas with the advent of cable transmission.

Big screen televisions, air-conditioners, guns and accessories pretty much made up their stock and trade now. In southern New England there are few retailers that deal exclusively in fire arms, especially handguns.

Pete found the first available clerk and presented his receipt for the initial transaction, some eight days prior. It was an unfamiliar woman who quickly summoned the gentleman who had waited on him the previous Friday. His smile and demeanor as he approached Pete while shuffling through some documents seemed a favorable indication. He began by informing Pete that the official paperwork from the ATF was indeed in order, and positive, and that the local police had failed to return their forms, period. Under law, that translated to a "go", since it is their responsibility to reply if, and only if, there is apparent justification to do so. One of the few occasions when a 'nothing or non-answer' is as good as a "yes": Pete thought such broad discretionary latitude was a little unusual, especially as it applies to fitness for gun ownership. He wasn't about to debate the issue. All the legal requirements had been met.

Pete smiled broadly as the clerk went about finalizing the transaction. Before he could finish, Pete interrupted him to inquire about the availability of the proper kit to both clean and then oil his used gun and also the correct ammunition to load it with.

Originally, the clerk had mistakenly identified the pistol as a .32 caliber; however, today while recording the required serial number, he discovered it was in fact, a Davis 380 cal. semi-automatic, a more powerful gun. It apparently had been sold new in the early 1990's and seemed more than adequate for what Pete had in mind for it to accomplish. After securing the cleaning kit, and a 50-round box of ammo, the clerk processed Pete's visa card and the deal was done.

Two minutes later, with the pistol back in its original box and everything secured in a plastic shopping bag, Pete was on his way home. He would spend the remainder of that day totally enthralled and gradually familiarizing himself with his new "partner". In the box were instructions and a schematic illustration of precisely how to go about disassembling this gun and putting it back together. Pete liked the way it felt in his hand and the way it looked - all chrome, with grips that were a dark shade of gray. It measured approximately six inches in overall length, and weighed he figured all of 2 ½ lbs. fully loaded. It held six rounds, with one in the chamber and five more in the magazine that slid nicely into the butt.

As evening approached, Pete couldn't wait to get started with his immediate task of cleaning and oiling his weapon. Unfortunately, it didn't come with any service or maintenance records. His firearm of choice, complete with kit and bullets, had set him back a modest $154.00. He was more than satisfied and, without a doubt, would have expended twice that amount, had it been necessary.

His adventures disassembling, cleaning and lubricating the pistol lasted well into the night. It came apart quite readily, but getting the slide or muzzle that fits directly over the barrel to cooperate, required some patience and persistence.

There isn't a whole lot involved in the construction of a pistol like this, but what there is has been calibrated to very fine tolerances and sturdily manufactured. The few springs, clips and the firing pin must be re-inserted in the exact opposite sequence employed to remove them.

After accomplishing this, and relatively certain all components were again functional, Pete was ready to load the magazine with copper-jacketed .380 cal. bullets. This was another challenging task for any novice because of the heavy spring-loaded tension that increases after each round is inserted. He could readily understand why: this is a semi-automatic, and after the first round is in the chamber and fired, the shell casing is ejected and the next round advances automatically. Squeezing the trigger is the key to this simple mechanism.

Pete had some chrome polish and wanted to shine it up as best he could after loading the magazine. When he finished and did slide in the clip, he began to experience the sense of empowerment this weapon could generate. Why it had such a scintillating effect on him, he wasn't quite sure. He did know that if prior to this moment, he had any personal safety concerns about living alone in a first floor, urban apartment, they were gone in that instant.

His thoughts now switched focus to where and when he might be able to inconspicuously squeeze off a few rounds. He needed to ascertain that it functioned properly, how accurate it was, and what kind of "kick" it might have. Inside city limits, all this can be a problem. There are laws against carrying a concealed weapon on your person or in a motor vehicle, unless you have the specific permit necessary to do so. He could buy a gun to keep in his home and keep it loaded. To discharge that weapon inside a dwelling for any reason other than to protect your life and property from imminent danger was more than likely a felony. To transport a gun in a car to and from a shooting range requires that it be broken down or disassembled and the ammunition stored separately. Pete was not about to take this gun apart again unless it misfired or wouldn't fire at all.

For now, it would be kept in its box, at arm's length in the living room where he watches TV and reads. It would be loaded with the safety "on", a very handy and critical feature.

The dealer had been legally mandated to supply Pete with a "trigger locking mechanism" free of charge. He fiddled with it briefly before finally discarding it as unnecessary.

The solution to where and when he might fire the gun came to him as he was lying in bed that night. He would wait until Monday-morning when the apartment upstairs would be empty and his one next door neighbor, an elderly gentleman who also lived alone, would most likely be gone for a spell. Meanwhile on Sunday, he would rummage through his storage room in the cellar to see what he could come up with to use for padding and some semblance of a target. He could ill afford to get hit by any ricocheting slug that could injure or kill him and fuck up his plans royally.

Pete was pretty satisfied as he began to drift off to sleep. He had the weapon, the ultimate intimidator, and probably the most vital element of the entire sinister scenario. He couldn't yet imagine actually pointing and firing at anyone, least of all Leslie, who he wanted and needed so desperately. The simple fact that he could brandish it in close proximity to her, should more than accomplish what he needed it to do.

He slept well that night for the first time in weeks. After breakfast, he fondled his 'newest ally' for a while and decided he should cruise the streets of the East Side for an hour or so, since this is where many doctors not only practice but also have their residences. Although it's a real longshot, he just might spot that ivory-colored Audi IV with the right plates attached. This could supply Pete with a major clue as to where Leslie spends her nights and weekends, just in case he needed a desperate last-minute option.

He figured that on a Sunday morning, the traffic would be light. Most people would likely be either in their homes or at church services. His efforts were in vain, and as he was heading home, he wasn't overly disappointed. He reasoned that even if he were to discover where she is laying her little head at night, there wouldn't be much rhyme or reason to when she might come and go, anyway. He would have to tie her movements exclusively to her work schedule, and one element of that he had already begun to focus on, and with all factors considered, it seemed more feasible in every respect. Also, it is considerably more difficult to surveil someone at any length close to their residence without being noticed or perceived as suspicious. It is less risky around offices and businesses where people are constantly corning and going.

The next morning, Pete focused on one specific endeavor: he was going to fire a weapon for the first time in his life. There were two contingencies that had to be met. First, he had to make sure that his makeshift target would be adequate. It consisted of flattened cardboard boxes and behind them, a one-inch-thick piece of scrap lumber. He had carefully placed them in a corner of his 8 x 10 storage room, allowing ample clearance for ricocheting bullet fragments. Secondly, his neighbor in the small house next door had to be gone.

The two dwellings are only fifteen feet apart and Pete wasn't about to fire this gun while it might be occupied. At about 10:30 a.m., all indications were positive, his car was gone, and all windows were closed tightly. There was nary a soul meandering thru the immediate vicinity.

As he hurriedly made his way down the cellar stairs, gun in hand,

Pete's adrenalin was flowing effusively. He quickly assumed the best stance he could near the half-open cellar, pulled the slide back and saw the first bullet enter the chamber. There was no hammer to cock, so it was just aim and fire. He had taken the precaution of wearing eye protection, but didn't have anything suitable for his ears, a mistake. He fired and the sound was deafening for a few brief seconds. The recoil was minimal, and the shell casing ejected and fell to the floor next to him.

He had hit the area on the target he was aiming at; in fact, the hole was within two or three inches of dead center. Now, where is the slug? It had pierced the cardboard with a whole the size of a pencil eraser and had traveled completely through the wood. It left an exit gouge or rip the size of a quarter.

Pete couldn't help visualizing for a moment the horrific damage this weapon was capable of inflicting on human skin, flesh and bone.

Just the thought of how much blood loss could be generated from a wound the size of that exit shred both amazed and sickened Pete. It was awesome and very frightening.

He was now ready to test the "automatic" capability of this weapon. He had to be sure that since it was used, and he had also taken it apart, it was going to function as it was originally designed to. After going outside and checking next door, walking around the house, and then ascertaining that the first blast had not attracted any unwanted attention, he returned to the cellar. Once again, in proper position, he fired and kept on firing, pow, pow, pow, pow, pow. The sound reverberated off the concrete walls. The cotton he had packed into his ears did little to lessen the disorienting blasts. The holes in the target at first glance, seemed to be bunched relatively close together, and shell casings were all around his feet.

There was no mistaking the distinct odor of gunpowder this time and the acrid blue smoke hanging ominously in the air all around him.

Pete was not overly concerned with these developments. He could simply open the two half-size windows often present in these old cellars. They usually swing inward and hang from a hook attached to a beam; these were no different. A can of strong air freshener wouldn't hurt either. As he proceeded to gather up all the expended shell casings, Pete couldn't help feeling this had been at the very least, an extremely enlightening and encouraging experience.

CHAPTER SIX

P ete would grow increasingly uneasy over the next few days. With a lethal weapon now firmly in his possession, he was plotting an abduction that could very well be life-threatening and most certainly a catastrophic, life-altering experience for two individuals. He had in effect, thrust himself into a realm that for virtually all of his life, he had fostered an unforgiving contempt for. To him, anyone who perpetrated any manner of assault, robbery or carjacking, had to be low-life and nothing more than a 'street thug' or 'punk'. What, when all was said and done, was going to make him any different? Certainly, in the eyes of the law and John Q. Public, he would be nothing better or special.

Would it matter that he was doing this for love, and out of desperation? Not likely. Perhaps because he had no felony record, and there were mitigating circumstances, he would only get fifteen years instead of thirty. Even entertaining such ludicrous questions, turned Pete completely off. To him there was absolutely no redeeming quality to any of it.

These sobering self-examination exercises served no useful purposes, so Pete decided to focus on the 'what-ifs' only as they applied to enhancing his preparation to go forward, and what the possibilities might be after he and Leslie were in the same car together, and on their way to far off places.

In that vein, Pete's response was more palatable. However, he couldn't help acknowledging that even after he had her in his possession, the potential existed for some disastrous and crushing disappointments.

He would be subjecting this accomplished and professional lady to the most harrowing and traumatic experience of her life. In return, he was anticipating she would somehow willingly take part in and help him fulfill this outrageous and misguided fantasy. What if she was so repulsed by him and his intentions that she spit in his face, just for starters? Suppose she hurled a few choice epithets his way such as, "you gutless fucking coward." or "you lame excuse for a human being."

Would Pete be able to let these kinds of reactions from her just roll off his back and not deter him? How much was he willing to hurt her to keep her relatively subdued and non-combative?

He fully expected to gag her or tape her mouth shut early on, but only long enough to get out of the city. Once on the open road, he would make her somewhat aware of what might happen, in general terms, and give her every conceivable chance to be grudgingly compliant. In this respect, the choices to a large extent, would be hers to struggle with. Pete could only hope that it didn't take Leslie long to accept that for once time would be on his side, and not hers to manipulate.

Once that situation was manageable, there were a few other vital considerations he had been wrestling with a little.

One of Pete's more curious ruminations was whether Leslie could still claim the status of a bona fide maiden. Pete, rightly or wrongly, had suspected all along that this was a distinct probability. If so, did he want to forcibly appropriate such an incursion, knowing its significance can never be restored?

Would the selfish rationale that his sick mind had concocted stand up to this degree of encroachment and trespass? Did he want to risk ruining her professionally, or at the very least, damaging her so severely that she could never feel comfortable with patients again, especially the male of the species?

These soul-searching questions, for the most part, were fleeting in nature. He could not afford to allow these complex dilemmas to infiltrate and undermine his resolve. Besides, he could make credible arguments both for and against when he got right down to any of them. He did not feel at all like a 'monster' or sociopath that is totally incapable of identifying and acknowledging another's feelings or pain. In fact, he was quite the opposite. When he turned some of these considerations around, which allowed him to feel somehow victimized, he readily found areas of responsibility where she could be found lacking, if not downright culpable.

He couldn't help feeling a distinct sense of callous disregard on Dr. Greer's part with respect to his most intimate sentiments. Pete had shamelessly provided her with copious amounts of undeniable implications, but she had ignored them.

Why had she failed to acknowledge at least the clues she had to be aware of in some humane fashion? Perhaps she could have found a way to placate or appease him and maybe validate him in some small manner as the worthy suitor he so desperately needed to be. Why was she so 'aloof' and seemingly content with the half-baked regimens of treatment that both she and the mental health system overall passively accepted as adequate? Fifteen minute med checks, a 90-minute group that never started on time and had to stop fifteen minutes early for more medication issues. Incidentally, once Pete was incorporated into the group, his 15 minutes alone with her ceased, and he became just another sap whose time was divided up with the other seven. It was like a cattle call. Speak up quickly, loudly, forcefully and keep it brief - what bullshit.

In deference to her, the "short cutting" did allow her to see a larger number of patients. But for what fucking purpose? It certainly didn't allow for any comprehensive give-and-take that just might lead to valuable insight and a more complete picture of the person supposedly being 'treated'. Pete knew all too well how overburdened the entire mental health system is, and has been for years; however, that is very little solace to the individuals who are 'short changed' because of it.

Pete had both worked and volunteered in psychiatric hospitals. In addition to that, whenever he wasn't drinking and while chronically suffering from depression, he tenaciously pursued whatever help he could find. He remembered on one occasion about ten years ago, when he was unable to afford even a minimal co-pay fee, and as a result, was told the agency could no longer schedule any future appointments, he was able to survive that offense, but hadn't forgotten its impact. He was well aware of exactly what these entities had to offer, and more importantly, what they could not. His experiences in this regard went back to when Dr. Greer was still a very little girl. Pete liked to think of it as a kind of 'wisdom' he had painstakingly accrued over the decades.

When he examined what he felt was his "truth" along these lines, it only exasperated him and cemented his resolve enough to act solely on his convictions. To him it all boiled down to this: the overall circumstances surrounding his requisite needs as they compared to hers when measured objectively. Whose had the utmost merit, and most importantly, the highest degree of urgency connected to them? It really didn't seem a difficult assessment to Pete. She was in her mid-thirties, with more than likely, another forty plus years to stabilize and fill out her life. If Pete was lucky, he might have one-third of that, and they won't be the "golden years" some might perceive them to be for him.

She had already 'pawned him off' onto another doctor, so in effect, he was "out of sight, out of mind" with regard to her day-to-day concerns. Pete was far from being that free of her.

Dr. Greer had dozens of other patients to occupy her mind with and just might have found it relatively easy to file her entire encounter with Pete under the heading of another practice or learning exercise. Perhaps in the very near future, Pete would be enlightened one way or another in this regard.

He, on the other hand, felt very strongly that his options were far more limited. It's a lot like trying to teach an old dog new tricks. He is what he is, and his feelings are deeply rooted. His desperation was not born of impulse and selfishness, but rather a by-product of life-long disappointments and frustrations. In many respects, he was indeed impotent and powerless.

Pete chewed on all of this for a few more days, and always seemed to end up at the beginning. What realistic alternative choices were available to him that he hadn't already considered? None, he concluded. He had been in practically the same position many times in his life, with one critical difference. Now, the all-important time, health and energy factors were significantly depleted, and he found himself infinitely more weakened and frustrated.

Pete had little trouble reaching the only decision he would be capable of living with. He needed to forge ahead with his plan and let the chips fall where they may. He was thirsting for the excitement and challenges that would unfailingly fuel his days and nights and allow him to feel alive again.

CHAPTER SEVEN

Pete was now in the right frame of mind to "move forward," at least with his interpretation of that axiom. To him, this translated to actually taking steps to realize his objective. There were numerous "tools" and amenities that need to be acquired that are relatively inexpensive anyway. There would be a rental car and some stolen plates needed. The former was a minor formality; the latter will involve some planning and careful execution. Any cinema, restaurant or bowling alley parking lot should provide adequate choices and opportunities to accomplish this. It was probably a good idea to secure the New York, Massachusetts, Pennsylvania or Ohio tags sooner than later. That way they wouldn't be as "hot" when it came time to actually attach them to the rental.

Pete also felt he needed to streamline his surveillance of the unsuspecting doctor. He was pretty much zeroed in on her "fees for services" office on the East Side. She kept what appeared to be irregular hours there - some mornings and some evenings. He was sure of that, but it's nowhere near being a schedule he could work with. Pete knew himself all too well; he didn't have the necessary patience to drive over there and wait indefinitely for her to appear.

He had to have more conclusive and reliable information at his disposal, and he couldn't wait months to get it. Why couldn't he just utilize the phone number he had already made note of weeks ago, when researching exactly that, in the business listings of the city phone directory. He could pose as a prospective patient inquiring about the possibility of making an appointment. He could always use a pay phone that would neutralize caller ID and explain that he is a salesman with unpredictable work hours and needs some flexibility. It sounded feasible.

Pete was charged up again, his diabolical mind was firing on all cylinders and the adrenaline was flowing through his body at near full tilt. This is when he feels he is at his best. It mattered very little what his objectives or motivations might be, and even less, what tactics he may have to employ to take him where he feels he needs to go.

He was now convinced it was just a matter of picking the right time to make this call. The weekend seemed most appropriate, for with any kind of luck, there might be a message left on a recorder that would provide him with the answers he was after. He had to be absolutely sure that neither he nor his voice can be detected snooping or stalking anywhere near Leslie. To Pete, being thwarted or exposed in any way at this point would be the ultimate failure and humiliation. He was convinced that Dr. Greer would not hesitate for one minute and pursue every legal resource available to keep him away, and out of her life.

As Pete examined his plot a bit closer, he reasoned that he could make this call any day of the week, as long as it was late enough at night or very early in the morning. The risks would be minimal; he would not be answering any of the standard queries such as name, referral source, insurance coverage, etc. These would only become a factor if he were forced to call during business hours. Pete was hoping that it would never come to that, for he didn't consider himself a very convincing liar or pretender. However, with the stakes this high, and over a phone line, he felt capable of pulling it off if necessary.

As fate would have it, the next day was the Fourth of July, an equally accommodating day to do some cruising through the upscale East Side and to make the phone call. At about 10:30 am, he set out to peruse the thoroughfares and parking lots that are set back among the manicured lawns and tree-lined streets of this affluent urban setting. There is also one medium sized hotel, The Crescent Manor, about eight stories high and smack in the middle of the 'ritzy' little retail district.

It reminded Pete a lot of Beverly Hills, only on a smaller scale. Occupying the western third of this locale are all the buildings that make up Brown University. Although the campus is not all that expansive, accommodating 6,000 students, it did occupy some serious real estate, going back well over 200 years, and the city is justifiably proud to have it right where it is as an important part of its history.

After about an hour of being as thorough as he could be and still remain relatively inconspicuous, he had yet to find the ivory-colored Audi IV with the right plates attached to it. There were countless Mercedes, Jaguars, and BMW's, but only a few Audis, and none of them ivory. Pete also made a pass by both her office and the parking lot in the rear on the remote chance that she is even more of a workaholic than he suspects, and might be there on the holiday. Not a trace. the whole block was virtually deserted. It was time to place the call.

Pete found a pay phone on his return trip home. It was not enclosed in a booth, making traffic noise a critical factor. He dialed the number and then deposited the requisite 35 cents. There were four rings, and then this sweet, articulate and unmistakable voice began to speak. It was Leslie with a pre recorded message informing the caller of her 'unavailability' right now, and then reciting her office hours. Tuesdays 9:00 to 1:00, Thursdays 9:00 to 11:00, and Mondays, Wednesdays and Fridays, 5:00 to 9:00. Pete scrambled to fill in the times on an index card he had written the days of the week on before he left home. There was a totally unexpected bonus as well.

At the end of the message, she rattled off her pager number to be accessed in the event of an emergency. He listened while totally astounded, for this would never happen at the Center, where all her patients are Medicare, Medicaid and co-pay status. Pete didn't know what manner of compensation package she might be contracted to at the Agency, which for all intents and purposes is a non-profit entity. What he did know from the statements he received from Medicare is that they have their own table of fees structure, and rarely disburse the full amount for any bill submitted to them by doctors, hospitals, clinics, or labs.

Apparently, this 'access as needed' contingency that Dr. Greer provides, is reserved for her more private and 'well healed' patients. The ones who pay 100% of her fees for fifty-minute hours, with cash, checks, credit cards (perhaps of the corporate nature) and top-of-the-line private insurance coverage.

Obviously, she could be reached for similar emergencies through the agency network. However, Pete doubted very much that it was handled with quite the same personal touch. Everyone had their priorities in this life, he cynically deduced, even doctors.

After Pete hung up the phone, he felt a sense of exhilaration. He had gotten the information he needed, and then some. Although he couldn't see her, it tickled his heart strings to hear her voice. He felt satisfaction in feeling it wouldn't be too long before he would have her all to himself, at least for a little while.

On his way back to his apartment, he stopped at the North eastern Horne and Auto outlet to pick up a few of the necessary items for his much-anticipated excursion with Leslie. The prices and selection here were the best in the area.

Pete spent about twenty minutes browsing the aisles and eventually ended up with medium sized roll of sturdy but *tearable* duct tape, 30 feet of rugged but pliable rope and a five-gallon container approved for gasoline storage. He felt the latter would provide insurance against having to stop when conditions may not be favorable or logistically feasible. For a little over $30, he now had three items he could eliminate from his list. He felt energized as he drove the mile or so back to his home base.

Pete spent the remainder of the holiday in his 750 square foot apartment. The living quarters are clean and more than adequate for his simple needs. He had moved here in May of '99' thanks to a tip he had received from his son-in-law Jeff, who is a distant relative of Pete's landlord. The place had been empty and recently refurbished but had never been advertised for fear of attracting undesirable applicants. It is located in a quiet, predominantly Italian section, and situated virtually on the Providence/No. Providence line. A half mile in either a southerly or northerly direction, the living conditions were appreciably worse. Pete was keenly aware of the stark differences in the two locales, having spent the previous eight years in a third floor apartment just down the road. Drug dealers, pit bulls, garbage, blasting 'rap' noise and dozens of unsupervised and disrespectful kids of all ages surrounded the house. Had Pete been in possession of a gun during those years, in all likelihood he would have used it, and been either in jail or on parole right now. The circumstances on any given day could have been that bad. However, like so many other ultimate realities, he didn't realize just how different things could be until he was away from that for a while, and relatively peaceful here.

This all became possible when after two summary rejections, he persevered and finally was deemed deserving and eligible for Social Security Disability benefits. A caseworker at the center who took a liking to him hooked him up with a lawyer who specialized in procuring these benefits for his clients.

It didn't take long once he became actively involved in the tedious procedural machination of the applications and appeals process the federal government has long been justifiably infamous for. Pete never actually met the principal attorney who was responsible for his good fortune. His team of subordinates handled all the interviews, paperwork etc., and for their trouble were paid the maximum amount allowed by law of 25% of the total retroactive benefit figure, which in Pete's case was close to $12,000. At the time, Pete began to doubt if he'd ever get approved, and after he did he couldn't help questioning why his application had been turned down on its merits twice, and once he had retained legal assistance, it was approved expeditiously. Anyway, the money did sustain Pete for quite a long spell.

Pete didn't splurge too much at all, other than buying an 86 Toyota Tercel which he still drives, and a new 32" TV along with some stereo equipment that continues to provide countless hours of pleasure. Prior to that, he hadn't bought anything of substance for years, either because of his drinking or his inability to work more than part time.

On this particular Fourth of July, he didn't have much in the way of plans. The weather was nice enough, sunny with temperatures in the low 80's was forecast. He also realized that many people find joy and fulfillment on this holiday by attending parades, cookouts or fireworks displays. When he was much younger and married, with the kids in tow, these activities held some appeal, but not anymore.

Pete at time couldn't help thinking of his former case worker, therapist and friend, Frank. They were only acquainted for about a year, but he was tremendously helpful and friendly to him. Frank had been to Pete's former apartment for breakfast, and they had met many times at a small neighborhood restaurant for chats and more of the same. He had come to the U.S. from Chile in the early 90's, and held degrees in psychology, theology and philosophy. He was perhaps 40, married and had one young son. His wife was a paralegal who formerly worked for Pete's disability lawyer. Pete had briefly met his family on one occasion. What made him so unique was the manner in which he reached out to his clients and treated them as equals, if not dependents.

When he came to Pete's apartment for breakfast early in their relationship, he remarked that it helped immeasurably to actually see where and how his clients were living. A picture is worth 1,000 words so to speak. Unfortunately, he eventually became overburdened with 'consumers' and the inherent paperwork, In essence, he was burning out. He spoke fluent Spanish, and as one of the few bilingual caseworkers, he was soon drowning under the tide of incessant referrals directed exclusively toward him. The last time Pete and Frank spoke about his work load, he had fifty-five clients, and that number was increasing every day. He gave notice shortly after that session and left on his own terms. That was over a year ago, and even though Pete had his home phone number, he had yet to utilize it.

Leslie was well aware of the budding friendship between Pete and his counselor, and she hardly put her stamp of approval on it. She made it plain that she had some reservations with regard to the potential problems that can develop within this kind of relationship dynamic. She was pretty much right on the money in a general sense, because not long after Frank left the Agency, Pete never missed a beat and started inviting HER to breakfast and suggesting other times and places that they might get together. She wouldn't allow that to happen then, and subsequently, it never did. As far as Pete was concerned, both his life and Frank's were substantially enriched by these so called, ill-advised experiences.

Even if Pete could have conjured up someplace attractive enough to make the effort on this holiday, it would have been difficult for him to enjoy himself. His back was radiating some discomforting and disconcerting pain. He had strained it cleaning out his car the previous Saturday and then aggravated it considerably the next day while helping his son Davis move furniture. Although Pete hadn't handled any of heavy pieces, the 70-mile drive and bending over repeatedly had taken their toll. He had no regrets whatsoever though; it felt good to be needed and useful for a change.

Another chronic annoyance that had evolved over the last eight or nine months was his addiction to nasal sprays. It began innocently enough the previous fall when after a few days of laboriously trying to breathe through his congested nose, he sought out the most effective remedy he could find. The most popular of these, Afrin, provided instant relief, but was also relatively expensive and habit-forming. For $5 or $6, he got less than an ounce, with explicit instructions to not exceed two doses within a 24-hour period. The difficulty arose when its effects started wearing off in ten hours, then eight, six and so on. A fervent believer in the "quick fix" approach to most problems, Pete found himself squirting this solution up his nose virtually every hour or two. Despite warnings from his primary care doctor, he could not scale back to any less than 5 to 7 doses a day. Simply put, an addict is an addict.

These not so minor additional irritants to Pete's already unstable existence usually manifested themselves in making it more difficult for him to maintain some semblance of an emotional equilibrium. He found it increasingly difficult to move about spontaneously without the pain in his lower back reminding him that he dare not risk doing too much or venturing very far from where he was. At times like this, it would take all the optimism he could summon just to ward off the all too familiar "dark and ugly" impulses that invariably would try to infiltrate his consciousness. He would usually resort to itemizing the few rewarding relationships and redeeming twists of fate that he had been granted. The list was relatively brief, but he always felt the quality of these gifts was most important: he is sober, there are his children and grandchildren, and he has been rescued from a ghetto apartment with a leaky roof and no central heat.

His most effective "fantasy" focused on his little sweetheart granddaughter, Hillary, all cuddly, curious and the epitome of innocence. As far as Pete was concerned there wasn't anyone or anything more capable of lifting his spirits. She represented a joy that just didn't exist in his isolated and bleak existence. Even the excitement and adrenalin generated when he played the sobering realization that in effect, he would ultimately be choosing to lose what he has with Hillary, for just a small measure of the unknown, in the person of Dr. Leslie Greer.

Pete had tried valiantly to transcend what he felt for his loved ones into an adequate sense of overall fulfillment. Unfortunately, it wasn't quite enough to sustain him. Leslie had touched and moved him deeply and his life was never going to be the same. The irony was undeniable and somewhat incomprehensible, for she, for all intents and purposes, had no desire to project herself in this manner at all. Pete couldn't help dredging up the philosophical term "existentialism," for it seemed to fit appropriately. He was exercising his freedom to both choose and decide the meaning of his particular reality.

Something Pete did indulge in occasionally were 'flightsof-fancy' in this regard. He disliked with passion the connotation of the term "fantasy". To him, his visions just had yet to materialize, but somehow, they most certainly would.

His images of Leslie, all 5 feet 3 inches and 105 lbs. of her, were deeply ingrained in his obsessive mind. She had very dark brown eyes and relatively short brown hair. It was parted neatly, and just long enough to cover her ears completely and fall almost to her shoulders. Her facial features are tiny and exquisitely proportioned, as is the rest of her. Her mouth, especially, is so small it might well have fit on a child or an expensive porcelain doll. She wore very little makeup, except on rare occasions. Pete couldn't help distinguishing at perhaps two or three meetings, a sensual burgundy lipstick that nicely accentuated her beautifully contoured lips.

Pete admittedly, often 'fantasized' how nice it would be to share an intimate kiss with Leslie, and while experiencing that bliss also be able to caress her little frame ever so tightly but gently. To him, her figure was also uniquely special: nice firm and full breasts for such a tiny lady. He had experienced observing them up close and personal when at the end of a group session a few months prior, she was writing her usual handful of prescriptions while half sitting, half leaning on a table where all the patient charts were. She had on a top that was cut a little low, and fit loosely around her shoulders, allowing Pete a full view of her entire chest. He was both amazed and a little bit aroused at what he processed in those few seconds. There was no oversized, padded bra as he might have expected after all these months of keenly observing everything about her. Only a gorgeous pair of breasts that he couldn't wait much longer to admire somewhat more intimately.

Her small waistline could not measure more than 20 or 21 inches. It was superbly in tune with the firmness and tightly curved linear features of her derriere. She wore a lot of pantsuits and pants coordinated with a variety of loose-fitting tops.

Whenever she did wear a skirt, there were always matching colored hose. Pete never once saw her bare legged or with flesh tone nylons.

Pete ultimately concluded that female psychiatrists, therapists, and clinicians in general make a conscious effort to not appear unduly attractive, seductive or sensual in any manner whatsoever. Pete couldn't help perceiving the irony in Leslie's presumed efforts in this regard. For if this indeed was her intent, how miserably she had failed where he was concerned.

Peter was now seeing his new therapist on a semi-regular basis, so far about every ten to fourteen days. His name is Wayne, and thus far Pete had been unable to connect at any level with what this guy had to offer. As a sounding board he was excellent. He listened intently to all manner of irrational fantasies, obsessions and dilemmas and invariably spit back something he felt was remedial and ideally suited for Pete.

There was no 'in between' or gray area or any hint of possible uncertainty. Much to Pete's astonishment, during their second session Wayne had volunteered that he had in the past been accused of being rigid and robotic. He never did elaborate with regard to the prevailing circumstances of that accusation, but so far, Pete felt it just might have been warranted.

This morning Pete would try again. His appointment at 9:00 a.m. would be Wayne's first of the day. Pete arrived at the reception desk ten minutes early. He firmly believed that his investment and commitment to treatment, regardless of how well or poorly it might be progressing, demanded priority status, and at the very least, punctuality.

A little after 9:0 as he was following Wayne back to his 'cubby-hole' office, Pete had his agenda firmly in place. His abduction plans would be discussed only in the past tense, if at all. He knew that if there were any indications whatsoever that the wheels of fate were still turning in that direction, all bets would be off, and Leslie would be informed in short order. These people operate with a code, aptly described as a "duty to warn," that was installed for their protection in these kinds of cases.

Pete had little doubt that Leslie would get the police involved, and the result for him would be a legal restraining order and additional parallel and undesirable complications would be forthcoming. Pete could not allow that to happen under any circumstances, "therapy be damned at this point," he muttered. It was the one truth he dare not share with another living soul.

CHAPTER EIGHT

It just so happened that today Wayne would have his own agenda and it would consume the majority of the hour allotted for this session. He needed to forge out a 'treatment' plan that both he and Pete could come to an agreement with. Pete had been through this before while he was under Leslie's care, seemingly at about six-month intervals. She had been much less definite and exacting with respect to goals and timetables, and as was usually the case, she was in a hurry.

Wayne explained that this procedure was a requirement of both state and federal guidelines, undoubtedly tied to funding, licensing and accreditation. It went relatively smoothly since they both agreed that a desirable goal needed to be some kind of assistance that would enable Pete to meet people, either through a part-time job or as a volunteer within an existing structured program. Wayne was gung-ho to get all this moving and offered to make some calls in the middle of their session.

Pete pooh poohed that idea, explaining that he needed some time to mull this over before deciding which direction might be most appropriate for him.

Deep down, and where it stayed, Pete really didn't expect to be around for the six months or year that Wayne had incorporated into his "plan" for this to happen. He had something very different in mind that would address all his critical needs in a much more direct and expedient fashion.

There were two other noteworthy occurrences during this session with Wayne, and Pete couldn't help, albeit for different reasons, be amused. The first came about through pure happenstance. Wayne as usual had Pete's treatment record or chart on his desk as their meeting began. However, twice within the first ten minutes Wayne excused himself – first to make a photocopy and then to procure a necessary form.

The file sitting exposed on the desk three feet away quickly piqued Pete's curiosity, for contained in those pages was information he felt could prove very useful. Primarily, he was interested in all the entries Leslie had made over the two+ years. It could undoubtedly provide him with valuable insight and direction when the time came to deal with her in a very different setting, and on a much more personal level.

Resisting the urge to probe hurriedly through what was a pretty extensive wad of documents, Pete instead waited for Wayne to return and inquired as to exactly what the guidelines were with regard to patient's accessibility to their own and the Agency's medical records. The answer was pleasantly surprising in that they were 'open' to him at any time. In fact, he could ask for and receive copies of everything contained in his file, except for documents obtained from an outside source, such as another health provider. Pete decided immediately that he was going to initiate such a request ASAP and that the 20-cents per page copying fee would hardly be a hindrance.

There was one additional qualification, and with a little deceit it was relatively easy to meet. All Pete had to do was deny that anything he might interpret from these records would exacerbate his "fixation or obsession" with Dr. Greer. He answered with an unequivocally negative response to that question, and Wayne handed him the chart. It was a good 2 1/2 inches thick. After briefly thumbing thru its basic form and structure, Pete handed it back to him. He wasn't ready just then to try digesting piecemeal fragments of information in a compressed time frame, and besides there was already an established agenda for that session. Pete submitted his formal request on his way out and would await their mailing supposedly within a week.

He was convinced that at home, he would be infinitely more capable of assessing and assimilating the contents.

The other manner of "bombshell" that was dropped during this session was Wayne's surprising and bizarre references to the similarities in motivational genesis between Pete and Jeffrey Dahmer: yes, the serial killer in and around Milwaukee, Wisconsin in the 1980's who, before he was beaten to death in prison, admitted not only to cannibalism, but to 'necrophilia' or engaging in sexual activity with his already dead victims.

Wayne's rationale stemmed from his dubious conclusion that

individuals who are so isolated, empty and desperate sometimes resort to gratifying their unrelenting, painful voids by justifying almost any despicable act of violence that can serve to provide them with a temporary satisfaction. Wayne had a different take on the motives of Ted Bundy, all of which left Pete with not much to offer with regard to either. He needed time to digest all of this.

Initially Pete felt that Wayne's "insights" into abhorrent human behavior had some validity. In fact, it was a subject that had always fascinated him, and he firmly believed in the classic cause and effect theory for almost everything not connected to natural forces. The only major and perhaps unfounded leaps Wayne was making were the degrees of violence and death that these guys had perpetrated, and that his "referential subjects" were deviant serial rapists and killers.

Pete couldn't relate to anything remotely resembling these extremes. He wanted to make something potentially rewarding develop in one continuous time frame that admittedly could get a bit ugly for brief moments. However, he didn't believe for one millisecond that he had it in him to intentionally Inflict serious and lasting harm to anyone, especially a petite defenseless female, like his Leslie.

Pete, after giving these comparisons some analytical thought, found Wayne's attempts at connecting all these dots a bit strange, and overall, his plans were not about to be altered in any way, shape or form. He would keep his appointments and continue with whatever dialogue was necessary until the time was right and he was totally prepared to make his move.

Pete's was able to extract some joy and enrichment from the first part of his weekend. On Saturday he met with his son Davis and little Hillary at Roger Williams Park. The weather was perfect, with sun and temperatures in the high 70's. The majority of their time was spent traversing the zoo where Hillary was very much fascinated and amazed at all she could see. The highlights were provided by extended visits to the polar bear and sea lion exhibits. The park was quite crowded, but eventually they were able to find a table and share an overpriced 'junk food' lunch. Following that, there was some horseplay on one of the grassy expanses and then unfortunately, the sweet sorrow of parting.

Pete cherished the time he got to spend with his son and his granddaughter more than just about anything else in his life right now.

This particular son, his youngest child, rep resented probably the only ongoing nurtured and selfless relationship he had cultivated with any degree of success in his entire life. He found it hard to a large degree to feel proud of this isolated accomplishment, for he had two other children and a wife of almost 31 years before they divorced. Those relationships remained for the most part cordial and caring. However, Pete's alcoholism and emotional immaturity during critical years were unyielding impediments to anything more substantial.

In spite of these shortcomings, Pete felt he had much to be grateful for. He was convinced that all of his children would have suffered had it not been for his long-suffering ex-wife's determination and commitment to their wellbeing during Pete's "lost years. Her ultimate gratification was seeing all three earn their college degrees and become productive, responsible adults and citizens.

Susan, the first born, witnessed and was probably the most negatively impacted by her father's alcoholism. She was at a very vulnerable age when Pete reached the lowest depths of his struggles. That said, she had managed to stay married for over 20 years and raise three wonderful children of her own. Her degree was in early childhood education, and she currently teaches in a Providence elementary school. She and Pete, unfortunately, have complex, residual relationship issues that understandably continue to linger.

His oldest son, who also carries his name, but is not a "junior", is a veteran of 20 years in the United States Air Force, retiring as a Master Sergeant in June of 2000. His specialty was encrypted messages, a highly sensitive and classified field. He spent the last four years of his tour stationed at the Pentagon. He currently lives and works in Virginia, where he is divorced He has two boys ages 14, 10, who he sees as often as is feasible. He tries to come up to New England at least once a year, usually around the winter holidays, and during 90's the entire family would rent cottages down in Florida, where Pete's ex-wife, who has remarried, currently lives.

In 1991, a year and a half after Pete's divorce, and while he was experiencing what he now feels was a mid-life crisis, he sold and gave away everything that wouldn't fit in a suitcase and went to Hawaii to live with his eldest son. His wife, the two boys and father and son, co-existed very nicely. They were housed in a duplex on an Air Force base called

Hickam Field. Pete swam and sunned virtually every day, pedaling the 3 1/2 miles to the private beach on a secondhand bike he bought soon after arriving. Their sightseeing during the six months Pete was there included Pearl Harbor, climbing Diamond Head, and the famous North Shore of Oahu, legendary among surfing enthusiasts for its awe-inspiring breakers. It's actually much too dangerous there for casual swimmers, but definitely a sight to behold. Pete has fond memories of that entire and all too brief experience. He left because he missed his other two children 5,500 miles away, and because he had yet to come to terms with all that he had left behind. It didn't take long before he climbed back into the bottle and stayed there for the better part of the next two years. His youngest son Davis and his fiancée, whom Pete moved in with upon his return from "paradise," eventually orchestrated getting Pete into a hospital for a desperately needed detoxification, and Pete is still nurturing the sobriety he gained there. That was in June of '93'.

Davis was fortunate enough to be barely seven years old when Pete put together the other significant and lasting period of "teetotalism" in his life. They shared a keen, if not obsessive interest in sports. Initially it began with baseball and basketball, and then football was added a few years later at the pre-teen level and on through high school, where he would eventually become the premiere quarterback in the state.

Davis was indeed a naturally 'gifted' athlete, and along with these talents, he also possessed the ego and desire to develop his skills and excel. He loved being in the spotlight. Pete had seen glimpses of his exceptional hand-eye coordination as far back as when Davis was only three years old. Although Pete had little or no frame of reference at the time, when he would take him to the park to play catch or pitch to him, it was obvious that his skills, although raw, were extraordinary.

Pete more or less 'fell' into coaching with the local Little League while living in Pawtucket in 1976. Davis was already playing as an 8-year-old and beginning to show signs of becoming a dominant player. The following year Pete would become a coach in the minor division, and a year later was recruited to move up to the major division by the Rossi's, a father/son coaching tandem who had an opening and also knew that in adding Pete, they would be acquiring draft rights to Davis for the next three years. Their combined efforts would lead to League Championships two of the three seasons, and were it not for an untimely injury to Davis' leg, could very well have been three. This partnership/friendship would also thrive through the ensuing Babe Ruth years, designated for 13–15-year-olds. There they competed against teams throughout the Blackstone Valley with increasing success each year.

Pete spent most of this period trying to practice, coach and mentor his youngest son as best he could. They spent a lot of time on the baseball fields and basketball courts together, and at home, the dialogue was usually related to sports. Toward the end of this period, Davis brought his talents to a small Catholic high school in Pawtucket, where he played three sports, and ultimately was recognized as one of the outstanding athletes in the state. Before graduation, he would receive numerous athletic scholarship offers from colleges throughout New England.

By then, Pete was quite busy trying to earn credits at the University of Rhode Island in their adult extension division, where he initially majored in Psychology. He later branched off to a condensed certification program being offered to the counselors of drug and alcohol abusers. He was successful in earning his certificate along with fifty-four credits, late in 1980.

During these years, Pete was content to be a proud spectator at Davis's year-round high school and summer league contests. Davis would eventually earn his degree in Physical Education, and soon begin his career as a teacher. He also initiated his own experiences as a coach, first at his high school alma mater, and then at a few distinguished but small colleges in central Massachusetts, where he still teaches and coaches today. Pete has continued to attend his games.

Chapter Nine

Pete was a very regimented individual. He attributed much of this to his learning experiences while struggling over the years to first achieve and then sustain sobriety. He needed to snack and drink at specific intervals all day long. The sugar intake seemed to alleviate the 'cravings', and the drink in hand, whether it be juice, lemonade, coffee or tea served as a viable substitute whenever he felt the urge. It had helped him put together fifteen years in one stretch, and currently, another eight and counting. To him, it was no less important than breathing, and he wasn't about to abandon either.

He was also very good at filling days with enough interesting pastimes. So good, in fact, that months and years would pass by, and very little would change. He often wondered if in one sense, he had in fact become a victim of his own survival when assessing his struggles and recovery from at least the acute aspects of his alcoholism. The bottom line was he had come to firmly believe that his worst days sober were still substantially better than his best days as a drunk. Well, at least ninety-eight percent of the time.

Pete now needed to get back to the task at hand. It would soon prove to be somewhat disconcerting, primarily due to two completely unrelated occurrences as the weekend approached.

One of these was in fact expected, and the other was completely out of the blue. The first came by virtue of a ringing telephone and the other via a regular mail delivery.

The phone call came late on Friday afternoon and was from Greg, a sporadic friend of sorts, who Pete had met at the Agency in a men's therapeutic group almost three years ago. In spite of Greg's inconsistent attendance and tardiness at the time, they somehow had hit it off in some fashion right away. He was a very bright guy, in his mid-thirties, with a history of hard drug abuse. He was now battling Hepatitis C and a myriad of other problems. He lived down the road from Pete in a federally subsidized hi-rise, where his rent was 30% of his Social Security, with heat and all utilities except cable TV included.

Pete had been somewhat instrumental a year and a half ago in motivating Greg to perhaps take another 'crack' at life. When they first met, he was trying to get around in a broken down Mazda pick-up that was not registered, insured or inspected.

He was pretty much a recluse who slept a lot and had virtually given up any hope of ever getting any quality medical care or finding any opportunities that he might be capable of embracing and hopefully taking advantage of. When Pete finally received his retroactive Disability settlement, he was in a position to help, so he offered Greg in the form of a loan enough money to at least acquire some decent transportation. There was no structured or urgent need for repayment, and once Greg had his $1100, a Pontiac Bonneville, he was in effect, on his way.

Greg quickly took full advantage of his newfound enthusiasm and enrolled full time at the state university, where he was currently maintaining better than a 3.5 GPA as an English major. He was also able to find part time work in their computer lab to supplement the grants and aid he was eminently qualified for once he applied his energies to exploiting these resources.

The loan was repaid appropriately and shortly after their men's group was disbanded, with Pete moving on to Dr. Leslie's group and Greg eventually dropping out of any kind of treatment completely, as far as the Agency was involved. Except for a few brief e-mail exchanges almost a year ago, neither of them had initiated any contact until now.

Greg was calling today because he was planning a rather lengthy and demanding trip across the U.S. to see some of the natural wonders that he so far had only read about. Pete remembered Greg saying he had never been any further west than Massachusetts or southerly than Connecticut. His itinerary now was to visit Niagara Falls, then head for Yellowstone National Park in Wyoming, and end up at Yosemite in California. He wanted Pete to accompany him and share the expenses. However, it was obviously an impulse-driven idea, with a plan to make all the preparations and leave ten days hence. His rationale revolved around the need for him to be back in time to ready himself for the fall semester, which was scheduled to begin in approximately 3 1/2 weeks.

Pete's initial reaction to the impromptu invitation was decidedly mixed. He did acknowledge that it might be nice to get away for a while, let his batteries recharge, and perhaps fine tune his perspective somewhat after utilizing Greg as the 'devil's advocate' and a sounding board for all the sinister ideas he had been cultivating. Greg could be trusted totally, and usually could come up with different slants on just about anything one might conjure up for discussion. Money was not an issue in any way shape or form.

The 'down' side to Pete seemed to be the actual logistics of a trip that sounded more like roughing it than Pete felt able to handle. Living out of a 1987 slightly altered Dodge van, while sleeping in tents and eating out of a cooler was not all that appealing. He needed to access toilet facilities much more frequently than is considered normal, and his back had just begun to function relatively painlessly, and he did not need to be sitting in one position for hours on end right now. Pete had undertaken similar treks on three previous occasions; once in a motor home, once on a Greyhound bus, and the last in a rental car. It is very long and tiring under the best of conditions.

Further complicating his decision was the fact that his Medicaid health coverage was in the process of either being renewed for another year, or summarily rejected. In the overall scheme of things, Pete realized that more than likely his eligibility or for that matter, the lack of it wasn't going to figure too prominently in his life one way or the other if he followed through with his diabolical plot. It was more of an ongoing chess match he had been engaged in with the state's omnipotent guidelines and their emissaries that challenged him most. He firmly believed he was entitled to a certain level of care and prescription coverage, without having to jump through hoops to get it.

Pete was covered with the federal governments Medicare Umbrella; however, they did not cover any medicines, and only paid what they deemed acceptable fees for any counseling. Their best endorsement was hospitalization insurance, if and when necessary. A nice ace in the hole to have, but to a large extent of little value to him.

He had decided long ago that he would never deplete any cash reserves he might have in an effort to keep up with the ridiculous costs of prescriptions (currently more than $500 a month and or counseling fees, (another $175) He reasoned that how can anyone's holistic condition improve while they are concurrently being financially devastated in this manner.

In deference to the system as a whole, it must be acknowledged that there are other programs that pick up those who fail to qualify for any kind of measured assistance. However, they are less than efficient at keeping their files active, and pharmacy access is considerably more restrictive. Pete needed a favorable decision, primarily based on principle, and if one was not forthcoming, he needed to be ready to contest or mediate it in an aggressive and expedient manner. It was part of what made him what he was, and he couldn't separate himself from his convictions even if the consequences in a practical sense, at this particular time, would be minimal at worse.

With his mind now made up, Pete called Greg that Sunday to decline the sightseeing adventure of sorts, at least for now. There would still be another week or so to reconsider, however unlikely such a scenario would have to be. He also offered Greg a $400 loan to help finance his trip. It would have no urgency to repay attached to it. In addition, he suggested a few articles that Greg was more than welcome to borrow that might prove useful on such a journey. Greg thanked Pete, and said he would try to come by on Monday with the van, and if Pete should change his mind, that would be great.

Greg had another untimely problem to deal with in the interim. His regular mode of transportation, a 1989 Isuzu Impulse, had died on him and had to be towed to a friend's garage. He suspected a fuel pump breakdown, and at this point was more than a little frustrated and didn't need to be spending money that he had other imminent plans for.

The other surprise of the weekend came on Saturday in the form of a large, manila envelope from the Center that subsequently proved to have Pete's medical records enclosed. According to the bill conveniently stapled to the front page for $25.00, there should be at least one-hundred pages of revealing material included within, and Pete was anxious to begin ingesting all of the details. To him it was a timely opportunity to acquaint himself at some level with Dr. Leslie and the other mental health professionals, who had sat across from him session after session and had made interpretations and formed conclusions based on what he had shared, and how he had presented himself.

The most current entries were on top and went back in sequence to the summer of 1998. It was all there except, curiously enough, all the letters Pete had written to Leslie over the past year or so. He had seen them in his chart less than a month ago, and he wondered for a moment why they were not also included. Perhaps that loophole that allows them to retain any documents that are generated by someone other than their personnel, or from another total entity, could be applied to his letters, by virtue of some nebulous legal application.

Pete was not overly concerned. He pretty much knew verbatim what the letters said, or at least their intent. He just wanted to refresh his memory as to the dates they had begun and get some sense of just how the progression had ultimately played itself out so far.

The first few pages of records were entries made since his transfer to North Main Street. They were essentially summaries, his treatment plan, and his new therapist, Frank, and Dr. Michael Andrews, his new doctor, had signed them.

Initially, the content was not all that informative or enlightening, except for two very notable perversions, each of which he felt compelled to examine over and over. The first dagger came in the form of a totally erroneous and inappropriate diagnostic label that had been assigned to him, and he wasn't yet sure how, when or why it had been deemed prudent.

The term "narcissistic" had been included as describing one of his so-called "mixed personality traits", along with border line and dependent. Its connotation is one that Pete was not only repulsed by but had contempt for. It was contained in all its repugnant implications as part of his treatment history, medications, and current diagnoses. Technically, it was part and parcel of his "Annual Psychiatric Summary", dated very recently, and signed by Dr. Andrews.

This specific and troubling conclusive judgement had Pete's blood pressure rising. He knew exactly what this particular personality trait implied. However, he felt compelled to research it again in a newer text, just in case it had inexplicably been amended somewhat. It had not! The definition was clear, precise and unforgiving: "excessive self-love, selfishness and self-centeredness," all characteristics Pete had found particularly loathsome and repellent wherever and whenever he perceived it to be apparent in others he might just be unfortunate enough to come in contact with. It was a description so inflexibly contrary and unequivocally in conflict with everything he had ever felt.

As much as Pete was rendered speechless and dumbfounded by what he felt was in some manner of interpretation a patently erroneous diagnosis, he was injured even more by what he read in one of Wayne's most recent progress notes. It stated, "Dr. Greer has declined any further updates re: patient's status, other a duty to warn."

Apparently, Wayne had been leaving her messages on her voicemail related to Pete's progress or lack thereof, in his new treatment environment. Leslie, for reasons only known to her, obviously didn't feel that was necessary. Pete was devastated, and could only ask himself why: what could her motivation and rationale possibly be for closing the door on him so abruptly and so finally?

Was it because she was fearful of a genuinely perceived threat to her safety and needed to distance herself as much as possible from that reality and any related reminders? Was it possible that she was capable of casually and stealthily moving on from an experience that she felt at some level might not have handled as well as she might have? "Out of sight, out of mind" perhaps? Pete couldn't bring himself to believe that she could 'care' for a patient, and then cease altogether, so suddenly.

Any and all of these mindsets were no doubt possible and even plausible, and all were equally difficult for Pete to accept, especially now that he had seen the undeniable and troubling result in black and white.

Pete needed to do a quick reality check, one that could help immeasurably in his maintaining his overall perspective. He had realized all along that there was a better than 50/50 chance of this blowing up in his face in virtually any manner conceivable, and these latest misconceptions from either parties' frame of reference were all but inevitable. Just because he couldn't let go didn't have to translate to her also struggling in any fashion with this reality. Her life was probably light years removed from being as barren and desperate as his, and the effects of this experience were hardly going to impact it as uncompromisingly as it had Pete's, at least if she could prevent it. Pete's all-consuming mission in life now was to bridge that gap by creating a scenario that would make it all but impossible for her to NOT acknowledge and afford due diligence to his unyielding needs. Bottom line, these perceived slights would only stoke the fire already burning within him and solidify his resolve even more.

The more he made his way through these tidbits of clinical observations and evaluations, the less he appreciated what he saw, especially from Leslie. Her handwriting, always applied with expediency in mind, and rife with coded and medical jargon shortcuts, was often difficult to decipher thoroughly. Pete, however, had some clinical experience of his own perusing the charts in detoxes and group homes, so he was able with persistence to successfully piece most passages together coherently.

Pete ultimately had to conclude that some of his assumptions about Leslie were ill-conceived, disappointing and in some respects painful to discover. He had yet to come across a single sentence in all of these notes that alluded too much of anything positive, endearing or promising in his regard. She couldn't find ONE admirable trait worthy of even small mention. Pete began to feel that all of his efforts, both on a professional level as a patient, and on a personal level, as a man, had not only been grossly ignored, but apparently had little value or meaning to Leslie.

Why was it so hard for her to identify or acknowledge even the slightest gesture of kindness or human tenderness however conveyed from one person to another? Why was it his weaknesses and shortcomings were deemed so important, they demanded exclusive focus and detailed documentation, and his strengths were conspicuously absent with respect to being noteworthy.

Could it be that her perceptions had become so jaded and saturated with the features described in the thousands of symptoms spelled out in her Diagnostic and Statistical Manual that she had been rendered incapable of recognizing and appreciating the simple value of the human spirit and its desperate need to be nurtured? Pete couldn't help asking: "What kind of doctor and healer can be represented in this fashion?" And even more troubling, "What kind of "one-dimensional" person had he naively fallen so hopelessly in love with?"

Pete couldn't help being flabbergasted and royally pissed off for the remainder of the day. He felt that by and large, what he was ingesting by· examining these so-called clinical entries was unadulterated garbage. He didn't feel that it in any way, shape or form came close to describing him, his immediate needs or what his possible motivations might be. He had on numerous occasions offered unsolicited rides to at least half the group members, and Leslie, since she wasn't deaf or blind, had to know that.

He had extended his willingness to pick up and accompany one guy to a much-needed AA meeting. He also recalled an instance where he brazenly took it upon himself to volunteer the entire group in an attempt to move one woman and her daughter from an apartment she had described herself as being helplessly stuck in. All the other clinicians Pete had interacted with over the past three years had recognized at least something positive or endearing that they felt worthy of mentioning as part of his progress notes. Could it be that they were all indulging in some manner of frivolity, or was it, Leslie?

As Pete threw the charts on the floor near his parlor chair, he was mystified and hurt. After a while, he also couldn't help being somewhat amused by some of the labels and conclusions these "professionals" were capable of arriving at. The clinical term being applied to his "attachment" to Dr. Greer had been boiled down for their purposes to: EROTIC TRANSFERENCE. It was all over his chart now, and virtually every entry over the last three months spelled it out, and sometimes even hinted at possible root causes.

Curiously, Leslie had never articulated this terminology (erotic transference) even once while all of this was clearly escalating and well on its way to spinning completely out of control. Later, when Pete pressed his 'new' therapist, Wayne, for his best clinical interpretation, he hesitated only briefly before coming up with: "When the patient's deepest feelings of emptiness and yearning for intimacy distort their sense of reality to such a degree of desperation, they can then become vulnerable to misinterpreting the doctor's accepting and understanding nature for signals that a loving relationship is possible." That supposedly explained the "transference" dynamic. The erotic element undoubtedly alluded to just about any description physical desire imaginable.

Pete, to a certain degree, accepted Wayne's hypothesis because he felt there was some obvious validity in its general premise.

His follow-up question was, however, why had it taken all these months, and eventually a crisis, to evolve from an attachment to this more problematic and grievous complication, one that had been addressed by leaving him out in the cold, and her apparently "washing her hands of it", seemingly just to save face?

A lot of what Pete was discovering for the first time about Dr. Leslie Greer appeared to fly in the face of what is believed to be most doctor's driving force and their last line of defense.

Pete had seen a Professor at Harvard Medical School during a "Nightline" interview describe most doctors as "competence junkies," who in effect find it very difficult to accept failure and undesirable outcomes with their patients. They are routinely willing to extend themselves to extraordinary lengths in an attempt to find solutions and remedies for the most challenging and unrelenting circumstances they might encounter. Pete had a hard time identifying anything resembling that effort with respect to his and Dr. Greer's dilemma. In deference to her, it must be acknowledged that she did seek counsel or advice from a 'supervisor' before the decision was made to terminate Pete.

Perhaps this situation had indeed deteriorated to such a degree that a line delineating her resources as a practicing psychiatrist from the one in which she was the object of an obsessive love became so compromised and blurred that it left her with little or no choice.

Maybe it is grossly unfair to draw parallel lines comparing the challenges and potential responses of a shrink with those confronted by perhaps a trauma surgeon or ER physician. It would appear that although the latter two may well function "optimally" while having 'life and death' hanging in the balance, the former must rely on the variables of specific dynamics being present, such as voluntary information, body language and emotional content in order to make connections and ultimately arrive at some manner of deduction.

Even with that distinction being clear, Pete had a difficult time accepting the lack of a "humanistic or holistic" element, which was conspicuously absent throughout his doctor/ patient relationship with Dr. Leslie Greer. To him, acknowledging attention and appeasing or placating misguided overtures, even with humor or perhaps flattery, could have been a worthwhile positive response that there was indeed room for, within the rigid guidelines of overall treatment. It should have been forthcoming and might well have been instrumental in soothing his sensibilities before any subsequent obsession could evolve.

Pete could now comprehend, even if he was unable to accept, why it had been an exercise in futility, trying to penetrate the impregnable "veil of elite professionalism" or clinical shell that Leslie and her world were enclosed within. He found it hard to acknowledge, at least on the surface, that she gave the appearance of being little more than some "android like" automaton, that processed perceived symptomology and spit out prescriptions with little more than just the most appropriately 'clinical' platitude.

If that assessment seemed cold and distant, Pete felt it was relatively fitting and accurate. She rarely if ever smiled in the presence of her patients, at least that he had ever discerned it was a 15 minute 'med-check' in her office, or 80 or 90 minutes in a designated meeting room for the group. Issues, analyses, prescriptions and one eye on the clock could fairly describe her overall "modus operandi". As Pete had pain fully come to discover, she curiously found it unnecessary to recognize and embrace the humanity and spirit of the individuals who sat across from her.

In spite of his burgeoning disappointment, Pete's hunger for this challenging little dynamo would hardly subside. His feelings of love, desire and tenderness if anything were intensifying. The more she attempted to distance herself from him and what he represented, the more he wanted her. These passions were now also being fueled and bolstered by some bitterness and contempt for her indifference and professional and personal slights.

Her willingness and obvious attempt to 'eradicate' Pete so callously only served to solidify his conviction that she was undoubtedly in dire need of learning a few painfully objective lessons. He was also totally convinced that he was equally deserving of a few sincere and legitimate answers that only she could provide.

This little lady who had successfully earned the privilege of adding an M.D. to her name had found her life intersecting with that of Pete Masters through simple fate and pure circumstance. During this encounter, she had been forced to make some considered, elective decisions. These choices and their inherent substantial impact on another had unwittingly placed her in an untenable position and rendered her quite vulnerable.

Dr. Leslie Greer has now become Pete's judicious and discriminating quarry. She would soon discover how it felt to be demoted from the omnipotent and powerful to the helpless and powerless in a heartbeat. Pete would soon become her absolutely worst fucking nightmare . . . come true.

CHAPTER TEN

The hunt was on. The only question seemed to be how much time was Pete prepared to devote to surveillance and all the other nuances that he had so meticulously incorporated into his plan. He could feel his patience and attention to all the minute details evaporating by the hour. He had to get hold of himself before his lifelong propensity to do something recklessly impulsive and poorly planned brought him to a place he could not afford to go.

His emotions were percolating to such a degree that he was now carelessly looking for shortcuts. He was starting to believe that, just maybe, all the tracking and amenities that he once felt were so vital to the perfect execution of this abduction were no longer necessary. Was this a dangerous and foolhardy mindset for him to be entertaining? Shit, the whole fucking idea, no matter how well it was dissected or examined, was dangerous and foolhardy. Just look at the end of it: he wasn't going to walk away from this, and that was as sure as the sun comes up. So, all the other bullshit was just so much foreplay.

Pete's fairytale visions of Leslie being somewhat under standing, emphatic and cooperative now seemed illusory at best. She would probably fight him tooth and nail every inch of the way. That said, Pete concluded that he would have to decide, once and for all, what objectives he would be willing to risk dying for. That, or at least be somewhat satisfied reminiscing about while he spent the rest of his days languishing in some shithole prison. This was going to be an "all or nothing" proposition if there ever was one.

What was running through his mind now, with ephemeral speed, was the notion of, "Why not just get the car and the plates, throw a few things in it, and pounce on her at the very first opportunity?" He felt confident that he could easily find her in the course of any given day, and if necessary, follow her to the most feasible location she might lead him to. It sounded unnecessarily reckless until he also considered the very real risks of being detected as suspicious on any one or more of his repetitious surveillance excursions.

That would be, in effect, a fate worse than death, for he could be exposed, humiliated and prosecuted before he ever really got started. Pete couldn't stand to live with that kind of failure. He would continue hashing and rehashing his options for the next day and a half. D-day was not going to be too far away.

Pete concluded that two of three critical elements were already in place to give him the optimal possibility of executing the initial phase of the "event."

They were the weapon and the car, and once the stolen plates were attached to it, the authorities would be hard pressed to connect it to him. The most opportune time and place could be so variable and unpredictable that he figured he would be just as safe getting everything ancillary in place and playing out that part as it might unfold. He could either go or abort on two or three consecutive ventures until the most favorable scenario presented itself.

He had played out the "grab" sequence over and over in his mind hundreds of times. He visualized it as lasting no more than a few precious seconds. He was counting on the gun to seriously neutralize any resistance she might be inclined to offer. Ideally, he would be capable of parking his car close enough to hers; however, a few more feet either way were not going to be too problematic. He had to get his right hand over her mouth from behind, while having the pistol in his left and pointed very close to her face. This had to be done in a millisecond. If she was able to screech out any manner of distressing scream, Pete's blood pressure, adrenaline and no doubt red-lining anxiety could threaten to blow a gasket and cripple his sense of timing and sequence, and that could not happen.

Strips of duct tape already cut and hanging inside the car would quickly immobilize Leslie once they were inside the car. The front door would already be partly open. Her first captive position would be with her wrists taped together behind her back while kneeling on the floor. Her head would be down on the front seat, which would be pushed back as far as it will go. Pete's plan was to rent a full-size car from Hertz, most likely in the Ford Taurus class.

The actual act of taking possession of Leslie could not last more than 15 or 20 seconds, which doesn't seem like much at all. However, it indeed could be when one was struggling violently with a female who might manage a loud enough sound even if it wasn't in the form of a scream. She could very well be successful in kicking the car or whatever. The chances were one or both of her hands would be clutching keys, a briefcase or purse. Presumably, these articles would end up on the ground. That was where they would remain until someone, hopefully much later, unwittingly happened upon them. The next morning would be ideal However, an hour or so would be OK.

As things stood now, Pete had no idea if there would be an acquaintance, colleague or family member that might be waiting for her or supposedly meeting her after 9:15 that fateful night. For his purposes, it would be better if that was not the case, but he did not see it as critical in either case.

His feeling now was that he was as ready as he was ever going to be, and with that in mind decided to target a series of three tentative dates, all within the same week, and two weeks hence. It would happen either Monday Aug. 13 or that Wednesday or Friday.

Leslie had office hours scheduled on all three of these target dates. The only possible glitch was she could be away for vacation. Pete would make another phone call on Sunday August 12 just on the chance that if she were going to be away, there would be a message left on her recorder in that regard.

He would also casually cruise over there this coming week and perhaps park nearby one night, just to get a sense of the layout at that time of day. By doing so, he could observe the lighting, the traffic, apartment windows open or air conditioners running and anything else he could pick up.

Also, during this week he could acquire everything on his list, trusting his initial instincts that they were all essential for one possibility or another. His plan now, precipitously accelerated, would require that he 'lift' the out of state plates as soon as possible, most likely the Saturday night preceding the week he had now set his sights on. Pete had a medium sized Italian restaurant in mind on the Rhode Island/Massachusetts border as the quarry for his fictitious plate acquisitions. As for ready cash, he had $2700 mostly in fifties and hundreds, which he felt was more than sufficient to meet any manner of improbability that might occur in a ten-day to two-week journey.

Undoubtedly, his most formidable hurdle now would be his efforts to maintain his resolve and to actually follow through with the plan. The dynamic that existed between him and Leslie, and his determination in that regard were not what troubled him.

It was the relationships with his children and one grandchild that, for all intents and purposes, would cease to meaningfully exist that Pete would struggle with. They were his primary motivation to continue day after day for quite a spell now, that is, until Leslie, with all her guile, aloofness and mystery bedeviled him and ultimately thrust him up to this point of obsessive desire and insanity.

Pete had now to find the means to find an acceptable way to rationalize and minimize the shock and dismay that his children would no doubt suffer because of this abhorrent and seemingly selfish act he had chosen to perpetrate. He would make every effort to see Susan and Davis, and of course, Hillary, as often as he could during the next two weeks. There could not be even the slightest hint that he would, in effect, soon be removed from their everyday lives forever. This would be an excruciatingly difficult experience for him, especially when he held and hugged them for the last time. It would be most painful, saying goodbye to his innocent and trusting Hillary, whose cheek he always planted a kiss on and say, "Grandpa will see you soon," as the visit is coming to an end. It would be all he could do to keep from completely breaking down emotionally.

Pete had decided that he could write letters to them individually. Perhaps in this manner he could give sense of insight as to how and why their father might be so desperate, and why he felt so compelled to make this choice.

His life insurance with a face value of $7000 should be in order and was paid up. It was enough to bury him in any manner they could agree on. He was trusting that there were no clauses within the small print of the policy that negated benefits for anyone killed in the act of committing a felony.

He knew that most policies cover suicide after they have been in effect for two continuous years. His policy was at least three years old.

There was not much materially to be divided, and Pete hadn't given any serious thought to leaving anything resembling a will. All three of his children could generally be considered "middle class salaried personnel", and already possessed at least one of everything he could leave them. Pete would be very disappointed if they were to squabble over anything of this nature.

Last but not least, there was Madeline, his ex-mother-in-law, who had come to depend on Pete, and considered him a friend. She would be forced to rely solely on the only son she had living in the general area. He was fairly reliable in emergencies, but other than that, he had not been overly thoughtful or considerate.

There was also a female 'tabby' cat that had been with Pete since 1988, and a tropical fish that he had had for about a year and a half. Would they become orphans?

Although that possibility certainly existed, his instincts dictated undoubtedly, they would end up being adopted.

These were all extremely difficult and heart-wrenching realities that Pete would somehow have to come to terms with in the next 10 to 14 days. "IF" he decided to spare them all this anguish, he would effectively be once again burying himself. He had had his fill of literally retreating to the background, and existing only on the periphery of anything and everything worthwhile in this life. For just once in his life, Pete wanted to embrace and realize an experience without fear and doubt, one that he could fully internalize, even if for all practical purposes, its entire concept could be regarded as "tabooed" and appear to be completely beyond his grasp.

The "moral" and unselfish choice outwardly might be a relatively tranquil one to arrive at; however, it would be dreadful to have to live with. The desperate and impulsive scenario by its very nature provided adrenaline, fantasy and purpose.

Are these the rationales of a sane, reasonable and altruistic person, or those of a thrill-seeking, selfish sociopath? After all his therapy and introspection, Pete was still not comfortable with what he dredged up from the depths of his tortured soul.

His conclusions and convictions unfailingly led him back to the same place. His isolation and emptiness were at the root of all his frustrations and unyielding desperation, and unless he took this bold step, nothing would ever change.

Pete was ill-equipped to start building any kind of worthwhile life at this stage of the game. He was not physically or emotionally stable enough. Even if one condition had a chance of marginally improving, the other was guaranteed to worsen. He was aging. The clock was ticking at what often feels like 'double time', and neither his children or anybody else had the power to stop it.

Surely, over the years there were attempts by loved ones to effect some positive and lasting enrichments on his behalf; however, most were fleeting and capricious in nature. Pete's life was his to deal with, and always had been. This impending and desperate episode would just be another chapter. If things worked out, it would not only be brief, but more rewarding, satisfying and redemptive than all the previous ones combined.

Pete often wondered how he might have fared, had he been born in 1842 instead of 1942. He abhorred the technology and the rat race of contemporary America. He was convinced that people's lives on the whole were negatively influenced by much of what unfortunately was current in this regard. There were just too many 'toys' that the masses were cleverly conditioned to believe that they needed, and the result was everyone ended up like a dog chasing its tail. The auto makers, along with the PC and software d developers, were the major culprits. Enough was never enough, was their stock and trade, and the results were laughable: a little innovation and lots of advertising of a gratuitous and expendable cycle of very expensive commodities--a capitalist concept, indeed.

Pete's lone exception to this onslaught of superfluous technology was cable or satellite television. Not surprising, in light of the endless hours he endured alone in his apartment.

He usually managed to find plenty of worthwhile programming without subscribing to premium channels offering repeat movies. He had always felt that the farmers of long ago were the backbone of this nation. They worked long, hard hours and essentially subsisted on what was harvested. Their children followed them and were much too busy to be preoccupied with CD players, cell phones or a vile assortment of violent and insane video games. Teenage drinking and drugging just didn't exist. Simply put, just because things change, didn't mean they got better.

As Pete awoke on Friday morning, he felt as though he had experienced some kind of 'rebirth'. His conflicts and doubts had somehow depreciated and found their own little niche in his overall scheme of resolution. He now felt a sense of absolute and total certainty about what he needed to do. He had read somewhere that a deep, uninterrupted sleep could often mysteriously sort out a particular dilemma and bring into focus what was indeed important, and ultimately the most expedient means of achieving that end.

His resolve was now more hardened than it had ever been. His preparation could now shift into high gear, unhindered by any measure of trepidation or self-doubt.

Strangely, since Pete's perception and resolve had been so acutely adapted, his course of action also became crystal clear.

After a brisk shower and some breakfast, he would check his list of necessary items and add a couple he had been considering: one was a new flashlight, the other a decent first-aid kit.

He was determined to acquire everything he needed today, regardless of how many places he had to go or what the cost might be. The only articles that could be a little awkward would be trying to buy a few changes of clothing for Leslie. He felt a couple of different styles of warm-up outfits would prove to be most flexible and comfortable for spending a lot of time in an air-conditioned car or motel room. A few extra tops that could be worn separately with pants or shorts would add to the variety of choices she would have.

He was counting heavily on the able assistance of female sales personnel with respect to the sizes and co-ordination of these outfits, and footwear as well. The underwear he could only make a calculated guess about. She is petite but not all that short, maybe 5'3" or 5'4". Her bra cup size, he estimated, is a full band either 32" or 34" around her bust. He could get a couple of each size just to be sure. Her panties would be fun to pick out. He would err on the small side when forced to make choices.

Pete could feel his levels of energy, excitement and purpose escalating by the minute as prepared to leave his apartment after stuffing $300 in his pocket. He was alive and on a mission.

Pete decided he needed to put together on paper a chronological checklist, so that every pre-event action and detail was properly attended to. On Saturday, he would call Davis, since this should be his custodial weekend with Hillary. He would be aggressive in his effort to schedule some time with them regard less of how when or where that might be.

Also, this weekend, probably Saturday night, he would attempt to pilfer the out-of-state registration plates he would definitely need. His thinking now was geared to two different states, preferably ones that designate only rear plates, as is the case in Massachusetts. His feeling was that changing to plates that are lawful in states they would be motoring across, would make it significantly easier to meld in with traffic. He fully expected that at some point there would be an "all-points bulletin" posted once the authorities were able to connect a few clues.

He had targeted two specific locations for this purpose. One was a moderately sized mall in nearby Massachusetts; the other a multi-cinema parking lot close by. These lots were usually vulnerable because of their size and proximity to thickly wooded areas in their furthest corners. Pete's friend Greg had offered to go along as a lookout, which should expedite the operation once the right plates were located, and considerably reduce any potential risks.

The entire weekend looked very promising to Pete, no doubt because he felt more comfortable with his newfound resolution and also, because he expected to be busy and productive. As it turned out, most of Friday and Saturday were spent getting everything on his list. That included all of the feminine articles, which he couldn't help shaking his head and smiling about, once he went about sorting them for some very special future use. He had spent approximately $190 on outfits, underwear, socks, and sneakers and felt he had purchased something for just about every potential scenario. He even threw in a small jug of laundry soap, so if necessary, some of their apparel could be rinsed in a motel sink.

The acquisition of the plates also went smoothly late on Saturday night, and Pete was more than satisfied with the results. He now had New York and Ohio tags, two states that were definitely on his itinerary to cross from east to west, most likely within the first two days.

Greg, who would be leaving in a few days on his own trek to Yellowstone did not try at all to dissuade Pete from going forward with his plans. Greg now was planning to visit his brother near Harrisburg, Pennsylvania on his way, and attempted to enlist as possible company his 15-year-old nephew. Pete thanked Greg for his assistance lifting the plates, and also for understanding that that the time for his particular clandestine journey was approaching rapidly, and he needed to stay on course.

Greg understood this kind of desperate commitment to longing or vision and would be the last one to make judgements in that regard. As they shook hands, and were then heading off in very different directions, Greg had the last words saying, "I'll look you up when I get back, no matter where it is I have to look, or what I have to do."

CHAPTER ELEVEN

Pete's Sunday turned out to be enriching and rewarding. He was fortunate enough to spend some time with Davis, his new wife Isabella, and especially Hillary. When he first arrived at their apartment, she was propped up on a chair with her little nose no more than a foot from their Gateway computer screen.

On one hand, it was exhilarating to see a child so young, with mouse in hand, anxiously exploring and absorbing whatever she was capable of, with a simple click. On the other hand, Pete saw it as a troubling sign of the times, as he wondered what this little girl's future might involve when she was exposed to so much "technology" at such a tender age.

Granted, there were some excellent teaching discs designed to enhance a child's thirst for information, experience and exposure to diversity. It just seemed all too instantaneous. How can they possibly retain anything of basic or permanent value, or even recognize it when they encounter it? Maybe Pete was just too "old school" to appreciate what this is all about. In many respects, he hoped his concerns were to a large degree unfounded.

That said, he would spend his time with her Sunday, reading from alphabet books, arranging and re-arranging stickers and simple coloring. As usual, there were snacks to be shared, and it was all great fun.

Pete decided that this week he would finally put to use his brand-new metal detector. He had acquired it in the spring by virtue of an impulse-driven order placed with a national catalogue that he had an open account with. His motivation, other than the obvious possibility of finding treasure, was rooted in the potential opportunities such an activity might present to get out of the apartment, and as a bonus, perhaps reap the benefits of some real exercise.

The saltwater beaches in Rhode Island and nearby coastal Massachusetts were, in a word, unspectacular, at least in Pete's judgement. He had seen some of the awe-inspiring beaches in Florida, California and even Hawaii, and these in his home state were sorely lacking. To make matters even worse, the sonsof-bitches that created statutory law had the audacity to charge fees ($10) to the taxpaying citizens who live here, to visit these so-called 'aesthetic treasures.' When Pete's kids were much younger, he didn't have many options, but now there was very little incentive to patronize them.

His plan this week was to hit them when the tides were low, either in the early morning or late evening, thus avoiding any fees and most of the traffic. Additionally, it would make for better conditions to walk and hunt. He had practiced with the functional components of his new toy when he first received it, but lately, it had been relegated to a corner of the kitchen, collecting dust. The summer was now two-thirds over.

Pete's plan was to start his series of treasure hunting/ exercise trips at the most distant location and work his way back on subsequent days to shorter treks. Today his destination would be Misquamicut, which is located on the very tip of southern Rhode Island, where it shares its border with Stonington, Conn. For his money, this is the jewel of Rhode Island beaches, if there is one, with consistently above average surf and a lot of white sandy beach. The biggest drawback is the considerable amount of kelp or seaweed usually present in the water.

Pete arrived there after the 45-mile drive at about 8:15 a.m. The tide was just beginning to make its way back in. He parked at the southernmost tip of the beach and figured he could walk a good two miles in both directions in a kind of staggering pattern near the water's edge. He always enjoyed having the remnants of the cresting waves gently lap at his feet. It felt good to be out in the salt air with some nice, gentle sea breezes. It was a lot like the trade winds he so fondly remembered from his experiences in Hawaii. It was also a good 10 to 15 degrees cooler here than in the city.

The time seemed to fly by. Pete struck up conversations with a few people, usually kids who wanted to know more about his detector and stopped periodically just to soak up the atmosphere and peaceful serenity of nature. The treasure for a day added up to $1.76 in coins, a key and a token from the Mohegan Sun Casino. No rings, gold chains or Rolex watches just yet.

With high noon fast approaching, it was time to get out of the hot sun. Pete had been wearing a baseball cap; however, he had discovered the hard way that heat could build up and sometimes precipitate a headache. He also needed a snack before heading back to Providence, so he began peeling an orange before slipping back behind the wheel. It was then that he decided on a slight detour that would take him by the Center, where Leslie should be at this hour. It would be only a slight variance from going straight home, since the building could be seen clearly from I-95, and it was only two minutes to the parking lot once he exited the Interstate.

Her Audi was indeed there, parked in a familiar spot, and Pete did nothing more than make a mental note, turn around in the driveway and head home. Right now, he needed a shower and a nap, and later that evening when he is refreshed, he would be ready to head over to the East Side and undertake some serious and consequential surveillance.

Pete had his customary summertime light dinner, in the form of the frozen version of a 'Healthy Choice' meal consisting of approximately two ounces of chicken and equal amounts of rice and vegetables. With cranberry sauce and a slice of bread, it was tasty and more than adequate to satisfy him. He rarely attempted any cooking in the heat, choosing not to impede the efforts of his one air conditioner to moderate the temperature and humidity throughout his entire apartment.

Pete's somewhat elaborate cooling system whereby he used fans to extend and redirect cooled air was capable of reasonably moderating the indoor climate regardless of how hot it might be outside. As he prepared to leave for the location where Leslie had her private practice, he couldn't help but behold the bright red sun beginning to set in the western sky. This phenomenon usually guaranteed another scorcher for tomorrow. His watch read 7:45 p.m.

Pete needed to find the most advantageous yet inconspicuous spot available to park as he approached the general area. He had to have access to a clear line of sight to where Leslie's car would be parked, the rear exit from her office and the path she would normally take to navigate between the two.

Lady Luck was smiling, and Pete was able to maneuver his little Toyota into a spot adjacent to Ives Street, directly behind a car near the corner of the block. For some strange reason, the fact that if he could observe her and her car, she obviously possessed a similar capability only reversed, but it wasn't major concern. He was operating on the total assumption that she had no idea of what make, model or color vehicle he normally drove. His plan was to be extremely cautious and as close to invisible as possible, just in case.

Upon settling in, he quickly confirmed that the Audi IV was parked, at least for tonight, in one of the middle lanes of the three-lane lot. It was positioned horizontally from Pete's vantage point. The lot itself when filled appeared to hold 14 or 15 cars. Right now, there were cars seven scattered about, and his best guess was that she would have to cover at least 40 to 50 feet to get to hers. He broke that down even further to somewhere between 20 to 25 steps. Knowing how fast she had a tendency to move, Pete felt that time lapse would be in the range of three to five seconds, not counting the second or two she could spend opening either one or two of the doors. The only illumination for this parking lot was supplied by a streetlight at the curb, relatively close by. On a scale of 1 to 10, with 10 being the brightest and 1 being pitch dark, it was about a 4 or 5. It wasn't going to be the most ideal conditions, but definitely a feasible scenario.

Pete watched a few cars enter and a few more exit the lot, and he concluded that at 8:40, it was now as dark as it was going to be on any moonlit night. All he had to do now was wait for Leslie. His watch read 8:57 as he visualized her inside her office, with some faceless patient, striving to bring her last session to a timely conclusion. Shrinks are very good at redirecting their patients' focus so that it is plainly understood that there are stringent limits attached to the length of each encounter.

As he anxiously waited, Pete carefully took note of some shrubbery located at both ends of the lot, for these thickets could prove to be critical in the event that her car was parked in one of the spots directly in front of them.

There were no assigned spots per say, only a sign which clearly stated "parking for 293-295 Grove Street." Pete wasn't overly concerned. He would find a way, no matter where her car was.

It was now time to focus on only one object, the rear door to the office, and he wouldn't be kept in suspense for too long. At exactly 9:12, the door flew open, and the stealthy, unmistakable figure of a woman made her way at a very brick pace to the Audi. He could hear the remote control release the door locks and turn off the alarm as she got close to the car.

What happened next would prove to be the most important observation he would make that night. She first opened the rear door on the driver's side to deposit what appeared to be a sweater or jacket and then her briefcase. It took only a few seconds, and Pete knew then that this mini-capsule of time was going to provide him with just the opportunity he was looking for. It made perfect sense.

When combined with the two other occasions he had casually observed her at the Center, she would park and proceed to remove the same type of articles in the reverse sequence that he had seen tonight.

Pete had to duck down as she quickly started her car and went about exiting the lot. This move had her for a split second directly facing him and his car. He could ill afford to be recognized in any form whatsoever, especially at this location.

He was excited and encouraged as he drove the mile and a half to his apartment in the north end of the city. He had established a fairly reliable time frame and had discovered a very predictable behavior of Leslie's, which was going to render her extremely vulnerable.

Pete found it difficult to sleep that night. Maybe it was the nap that afternoon, although all that should have accomplished was a measure of compensation for all the driving and beach combing he did earlier in the day. More than likely, it was a combination of his adrenaline pumping and his lifelong penchant for wanting to short cut his way to his objectives. The question he entertained most prominently and repeatedly was, "How many dry runs are enough?" Why couldn't he just rent the car on Wednesday, throw everything in it, and if conditions were similar to Monday, let the plan and himself breathe some exhilarating Life? This waiting was nothing short of fucking torture.

He twisted and turned for a while longer and finally, at 1:30 am, got out of bed, lit a cigarette, and started examining his list of things that could stay in the car indefinitely, as opposed to those of a more perishable nature.

The latter would have to be replaced or at least refreshed if he had to abort on Wednesday and try again on Friday. What it filtered down to where the food items in the cooler, sandwiches, ice, salads, and a few other dry foodstuffs that wouldn't survive too well inside a parked car during a heat wave.

To Pete, these 'snacks' were every bit as essential as any of the other necessities, for two important reasons: most importantly, they would eliminate impulse driven stops along the road that he felt very strongly should not be unnecessarily risked. Secondly, they would go a long way toward keeping the stress quotient from boiling over, at least for him, as they made their way into the night. He also was positive that at some point Leslie was going to get thirsty and even hungry, no matter how much she might try to be uncooperative and, in effect, hold out.

After about an hour of hemming and hawing with these critical choices, Pete went back to bed with a decision he felt reasonably comfortable with. He would continue in his stakeout mode for one more night, and barring any major surprises, be fully prepared to make his move on Friday. Meanwhile, he would continue with his agenda of walking the beaches for what he felt were a variety of sound reasons. It helped him to relax, it was healthy, and it allowed him to fine tune his focus, far removed from the apartment where it was conceived, nurtured and where all the accoutrements were right under his nose.

Pete's restless night necessitated an adjustment in the next day's activities. He didn't wake up until 9:00 and wasn't about to drive to the shore in the blazing sun of midday. So, while shaving and with his sad reflection peering back at him, he asked himself, "Why not do the beach this evening?" "Absolutely no reason not to," he answered. Taking his conviction a little further, he added, "maybe I'll also sleep better tonight as a result. Besides, there are a few details that he wanted to tend to, such as calling Hertz to reserve a car, and at least beginning to pack some of the clothing and toiletries.

Pete's first inclination was to bring along both of the coolers he had. The larger one could be filled with ice and stored in the trunk. It could then be accessed at the rest stops all along Interstate 90 in Massachusetts and then New York. Pete had lots of plastic containers that would enable him to bring along a variety of fresh snacks. The smaller cooler had to be in the car and no further away from Pete than arm's length. He must have his drinks, throat lozenges and chewing gum to neutralize the harshness of what will no doubt be a marked increase in his anxiety-driven smoking addiction. Under normal conditions, he succumbed approximately hourly; however, when stressed, that could easily double in frequency.

How much of an annoyance or burden this would effect for Leslie remained to be seen. Given the overall magnitude of her plight, one might easily consider 'second-hand smoke' rather trivial.

Pete was convinced that all the accommodations of this encounter would have to be 'tailored' to his needs. Any major compromises could severely impede his ability to function efficiently. Today, he also needed to do a moving check of his quarry, who was supposed to be on the east side from 9:00 to 1:00. He had to confirm that her schedule remained predictable, although an isolated 'sick-day' would hardly alter his plan to move on Friday.

His initial task for today involved nailing down an appropriate car. He decided on a Mercury Marquis, which is supposed to have the most cargo space in its class, and an above average fuel capacity. Technically, he reserved the car for ten days, with some flexibility after that, and his Visa card confirmed enough available credit for such a contingency.

The clothing he managed to fit comfortably in one moderately sized suitcase. Pete couldn't help smiling as he separated all the apparel into neat "his and hers" designations. The experience filled him with a warm glow and bountiful anticipation.

There was good news on the observation front as well. Leslie was where she was supposed to be at 12:15, although her car was parked a little closer to the building. This made sense to Pete, since she probably arrived before 9:00 and had her choice of spots, which more than likely would not be the case when she arrived at 5:00.

As evening approached, Pete narrowed his options for beach combing to two. There was Horseneck on the other side of New Bedford, Massachusetts, or Scarborough Beach in Narragansett, Rhode Island. Both were about 35 miles away, one due south and the other east toward Cape Cod. The traffic would probably be lighter going east that beach had fewer punks raising hell, so it was not contest. He grabbed his metal detector and a frozen bottle or water, and he was on his way.

The beach was shorted here and not as nice, but the treasure hunting was a hell of a lot better. After about 45 minutes of scanning, Pete got a different kind of beep than he was used to getting with coins, bottle caps and other kinds of trash.

He moved a little seaweed and a few shells and began to trowel up some sand. As he shifted through his second scoop, he discovered what appeared to be a gold chain, maybe 7" or 8" length. He brought it over to the water's edge and rinsed loose the small granules of sand still encrusted to it. There was a clasp that was still functional, and Pete determined that it was a herringbone styling. It has, no doubt, fallen off someone's wrist or ankle. Pete was ecstatic and couldn't wait to get it home for closer inspection.

On the way home, he couldn't help envisioning a moment in a motel room somewhere, where he could gently fasten his special piece to one of Leslie's sweet limbs, perhaps while she slept. When he got home, he cleaned it thoroughly, and his magnifying glass revealed a tiny 14K stamp. For the first time in a long time, he felt lucky. Could this be an omen?

On Wednesday, any treasure hunting would have to be done early in the morning. In the evening, he had to monitor Leslie, her critical hours and the Audi, hopefully for the last time.

He set his alarm for 6:30, and enthusiastically rolled out of bed. His destination today would be Newport, or more precisely Middletown, Rhode Island, the next town over. There were two medium size shorelines there aptly named First and Second Beach.

That whole area, especially Newport, is commonly referred to as the "playground of the rich," with a lot of old money and some of the most opulent mansions ever constructed anywhere and opulent and the United States. Pete had toured most of them over the years, and when you consider that these were exclusively summer homes for people like the Vanderbilts and Whitneys, it all seemed kind of obscene. He did appreciate the extraordinary decor, artwork imported from Europe, and the exquisite craftsmanship that just doesn't exist anymore. The Historical Society had these mansions endowed to them years ago, with the only provisions being that they are maintained and open to the public.

The two sandy expanses were relatively small, and Pete was able to scan them in both directions by noon. There were a lot of false alarms but only a meager booty of $1.35 in change and another casino token from Foxwoods Resort and Casino, a huge gambling operation in nearby Connecticut run by Native Americans or "Indians." Their revenues are in the tens of millions per month, and they are constantly lobbying to expand into Massachusetts and Rhode Island. Pete found it amusing that ten or twelve years ago they didn't have a pot to piss in; however, to their credit, they went all the way to the US Supreme Court to claim their Constitutional sovereignty and birthrights. This ultimately led to granting them the freedom to build and earn a living on it. Technically, they are the Pequots tribe, and if one can prove as little as a 1/16 blood lineage, the entitlements are now capable of transforming a life of poverty to one of financial security. Pete found this astonishing.

He headed home to rest for the remainder of the day. He wanted to call Madeline later to make himself available for the last time if she needed anything. As far as beachcombing was concerned, he was done with it.

As early evening approached, it was still oppressively hot. The heat index had peaked at 102 degrees, and had relented very little since then.

His little Toyota was not air—conditioned, so he jumped into the shower to freshen up before heading over to the east side for what he expected would be his final excursion. Madeline did need some things rather urgently, so he set up a meeting for tomorrow at 9:30 a.m.

As Pete made his way over to Leslie's workplace, he began to feel a sense of confidence and comfort with his resolve and how things were falling into place. In a lot of people's eyes, his desperate transgression would undoubtedly be seen as some lame rationale, palatable only to a twisted predator. He would never internalize that judgement, especially from individuals lacking in any intimate knowledge of who or what he is. As for loved ones, he could never see himself abandoning them for virtually any conceivable justification. He strongly believed that understanding and support are not meant to be arbitrary quirks to be withheld in discretionary reserve. They must be much like love, offered unconditionally.

As he turned down Ives Street to see what vantage points were available, Pete experienced another one of his pangs of impulse. He asked, "Why can't I just pull into the lot over in the far corner as any other patron who just might be coming and going?" Strategically, there wasn't a better spot to observe and discern what he needed to establish. It was dark, and why couldn't he be ostensibly waiting for someone to finish with an appointment in the building? Before he could dissuade himself, he was in the lot and backing into a spot near the shrubbery.

Leslie's car was in the middle again, only this time it was one spot closer to the exit door. He estimated her car to be no more than 25 or 30 feet diagonally from where he sat.

It was 8:40, so Pete probably had a half-hour or so to visualize what course and sequence of events would be the most feasible and expedient come Friday.

He still hadn't decided on whether to force her into the strategically positioned rental car, or alternatively, 'car jack' her with the Audi, and either of them drive it to a pre-arranged spot, where the rental would be packed and ready to go. Pete had already discovered a very attractive location that would accommodate a switch of this nature very nicely. It was a family restaurant called Goulet's that was open and busy late on Friday evenings, and very accessible to both Route 146 leading to the Massachusetts Turnpike, and I-95 in either direction. The lot is extraordinarily spacious and in its furthest corner, not very well illuminated.

Utilizing her car for this initial segment of the plot would also probably extend appreciably the time lapse before Leslie would be reported missing. Her car would then, would not be at any location the investigators would undoubtedly look first, leaving them virtually clueless as to where she might have gone. In that scenario, chances were it would be quite a few hours before they might stumble on it, in one of their routine checks of a seemingly abandoned car in the middle of the night. Pete and Leslie could easily be somewhere in New York state by then.

He wasn't crazy about the idea of having to execute two separate transfers involving the cars, and likewise with Leslie.

Pete's feeling was that the actual abduction scene in that parking lot come Friday, would by far be the most critical; and if things unfolded in anywhere near the fashion he anticipated, it would also be over very quickly. Once Leslie fully realized that he was armed and not going to be denied, total control of the situation would immediately be his.

As he sat there with a baseball cap pulled down over his eyebrows, a surge of confidence filled his consciousness. His focus remained as sharp as it needed to be, and any doubts or trepidation once again had evaporated. It was crucial that Leslie not sense in Pete any hint of feebleness or hesitation, for she was certainly capable of exploiting any weakness and neutralizing him in a heartbeat.

Hopefully, there would be occasions to be sensitive and tender with her; however, it wouldn't be in that parking lot Friday night. Pete checked his watch once more. It was 9:12, and there were still four cars in the lot, excluding hers and his, when she finally burst onto the scene. She was running more than walking and was at the Audi in what seemed like a flash, but in reality, it had to be two or three seconds. Once there, she quickly repeated the same sequence of maneuvers she had executed on Monday. Rear door first, deposit some articles and then the front followed by a hasty entry behind the wheel. She never bothered to scan any of the cars left. A few seconds later, she was gone.

Pete, for an instant, entertained the impetuous notion of following her, but dismissed it just as quickly. This parking lot in approximately 48 hours was going to be his primary target location, and it couldn't come soon enough.

Chapter Twelve

For the remainder of the evening, and as he lay in bed waiting to drift off, Pete found himself embracing more and more the option of removing both Leslie and her Audi from the actual abduction scene. The critical problem that would present was arranging transportation from where he left the rental for a rendezvous, to her office. There are buses that run direct routes, so that leaves a taxi ride. Could he count on them to deliver him within the prescribed time constraints? It would be a relatively small fare, $5 to $7. he figured; so perhaps the promise of a sizable tip when he called would appreciably expedite their motivation. It sounded feasible enough, especially if he made his request early, although arriving on that scene with too much time to kill could very well be anxiety provoking and risky. A preliminary phone call was definitely in order.

He would also key in a 'fail safe' cutoff time of perhaps 8:45. The Merc would be right there should he be stranded, and he could scramble over there and switch to plan #2. He had enough faith that either option could be successful if he executed according to plan. Leslie was the unknown factor, and Pete was prepared to impress severely on her the futility and danger of her being combative, and even excessively resistant. She would quickly have to realize her 'life' was in imminent jeopardy.

The next critical element of the mission that Pete would be counting on was the parking angle and overall positioning of the Audi. Apparently, Leslie had developed a fondness for habitually parking in the middle lane and at a right angle. Perhaps it was because of the easy access it afforded, as she exited the building with both appropriate doors facing her as she hurriedly approached her car. In each and every casual or serious surveillance trip he had made over there, he had never seen the Audi positioned any differently.

This was so important because on the opposite side of that car she could not possibly detect anyone who did not want to be encountered. Pete, on the other hand, would be relying on two distinctive cues to spring into action. The most significant would be her remote control disarming the alarm, and then unlocking the doors as she approached. That failing, which was highly unlikely, his secondary prompt would have to be the sound of her feet approaching, or when she opened the front or rear door of that car.

Pete had approximately 36 hours to come to a decisive resolution with regard to what would ostensibly take place next. It was a choice of whether she would be forced to drive her own car to the restaurant, or if he would have to 'muscle' her into the Audi, and somehow immobilize her in the passenger's seat. He wasn't overly concerned - whichever tactic he employed, and no matter how it went down, he would, with sheer determination, tenaciously realize his objective.

The next morning, Pete completed his errand run with Madeline, unobtrusively wished her well, and was back home slightly after noon. It was still oppressively hot and humid; however, the forecasters were predicting the passage of a cool front by late afternoon, and were issuing warnings of torrential downpours, wind and possibly some hail. The weather picture for his rendezvous with Leslie tomorrow was mixed. The prognostication was for cooler temperatures, variable skies and just a slight chance of showers. Not bad.

As he went about whatever final preparations he could make at home, including writing rather brief, but poignant letters to his children, Pete couldn't help but reflect on some of objects scattered throughout his apartment. There were pieces of refinished furniture that he had labored considerably over, now remnants of his futile efforts to give most of away. Then, there were the countless brass and silver relics of every description that he had spent hours upon hours restoring to their long-lost luster. Half of them ended up in his grungy cellar, and the remainder continued to occupy space upstairs. Sadly, their shine had long since faded, and for months now, the dust seemed to accumulate on their surfaces by the hour. These objects represented a large portion of what his life had mainly consisted of for the past few years, and when he off-handedly tried to sum it all up, it mournfully didn't translate to very much.

Undoubtedly, the most cherished of his possessions from these years were his photographs. There were many of Hillary beginning with her at one day old and progressing to some taken just a few months ago. Pete had many of these enlarged to fit frames he had restored, and they never failed to lift his spirits when he needed it most. There were others also, especially one particular collage put together by his ex-wife of special events and extended family through the first 15 years or so, of them as a family unit. These were the 'best' of times.

The letters he was going to leave for his children would not detail any of his frustrations and disappointments. They would be a simple declaration of his love for each of them and a plea for some kind of understanding and compassion. Pete could not appreciate the need to say much more, and to even try would be extremely painful and difficult for him.

It was time that he went about procuring the perishables that he felt were necessary for the trip. That would leave only the ice for tomorrow. On his way to the local supermarket, Pete wondered what Leslie might be partial to with respect to food and beverages. He wasn't planning to buy any bologna and felt there were not many people who couldn't enjoy a ham or turkey sandwich, if they were hungry enough. He couldn't help getting more and more enthused as he strolled the aisles of the Super Stop & Shop in nearby North Providence. At times, he would silently whisper to himself, "She might like this, or maybe that".

It was kind of surreal, food shopping for someone he had never engaged in any manner of 'personal' conversation or preference in this regard, and additionally not a hint of concern for what anything might cost. It was definitely more of a 'lark' than a chore on this particular trip.

Pete was totally confident that if he could spend enough continuous, uninterrupted time with Leslie, she would not only eventually agree to eat, but she would also come around in some other respects as well. He finished his shopping and was quite satisfied with both the variety and quality of his selections. He had no way of knowing how many days they might be depending on this food to subsist. There were just too many variables. He expected to have to buy some takeout meals, and hopefully, as time went on, he could consider a restaurant a safe enough place to escort her to.

In the meanwhile, Pete had it all, or would have once he prepared some of it. He had macaroni salad, fruit salad, sandwiches, cheese, crackers, fresh fruit, a variety of soft drinks and sweets. If it wasn't here, they probably wouldn't need it.

The flow of adrenaline in his body was beginning to increase. He would pick up the Mercury in the morning at 9:30, allowing him ample time to familiarize himself, pack it and place all the amenities and necessities exactly where he wanted them. For now, everything non-perishable was grouped together in one corner of his kitchen, awaiting its ultimate designation.

Pete felt it necessary to ensure that a decent night's sleep was at the top of his list of imperatives as he went about last minute preparations. Two Flexeril muscle relaxants should do the trick, as they usually elicit a fairly potent sedative effect on him. They were leftovers from a recent episode of back pain. He felt opportunities to sleep would be elusive and fleeting, to say the least, after approximately 9:15 tomorrow night.

In the interim, he was committed to not allowing himself to be adversely impacted by dwelling on any or all of the ramifications of what was about to happen. He was convinced that adequate examination and dissection had been 'duly' processed. His ultimate choice was to perceive the entire experience in strictly abstract 'human terms'. Undoubtedly, two people's lives were going to be turned upside down. He was staking his freedom and future that what he derived in satisfaction, would be more than worth all the risks and consequences he would be inviting.

As for Leslie, she in no way, shape or form could be characterized as your 'average housewife'. Pete was convinced she was inherently capable of a lot more than "marginally" surviving an episode of this nature. It might take time and some assistance but she would ultimately find the means to extract something positive from her encounter with fate, and eventually find a new source of strength from the effort.

Perhaps most difficult for her would be the accepting and adjusting to 'polar' opposite role reversals.

Assuredly, Leslie would be forced to endure some painful object lessons. Abject desperation for starters was certain to be agonizingly ingrained into her psyche, perhaps forever. This would not be some clinical challenge or case history she might be consulting on or researching; it would be the most critical and threatening dilemma she would ever have to reckon with, her own.

Pete was relying heavily on his calculated assumption that the vast majority of what she faced would ultimately fall under the umbrella of her professional expertise; and that she would, for the most part, react in accordance with all her training and related instincts. This had better be the case, because the next week or ten days were going to be a prime example of the "human condition run amuck", with all its inherent danger and unpredictability. Would she get caught up in the electricity and desperation of her situation, or would she resort to attempting her more familiar role as the reserved and objective practitioner? Pete could not envision her doing anything but placing her complete faith in the latter.

He hadn't for one minute tried to dismiss or minimize the fear and terror that would be brought to bear on Leslie. As much as he would like to circumvent this horror for her, he felt it was all but impossible. He would anxiously await the opportunity when the time was right to shift gears and become her 'doting' caretaker. Hopefully, that would be sooner than later.

No matter how this incident played itself out, this young lady was going to feel more vulnerable and exposed than she had ever imagined could be possible.

As planned, Pete took his sleep-enhancing muscle relaxants just after 11:00 pm and was fast asleep before midnight. His alarm clock was set for 7:45 and he must have slept well through the night. He couldn't remember anything from when he turned on his side and firmly closed his eyes, other than the usual romantic fantasies that danced in and out of his conscious ness until he drifted off. The incessant buzzing of his trusty Westclox brought all of it to an abrupt halt.

As the sun slowly rose in the eastern sky on this most momentous of days, Pete was feeling a little groggy. This was relatively predictable and usually dissipated in a few hours. After a long shower and some breakfast, he set out to walk the 3/4 mile to the local Hertz auto rental facility. It was a small satellite operation that had sprung up two or three years ago. At most, they kept 25 cars there, servicing primarily the hotel downtown and the Amtrak train station close by.

The weather had improved considerably with partly cloudy skies and temperatures in the mid-70s expected. Pete was able to cover the distance in less than 25 minutes, and once there everything went smoothly. He signed his life away, as is usually the case in these kinds of transactions, and once that was done, they handed him the contract and the keys.

Pete was eager to finally take possession of the vehicle that would transport both Leslie and him far away from Rhode Island, and to places where the only people known to them would be each other.

He was definitely pleased with the selection of this car, a 2001 Mercury Grand Marquis, with less than 5,000 miles on the odometer. It is a metallic silver-gray with a little darker gray cloth interior. It was roomy inside, and quiet and comfortable to drive. For him, used to driving a tiny, 5-speed run about, this was like going from a Yugo to a 500 Series BMW or Mercedes. The luxury was all fine; however, Pete was most interested in the practical advantages and anonymity this car offered, especially once he attached New York or Ohio plates to it. For now, he would park it behind his house, away from prying eyes, and just bide his time before loading it and springing into action.

The afternoon would be spent preparing some last-minute food items and placing in the car everything else not perishable. A liquor store two blocks south would provide the necessary ice a little later on. As late afternoon approached, Pete could honestly say that he felt only an expected degree of trepidation and apprehension with regard to his mission. He felt as prepared as he was ever going to be to get underway.

His pre-event meal would understandably be relatively light, for there were a few inevitable butterflies in his stomach.

Pete did manage to get down pretty much all of a 'nuked' meal of frozen lasagna, garlic bread and a salad. He felt even more relaxed after finishing, hopefully a good portent of things to come a little later in the evening.

It was now 6:15, and as he stepped outside to enjoy an after dinner cigarette, a sense of melancholia swept over him. This was going to be the last time he would ever be standing on this spot enveloped by familiar surroundings. His apartment in this quiet neighborhood, his little Toyota that had served him so reliably, and all his neighbors, none of which he had experienced much contact with, but also had not aggravated him either. The bottom line quickly became crystal clear to Pete: he was standing there 'alone' and that wasn't going to change significantly as a result of anything he could initiate here.

While there, and for reasons unknown, he locked up the Toyota and decided that instead of walking the two blocks to get the ice, he needed to incorporate it into a quick trip over to the east side to confirm that Leslie has indeed shown up for her Friday appointments. It would be pointless to take his plan any further today if she was not where she was supposed to be. He still had plenty of time, so he jumped into the Mercury and zipped over there.

Surprisingly, the lot was nearly filled to capacity, causing Pete to come to a complete stop for a few seconds, so he could scan effectively, and hopefully find the ivory-toned Audi IV.

It was there, and as Pete breathe a deep sigh of relief, he was quickly able to discern that although it wasn't parked in its usual space, the angle was exactly the same. At this juncture, he remained steadfast in his conviction that even if it were located in the street or a block away, he would find a way to pull this off. On the way home, he picked up 20 lbs. of ice for the coolers. This left him with only two critical details to put into place, switching the license plates and arranging the taxi transport.

It was now 7:30 and dusk was rapidly descending on the smallest state in the union. As he finished tightening the screws on the antique white-with-black lettering New York registration tags, Pete felt comfortable with his resolve and completely in tune with whatever destiny might have in store for him.

His cat and tropical fish needed some last-minute attention to ensure their best chance of surviving. This included extra food for both and clean water for the fish. The cat had long ago adopted a slow-dripping spigot in the bathtub for her source of drinking water.

After they were tended to, it was approaching 8:00pm and time to call the Yellow Cab dispatcher to try confirming a pickup at Goulet's restaurant sometime after 8:30, but no later than 8:45. He was assured that this could be executed, especially after Pete told him he was willing to pay at least twice whatever the fare might be.

Pete now had to hurriedly transfer all the chilled food from the refrigerator to the coolers and then place everything in their designated strategic spaces in the Mercury. He also needed to look around for any possible items or detail he might have overlooked. There weren't any, leaving him only to plug in the night light, tape his farewell letter to the fridge and lock up the apartment.

The drive over to the restaurant was a short one, maybe five to seven minutes. Pete needed to find a spot to park that had a favorable chance of having a prolonged empty space directly adjacent to it. He would need to pull the Audi alongside in another hour or so, and his best chance of assuring that appeared to be in the furthest southern corner near a dumpster type container. His reasoning was no one would park there unless every other conceivable spot was taken.

This placed him at least 50 yards away from the restaurant entrance and in an area that was not too well lit. After he backed in and shut off the engine, his watch read 8:25, leaving him just enough time to scurry across the street and wait for his hopefully imminent taxi cab. So far, so good.

It arrived all right, heading in the wrong direction at approximately 8:38, and proceeded to turn around when Pete whistled and started frantically waving his arms. The lightweight jacket he had on was primarily to conceal the pistol he had slid somewhat uncomfortably but securely into the waistband of his chino trousers.

He had considered buying a holster when he bought the gun but didn't see one he felt was appropriate for his needs.

As the taxi made its way over to the east side, Pete initiated some chatter with the driver, mostly about the weather, and how beat up all cabs eventually become. His timing was still right on schedule as the driver slowed at the corner of Angell and Ives Streets. Pete gave him $20.00, $8.00 for the fare, and a $12.00 tip. It was now 8:54, allowing ample time for him to walk quickly around the block, and then zero in on a choice position in the lot.

His adrenaline was really beginning to percolate causing him some concern. It was a little too early for him to be this edgy, he felt. As he approached the lot from Ives Street, he needed to get to his vantage point and settle down some. He got an unexpected break of sorts, when he spotted where Leslie's car was now positioned. For some reason, it had been moved within the last couple of hours and was now backed into a space on the north side of the lot, close to the shrubbery, that Pete had hoped all along might come into play.

It didn't take him long to take advantage of his good fortune, and after briefly scanning the neighborhood, he made a beeline to a spot behind the Audi, where he wedged himself in between the car and the bushes. He had an unobstructed view of the door from which she would be leaving the building, and as he crouched down and checked his watch, it was 9:07 and counting.

CHAPTER THIRTEEN

Pete decided he needed to check his gun to be absolutely certain that the safety was firmly set. It was, and as he was about to finish exhaling the last of three deep breaths to calm down, the rear exit door swung open.

In a flash, there she was - his beloved Dr. Leslie Greer. She was coming straight at him and closing in fast. It was now or never, and as Pete silently whispered to himself "God help me," he felt a sudden burst of courage that seemed to elevate his whole body. He felt perfectly poised and ready to strike.

As she came around the front of the Audi, Pete heard the unmistakable beep followed by the sound of door locks releasing. In another instant and with the sound of her footsteps getting dangerously close, he heard her pull the rear door open, exploding Pete into action. He was all over her, rendering her unable or unwilling to scream, as his left arm and hand were quick to apply considerable pressure to her neck and mouth. With is right hand, he jammed the gun into her face while softly saying, "Don't make me fucking use this."

By now, Leslie's keys and briefcase were on the ground, forcing Pete to get even rougher than he had ever envisioned he could be. He had to twist her tiny body and pull her down with him so that he could retrieve the keys. Once upright again, he proceeded to open the driver's door. The gun was now briefly in his jacket pocket so that he would have both hands free to push and maneuver her into the car.

She was mumbling something into the palm of his left hand and struggling mightily to break free of the grip he now had on her right hand. He was twisting her right arm behind her back. Pete had to get her into the car fast, and he literally lifted her off the ground to move her closer to the front seats. With the next violent thrust of her body, the unthinkable happened.

Leslie hit her head on the top of in the doorframe, and millisecond, her whole being went frighteningly limp. There was no sound, no movement, nothing. This left Pete in a fleeting state of helpless panic. His mind, already racing almost out of control, wasn't capable of processing this. There wasn't time to adjust his perspective even slightly.

He had to move strictly according to what he had so carefully plotted out.

Pete placed Leslie in the passenger seat, where her lifeless body slumped over half on the backrest and half against the door. His hands were now shaking almost uncontrollably but that didn't stop Pete from finding the right key and somehow getting it into the ignition and starting the engine.

As he pulled out of the lot and onto Angel Street, Pete was numb. He didn't know what to feel. He had his unrequited love right there next to him, but she was, at the very least, distressingly injured. What the worst-case scenario might be he didn't even want to think about. He had to concentrate on driving within the speed limits and pay attention to all lights and stop signs. Paying such close attention was keeping him from doing anything more than making the briefest observations of Leslie as the Audi made its way toward Goulet's.

He hoped he would be able to determine a lot more once they had arrived over there. He could check her pulse and her breathing, for starters. He was hoping against hope that he would be able to detect at least a measurable degree of both. He had taken vital signs dozens of times in his years working first in a detox, and later in group homes.

As he pulled into the lot, he was thankful that there was room to pull in alongside the Mercury, which would make it a lot easier to effect the necessary switches. He could not afford to remain there more than two or three minutes, yet he desperately needed to know that Leslie was still alive. For now, all he had for lighting was what the interior lights of both cars could provide. His flashlight was in the trunk, and there wasn't time for that. He decided he needed to gently move her into the back seat of the Mercury so he could attempt at least a cursory assessment of her condition.

As he lifted her, he held his forefinger on the inside of her wrist. He was more than pleased to find a slow but steady pulse. As he laid her down, he was also quickly able to ascertain that her chest was rising and sinking, at what rate he didn't know yet. At least it indicated an observable respiration. He had yet to locate the wound, and before he closed the door to the Audi, he tried briefly, but he couldn't see any signs of blood where her head had been resting on the drive over.

Pete felt they needed to get moving quickly away from her car and to one of the larger rest areas on the Massachusetts Turnpike. His feeling was that once there, he could examine her in more detail. With any luck, he could try some things that hopefully might revive her.

Before sliding behind the wheel of the Mercury, Pete elevated Leslie's head slightly with a pillow and covered her with a light blanket. She looked so helpless and innocent, his heart sank as he asked himself, "In God's name, what have I done?" As he turned the Mercury onto Route 146 for the thirtyfive-minute ride to I-90, he turned off the radio and set the air conditioning on low so that if she were to generate any sounds at all, he'd have a much better chance of picking them up.

The irony of what had just taken place was now becoming painfully evident to Pete. He had envisioned this particular segment of their encounter as being the most difficult and challenging, with Leslie bound, gagged and struggling, at least the first hour or so. Instead, she was unconscious, and paradoxically, he was left longing for even the slightest sound or movement from her.

Now, he had to force himself to nurture only the most positive and constructive of possible scenarios. It had only been thirty minutes or so, there were still many things he could try once they reached safe rest area. The traffic was light, and although the road is pitch black for long stretches, it is a divided highway. With the hi-beams lighting the road a good 300 feet ahead Pete felt comfortable enough urging the Mercury up to 70 mph. He knew this road well, and rarely, if ever, had he seen the local police or state police patrolling it.

His mind now shifted focus to what remedial type item she might have at his disposal and how he might best utilize them. He had ice and water and the first aid kit he had bought for $30.00 appeared to be capable of dealing with a large assortment of injuries. He was positive it contained at least one of those "gel type" ice packs and provisions for abrasions, contusions, cuts, burns and who knew what else. Would there be any smelling salts or ammonia? Pete could only hope so at this juncture.

As Pete swung onto I-290, he knew it would be another 30 or 40 minutes to a decent rest area, and the revelation of a lot more discerning information that would, no doubt, weigh very heavily on Pete's and Leslie's immediate future.

As much as Pete tried not to, he couldn't help feeling a staggering sense of guilt and failure as he headed west on I-90. For the first time in his life, he had committed a premeditated act of violence and had hurt not just some random victim1 but someone he cared for more than life itself.

Pete steadfastly refused to beat himself up over his transgression of not taking a split second longer to make sure her Head would safely clear the roof, and it didn't take him long to accept that now he would have to deal with this consequence as best he could. He had to have faith that somehow, some way, her condition would gradually improve, and if it didn't, that scenario would have to remain inconceivable.

It wouldn't be long now, as he passed a sign that informed motorists that a full-service rest area was a mere 18 miles ahead. Pete now, relenting just a bit to the anxiety and ever-increasing sense of desperation, applied a little more pressure to the gas pedal. He fully realized that by the time they arrived at the rest area and he began checking Leslie more closely, more than an hour would have passed since she lost consciousness. That in itself was cause for serious concern.

His mind started examining some of the unpleasant and daunting possibilities that could result from Leslie's injury. Did she have a skull fracture which could present frightening obstacles, or hopefully a concussion, which with time and patience should lend itself to being somewhat manageable? As he approached the rest area, Pete couldn't dismiss the extremely troubling reality of how long she has apparently been "out." Alleviating his fear only slightly was the fact that he couldn't be absolutely sure that was the case, since he hadn't been able to really observe her since they left the restaurant parking lot.

It had only been an hour, but with her injured and Pete not yet able to discern how seriously, it seemed like much, much longer.

At a little after 10:30, Pete exited I-90 and slowly made his way through the huge rest area to a far corner where only a few parked cars were scattered. It wasn't surprising, given the hundred plus yards one would have to walk to access the facilities available at either the Roy Rogers eatery or the Sunoco service station.

First of all, He needed to access the flashlight from the trunk, which would prove invaluable in his efforts to assess the nature and severity of Leslie's condition. Over the years he liked to think he had accumulated something more than a "pedestrian" awareness of at least the symptoms of a variety of injuries. What he wanted to observe most was what, if any, reaction her pupils would have to a direct beam of light. They should either dilate or shrink when stimulated. No discernible movement would not be a very good prognosis. The result he would equally dread encountering would be traces of blood in her nose or ears. A severe skull fracture can damage the veins and arteries that surround the brain and cause a 'bleed'.

Pete prayed silently that neither of these conditions existed. The next few minutes were going to be more critical than any he had ever anticipated facing in his entire life. He had already taken a bold step that has placed him beyond the point any return. He had perpetrated a kidnapping, and the victim was not only still with him, but was incapacitated. This made him a fugitive. If all that wasn't distressing enough, the fact that it might have all been for nothing was Pete's worst possible nightmare. Suppose Leslie was in dire need of emergency medical attention? Would he be able to access that for her without leaving himself completely vulnerable? He could not fathom how this could be a viable, acceptable option.

It was time to get some tangible answers, so with flash light in hand, he climbed in next to Leslie and straddled the backseat as best he could. He purposely closed the door behind him cutting off the interior lights momentarily so that the effects of the beam could be maximized. With a thumb he gently lifted Leslie's left eyelid and took a mental picture of her pupil's size and bearing and scrutinized intently any discernible expansion or shrinkage.

The result was encouraging, for Pete was certain he had seen a constrictive reaction which is what he had hoped for. With his spirits now lifted, he repeated the procedure on her right eye. This time it was even more apparent. Both her pupils had reacted in a normal manner to the light.

Pete followed up with a close inspection of her ears and nose ·for traces of blood and breathe a deep sigh of relief upon not finding any. He felt reasonably confident now in concluding that this injury probably had sufficient indications to suggest a rather severe concussion. Ideally, Pete could seek out some measure of confirmation, treatment and prognosis at the nearest ER; however, that wasn't in the cards for now.

He now needed to find out exactly where on her head she suffered the blow. He knew that clearly visible outward signs of physical injury are not always present, but he thought it had to be in the frontal or top sphere of her skull. He began to feel around and through her hairline and upper forehead, and it didn't take long before two of his fingers came upon a lump just above her hairline, pretty much aligned with her right cheekbone.

Further inspection with the flashlight didn't reveal any breaking of the skin or scalp, but there was definitely a pretty good-sized lump there. With what he had discovered so far, Pete felt a renewed sense of optimism, and he was far from stymied yet. He was determined to try everything in his power right here and now to bring Leslie around, at least somewhat. His degree of success, or the lack of it, would very much dictate what his next move might be.

First, Pete went back to the trunk to access the first aid kit, along with some water, ice and a clean cloth. He placed them on the floor in the back of the car. He now would need the interior light on, and with the flashlight, he was ready. He wasn't sure where to begin, so he gently lifted Leslie and cradled her on his right arm and shoulder. With his left hand, he slowly and softly dabbed her face and forehead with the cloth he had dampened with ice water.

In Pete's opinion, she didn't feel abnormally warm to the touch, and her skin color didn't appear flushed at all. She was wearing a three-piece pantsuit, either dark blue or black, with a printed, loose-fitting teal top. On her feet were a pair of above the ankle, black dress boots with a heel of about an inch and a half. Next, Pete resorted to some soft cajoling and pleading into her left ear while gently rubbing her neck and upper chest with an ice cube.

As he was about to finish with the second cube, Pete was sure he had detected a slight moan or groan and slight movement of her arm and upper body.

He was now even more eager to continue and felt that this may be an appropriate time to attempt to get a small amount of water into her. As he reached for another cube, it happened again; she released a distinct whimper as he gently slid the ice across her lips in a slow and deliberate side to side motion. Pete continued to verbally spur Leslie on, and she responded with a slight cough when some melted ice trickled down her throat.

It was now time to find out if he had any consciousness-enhancing inhalants, such as smelling salts, in the first aid kit. Pete gently laid her down on the pillow so he could begin his search in earnest. The gel ice pack he found right away and put aside, for he definitely wanted to apply ice to that bump on her head. The kit seemed to have everything, all kinds of bandages, antiseptics, ointments, tape and even some eye drops.

Before he could finish his search, he was interrupted by something he had only caught a glimpse of. There was a vehicle with bubble lights moving very slowly through the parking area. It was still a few rows away, and as Pete exited the car for a better view, he was able to identify it as the blue and gray colors and unmistakable emblem of the Massachusetts State Police. There appeared to be only one trooper inside, but that was enough for Pete to decide he didn't want to stay there any longer than it took for him to slide behind the wheel and get himself, Leslie, and the Mercury out of there.

It was much too early for them to be the focus of any search by the authorities, but it could definitely be easily perceived as suspicious for Pete to be observed in the back seat of a car with someone in Leslie's less than responsive condition. Pete hastily made his way back to the turnpike, still heading west, and as well as he was able to determine, with no vehicles of any kind following them.

This latest development had rattled Pete a little, causing him to now think in terms of distance and lodging. He figured it was maybe 80 or 90 miles to the New York border and another 60 or 70 to the other side of Albany.

Pete hoped he could find a suitable motel a little removed from the "beaten path." A check of the dashboard clock told him that it was now 10:55, and he quickly calculated that he could cover the 160 miles, even with a short stop to check on Leslie, in less than three hours.

Feeling somewhat comfortable with his decision, Pete set the cruise control on 72 mph and spontaneously started talking loudly to Leslie, hoping to penetrate and awaken her senses in a more conventional manner. He still had the car stereo that he could crank up if and when he got tired.

As the Mercury hurled through the central Massachusetts night, it came upon some thick pockets of fog draped over the lowlands. This demanded that Pete slow down some and concentrate solely on what was in front of him. This momentary diversion, however, didn't prevent his thoughts from meandering ahead to what genre of possible scenarios might unfold once they were in New York State and had found an appropriate place to spend the night.

Pete was now fairly confident that he would be able to revive or resuscitate Leslie to a reasonable degree of consciousness; however, that could prove to be only one of the ensuing dilemmas he might find himself facing. She most likely would endure a plethora of residual symptoms from this injury. Although some could be relatively brief in nature, others could linger for much longer. He couldn't help visualizing a Leslie who was woefully lethargic, abnormally sleepy, confused and maybe even dizzy and forgetful. In short, she might not be anything like the spitfire he had anticipated locking horns with.

If Pete's concerns in this regard ultimately proved to be justified, his plans and objectives for this journey would have to be altered dramatically. His first impressions of how all this may all eventually play out were not too positive. He didn't see how it was possible to share any meaningful or tender experiences with a woman that he had not only taken by force, which in itself would be something to overcome, but someone he had injured physically and emotionally debilitated in the process.

Pete began to feel sick to his stomach as all these probable ramifications slowly started to shape themselves into this perception of what his reality could become.

This would require some piecemeal digesting by Pete. He turned on the stereo, cranked it up a couple of notches, and tried hard to envision what he might possibly be able to extract from such an uncompromising scenario. For starters, she would be incapable of being combative and inclined to attempt escapes at every turn. Perhaps, she would come around enough to recognize him, but not remember how or why she is where she is. Pete would then be able to hold and cuddle her virtually at will; he couldn't imagine that being too difficult to deal with.

For the time being, there was a toll coming up in Stockbridge, the last town in western Massachusetts. He felts a slight sense of relief as he paid the $4.20 and speeded up toward the access road to the New York State Thruway. He had decided that his only additional stop now would be very brief, just long enough to scan his National Geographic Road atlas and find a half-decent size town on the other side of Albany. He was a bit irritated with himself for not researching this much earlier, and it was too dangerous to try now, with the car moving.

As he slowed at the next booth to grab his ticket, it was 12:20 a.m. and the official beginning of his and Leslie's first full day together. In spite of the troubling setback, they had both suffered, that fact had a stimulating feel to it, at least for Pete.

Before accelerating away from the stop too quickly, his field of vision spotted an area where he should be able to stop inconspicuously and pick out an imminent destination. These huge interstates are usually conveniently funnel shaped so that 8 or 10 toll booths are channeling traffic to a normal 4 to 6 lanes.

After a slight pause to allow a few cars to clear, he nimbly maneuvered the Merc over to the safety of the paved stopping area.

After turning on the interior lights, and making a cursory observation of Leslie, he quickly fingered through all the urban/ suburban cities and towns surrounding Albany, until one jumped up at him. It was Amsterdam due west of the capitol city with a parallel road, State route #5, that would provide easy on and off access. With that taken care of, Pete hit the gas with such force, the tires squeal and propel the Mere up to turnpike speed in no time.

His mind now shifted focus to what kind of requirements any decent motel would have to offer to accommodate what Pete and Leslie would need. Without question, it would have to be a room on the lower level so he could carry her in easily and transfer all the food and luggage without undue strain. A refrigerator and kitchenette would be great and as far as sleeping or resting, either one king or two queen size beds would suffice.

This establishment would also have to accept cash, and if that is a potential problem Pete was prepared to offer a sizeable deposit to mitigate the issue. His plan was to register under the alias of Mr. and Mrs. Michael Andrews of Buffalo, N.Y. He has already committed the plates on the car, BEF 9642, to his short-term memo.

Pete's adrenaline was once again starting to bubble, and he was edgy and hungry. The excitement and cumulative stress leading up to, and including, the last four or five hours had been taxing for him. He really hadn't been able to eat, drink and relax enough to keep his metabolism from going off kilter. As for Leslie, what was done was done, and all he could do was pray that she hadn't suffered any lasting or permanent damage.

His train of thought was suddenly interrupted as he spotted the sign for the Route 5 exit. He was pleased to see the familiar icons that indicated access to fuel, food and lodging. A quick check of his gas gauge shows it was more than one-half full and not an immediate concern. As he made a careful left onto a winding and hilly state road, he needed only to travel a mile or so before his eyes made contact with just the kind of large neon sign he was in search of. Its name was quite fittingly The Adirondack Motor Lodge since it is located at the foot of the Adirondack Mountain range. Their vacancy light was a welcome sight and shined brightly into Pete's longing eyes.

As Pete swung onto the property to get a sense of the layout of the buildings and grounds, he liked what he saw. He pulled into a spot near, but not right next to, the office. After he made sure the Mercury was locked up tight, he paused momentarily to whisper a soft prayer: "Lord, please help me to restore Leslie to some sense of normalcy and guide me as I try to make the best of this unfortunate situation."

CHAPTER FOURTEEN

It was 1:40 a.m. when Pete pulled open the plexiglass door of the motel office and made his way to the counter. After being greeted by the elderly gentleman on duty, he inquired as to the availability of a room, preferably around back, away from traffic noise. There was no upper level, so that concern had evaporated. The clerk scanned his key pegboard for a moment before announcing, "I've got one on the other side #138, with a king-size bed, kitchenette and full-size refrigerator, but those units are only rented for two-night minimums." Pete didn't hesitate, and shot back, "How much?" The gent replied, "$89 per night and Pete answered, "I'll take it, but it's got to be a cash transaction, I'm not carrying any credit cards this trip." The clerk pushing the registration card toward Pete said, "That's fine, as long as you pay in advance", and then jokingly added, "We can't have people sneaking out, leaving us holding the bag."

Pete chuckled as he offered, "I understand completely." The total with taxes came to $191, so as Pete finished registering, he laid four $50 bills on the counter. The clerk gave him his change, the keys and stressed that check-out time would be 11:00 am Sunday, unless they decide to extend.

As he returned to the Merc and stood alongside it for a brief moment, Pete was struck by how clear, crisp and quiet the night could be at the foot of these mountains. It had a distinctly soothing effect on his frazzled nerves.

He now felt, having just secured a safe room for Leslie, just a little bit better about facing the challenges that without question, he would be facing.

The timing, at almost 2:00 a.m., could not have been much more conducive for the transferring of Leslie from the car to the room. The lights were off in all but a handful of rooms, and there wasn't a soul on foot anywhere in the parking area. With conditions so favorable, he backed the Merc up to the room entrance, and went inside to get a sense of the layout. After a quick walk-thru, he proceeded to unload the food and luggage, and last but not least, the limp body of his unrequited love.

Pete was pleasantly surprised by how immaculate and spacious it was, including the bathroom, which had both a shower and bathtub capability, a feature he planned on putting to good use, very shortly. Once Leslie was placed on the bed and covered with just a spread, Pete began putting all the perishable food in the fridge, which thankfully had been left running and was immediately capable of keeping everything cold. The room was just a little 'musty' smelling, so Pete decided he'd best put the A/C to work at a low setting, if for no other reason, than to just circulate the air. The clothing could be sorted out later, for right now, he wanted to concentrate solely on trying to bring Leslie back to the "living".

Pete emptied the entire contents of the first-aid kit onto the floor and began foraging through it piece by piece so he would know exactly what he had at his disposal. Whatever might be missing, he would have to seek out in the morning. As everything scattered around him, Pete's eye immediately felt an 'inkling' that maybe his little prayer of twenty minutes earlier may just have been answered.

As he sat back on his heels while kneeling on the carpet, there was no mistaking these two little cloth capsules that had rolled off in two different directions. He had a good idea what smelling salts looked like, and these little 'babies' fit that picture. As he grabbed one, and turned it over to read the miniscule label, it was clearly marked 'ammonia inhalants', 0.33ml, causing Pete to smile broadly, as he whispered to himself, "These will do the trick just as nicely."

Pete was happy as a 'pig in shit.' He now had a double dose of potential remedies for Leslie: some ice-cold water in the bathtub to attack her body from the outside, and these powerful agents to infiltrate her inner neurological reflex senses.

He couldn't wait to get started as he hurriedly stuffed all the other first-aid stuff back into the kit and made a beeline to the bathroom to start filling the tub with the coldest water the tap could furnish. He concluded that once it was 3/4 full, he could even lower the temperature more by adding the ice left in one of the coolers, just before easing her in.

It briefly became a concern that this icy water might have the potential of dangerously shocking her system; however, he felt he had few options other than risking this 'all or nothing' attempt. He knew he'd be right there to lift her out after just a few minutes.

Before he began removing her clothing, Pete felt a visceral inclination he just couldn't resist. It was the perfect moment to just lie down next to Leslie and hold her while whispering close to her ear, "Fear not my sweet, I'm going to make you feel a whole lot better very shortly."

Undressing her proved to be a 'captivating' experience for Pete. He couldn't help wondering how wonderfully exhilarating it might be under more favorable circumstances. However, for now it wasn't, and that fact required that he focus exclusively on the task at hand, reviving his sweetheart.

After gently removing her top and bra, and lying back down, Pete's intuition directed him to try listening to Leslie's heart. That little effort proved extremely encouraging, as he had no difficulty picking up what undoubtedly was a strong beat, in a very steady rhythm.

The bathtub was now full enough, and after he dumped about 5 lbs. of ice from the cooler in, it was definitely cold enough as well. It was time to lower her in gradually, and see what if any reaction this might bring. He had already brought a pillow from the car into the bathroom1and placed it on the edge of the tub.

He also had the inhalant capsules in his shirt pocket in an attempt to optimize this all-out effort.

As he approached the tub, Pete was holding Leslie in much the same manner a new groom would as he was about to carry his bride across the threshold of their first home. Once there, he slowly bent his knees and leaned forward until her feet, legs and then her buttocks were in the icy water. An instant later, he was sure he felt her left hand and arm exerting some slight but distinct pressure on his neck and shoulder. It was unmistakable. She was instinctively trying to hang on, a reflex response against the sensation of falling or being weightless.

It was definitely a huge positive sign, so as Pete continued to lower her, he loudly called out her name, "LESLIE, DR. GREER; IT's PETE MASTERS, AND I'M TRYING TO HELP YOU; YOU ARE GOING TO BE ALL RIGHT." With this stimulus and her whole body now virtually submerged, her eyelids began to lift slightly, and goosebumps began to sprout up all over her torso and limbs. Pete knew he couldn't leave her in that frigid water more than a few minutes, so as he gently leaned her head on the pillow, he reached into his pocket for one of the ammonia capsules.

As he cracked the first one open, he brought it up to within two or three inches of his nose to make sure they weren't stale. He quickly and shockingly discovered they were anything but.

In fact, they were so potent his nostrils were burning so much that he had to check for a nosebleed while his eyes filled with water. Quickly, Pete began moving the stinging aroma in a side-to-side motion, again about two or three inches from Leslie's nose, and within a few seconds her head lurched back and to the right. Her arms and legs also started recoiling uncontrollably in the water. She was indeed on her way back, he couldn't help believing.

Her eyes were now more than half open, but she was still very much dazed, eliciting from Pete as he took her little face in his hands and looked in her eyes, "Leslie, I'm here for you", he professed slowly and forcefully. "There has been an accident, and I'm going to take care of you, please trust me."

All Leslie could manage was to whisper ever so softly, "water" as Pete tried to facilitate his comprehension of her effort by focusing on her lip movements. He asked, "Are you thirsty?" to which she slowly nodded her head up and down. It was time to get her out of that water, dried off and into something warm and comfortable she could sit up in bed for a spell. He felt it was imperative to maintain any and all manner of stimulation, at least for a while, and maybe much longer, if necessary.

As Pete lifted Leslie out of the tub, she made, with only minimal prompting, some effort to hold onto his arm and shoulder. To him it felt good to have her willingly dependent upon him, even if it was only a gesture as simple as a safe carry from the bathroom to the bed. He knew she really wasn't capable of making a conscious, considered choice in the matter at hand, but so what: the whole theme and purpose of what was happening now was largely predicated on that same dynamic. She hopefully would be doing lots of things she might not otherwise find in harmony with her sensibilities.

Pete proceeded to dry Leslie off thoroughly and then slip her into some sweatpants and a matching jacket. As he was about to finish zipping it about half-way up, she once again made a weak attempt to pronounce what sounded like "water". Pete in a flash was back from the fridge and at her bedside ready to spoon feed her, much like a baby, and see where that might go.

She looked reasonably comfortable, propped up on pillows at the head of the bed, but still very drowsy and only capable sporadic slow and seemingly involuntary muscle movements. She seemed able to swallow without distress, and with Peter squeezing the bottle for her, managed to slowly ingest a good 4 oz of water. By then, Pete was starving and glad he had prepared some macaroni salad to go with the turkey sandwich he brought over to the bed.

The pasta also might be something Leslie would be able to get down, if not enjoy just yet, he felt, as he grabbed the TV remote from the nightstand and clicked it on. The constant sound in the room would be a plus, especially while he was busy trying to eat.

Pete, after finishing his meal and lighting a much-needed cigarette, was in dire need of at least some sleep. He had succeeded in getting Leslie to nibble at a few bites and a soft drink; however, she remained quite groggy, thus reinforcing his notion that she too, could benefit from a prolonged nap.

It was 3:15 am when he slid out of his chinos, climbed into bed next to her and prompted her into a position on her side, enabling him to slide one arm under her pillow and with the other hold her close. Once that was accomplished, he couldn't help kissing her softly on the cheek and rapidly drifting into some much-needed slumber.

Pete didn't hear or feel anything until sometime after daybreak, when he heard voices and door slamming from the room next to theirs. It startled him some, so he jumped up and peeked through the drapes to see a couple loading their SUV in what apparently was an effort to check-out. A glance at his watch informed him it was a little after 7:30 a.m. and a little too early for either he or Leslie to get moving. It felt wonderful to just lie next to her and cuddle for a while and let her hopefully stir herself to consciousness in a more normal fashion.

After twenty minutes or so, she did awaken on her own, and although her back was to Pete, he felt a strong sense that she knew who was lying next to her and holding her. Perhaps through some integrating process that had transpired since last night, he had that feeling. Or perhaps it was merely wishful thinking!

Leslie did manage to ask two pertinent questions while they lay there, and before she moved at all Pete didn't hesitate to answer them. First came, "Where am I?", to which Pete responded, "New York state," and then "How did I get here?" His reply was, "I drove you here." There was no discernible emotion or sense of desperation in either her body or voice. She apparently needed answers only to those specific curiosities for the time being.

Pete had answered truthfully, but did not volunteer any Details or additional insight into what was really happening, yet. He needed to assess if and how she might assimilate each morsel of information as it was offered to her. As he turned her ever so gently towards him, he could clearly distinguish that her eyes were still glassy, and there was no way right now of gaining even a vague sense of what might be going on inside that pretty little head.

Instead, he asked if she needed to use the bathroom, and she slowly but surely nodded a yes. Pete helped her to her feet and walked her over to the toilet. After a few minutes, he heard the flush, the door open, and saw Leslie leaning against the door frame, obviously disoriented. Pete sensed that she needed some assistance, walked her over to the bed, sat down next to her, and began stroking and grooming her tousled hair with his fingers. At the same time he said softly, "Leslie, we need to eat something. They have a continental breakfast here."

Pete continued, "I'm going to run over to the office and see what they have; it shouldn't take me more than ten minutes, OK?" Leslie nodded slowly but approvingly, so Pete quickly kissed her on the lips and leaned her gently on the pillows he had propped up for her. The TV was already on, so he turned up the volume a bit, and left.

He wasn't comfortable with the idea of leaving her alone but felt reasonably certain she was in no condition to either plan or execute any manner of escape.

At the office he was able to make off with two coffees, a bagel and a Danish. They also had orange juice, but Pete wanted to use up what he had brought along. When he returned to the room, Leslie was dozing. She stirred some as he closed the door behind him, and promptly opened her eyes upon being addressed somewhat aggressively.

Pete placed the breakfast items on the little dinette table, quickly moved over to where the suitcase was perched and removed a good size leather bag filled with toiletries. Displaying what he had, as he once again sat on the bed next to her asked her, "Maybe you will feel better if you freshen up; I have a new toothbrush, deodorant, some mouthwash and a comb and brush just for you." It took time for her to respond, but she did answer "Oh", and slid over to the edge of the bed, so Pete could help her to her feet. Once in the bathroom, and with everything laid out in front of her, she managed her tasks quite well.

From the bathroom it was only a few steps to the kitchenette where Pete pulled a chair back and carefully guided Leslie to it. With the OJ already there, Pete placed both the bagel and Danish in front of her, hoping she might choose one. After a pause, he slid his chair over next to hers, broke off a piece of each and held them in front of her. She responded by taking first the bagel, chewing and swallowing it, and then reached for some Danish.

Leslie was making slow but steady progress, and after drinking about half her coffee, she had another surprise for Pete. While leaning forward and with her chin resting in the palm of one hand, she uttered quite distinctly one very significant, six letter word: "Doctah." He was taken aback, somewhat; however, he didn't hesitate to acknowledge or confirm her declaration by responding very explicitly, "Yes, that's what you are, but right now you are out of commission". Given her subsequent silence and bewildered appearance, Pete had no way of knowing how much if any of his answer had been duly processed.

Apparently, some fragmented facts, at least subjectively, were beginning to emerge from the fog that had shrouded Leslie's consciousness since she suffered that injury. Pete was keenly aware that many symptoms associated with 'post-concussion syndrome can mysteriously clear up in hours; for others, it can be much longer. He didn't fret, for his original expectation had always been geared to dealing with a feisty, cerebral Leslie, and he looked forward with great anticipation to hopefully being favored with the opportunity to experience that challenge. Right now, he couldn't think of any possible scenario that would please him more.

CHAPTER FIFTEEN

Pete needed to step back and reexamine his logistic objectives and perhaps gain some sense of a new perspective as it might relate to the immediate future. He had this perfectly appropriate room for another twenty-seven hours, and in all likelihood by now, Leslie has been unaccounted for and the authorities have been alerted. So far, Pete had only distanced himself from the crime scene by a scant 160 miles. He wondered whether his chances were better on the move or holed up here, regardless of Leslie's condition.

As he gazed across the table at a lethargic and confused hostage, he had to concede that there was no possible way of assuming if, and when, she might recapture some of her 'spunk' and 'vitality'. After mulling this over for a few minutes, Pete decided on an aggressive, proactive strategy to address the most daunting dilemma he faced: Leslie's restoration.

It was time for the two of them to hit the shower together, and after, he would attempt to engage her with some pertinent question and answers. At the very least, this would supply her with some truths and facts as she tried to piece together a picture of herself, Pete and the situation as a whole. From now on, he would be virtually a non-stop source of verbal stimuli and see where that approach might lead them.

With that mindset firmly in place now, he stood up and announced to a startled Leslie, "Come on, we are going to indulge in a rejuvenating shower", while simultaneously taking her hands in his and leading her to the bathroom. If she had any qualms about sharing this experience with Pete, they went unnoticed; in fact, it seemed to energize her in ways nothing else had. She was able to suds up and even shampoo her hair successfully, without wobbling too much at all. Pete was close by and managed to suppress a moment of unadulterated "lust" and a brief but intense erection that he quickly squelched, and she never got to see. Pete could only find solace in repeating to himself, "There will be more appropriate chances".

After showering himself and then helping Leslie dry off and slip into her sweatsuit, Pete again took her by the hand and led her to the dinette table. After warming up the coffees in the microwave, Pete sat down across from Leslie and began his 'probe and disclosure' exercise. He started with, "Do you know who I am, Leslie?" After a brief pause, she haltingly replied, almost as if asking a question "a patient?" Pete continued, "Can you remember anything at all about our relationship at the Center?" She answered, "Not really, just your face." Pete again, "Are you afraid of being here with me, Leslie?" Obviously – perplexed, Leslie answered, "I don't know yet." Pete then in his most reassuring voice offered, "If I were to tell you that I care for you very much, would that put you at ease somewhat?"

Leslie tried to process what Pete had just said for a few seconds, and responded with, "Somewhat, I guess." Pete again, "Well, I do care and promise that you will be safe with me."

Surprisingly, Leslie then took the initiative and asked, "Why are we here in this room?" Pete hesitated momentarily, and while holding both her hands in his, replied "We are here because I wanted to be with you more than anything else in this world, and while trying to make that happen, there was an accident, and you bumped your head." Leslie appeared to be trying hard to understand all that Pete's explanation might imply; however, her focus persisted on the question she had just asked, compelling her to appeal once again, "But why are we here?"

Pete finding himself utterly incapable of sharing anything less than the outright truth with Leslie at this point, blurted out, "I brought you here so we could be together, and as God is my witness, I had no intention of hurting you. I am now a fugitive and need you to cooperate as best you can for the time being. Can you understand and accept that for both our sakes?" Leslie obviously had difficulty grasping the implicit desperation in Pete's voice, but did manage to offer, "I don't think I can answer to all of that, right now,"

Pete, without making any effort to construct a more appropriate, less threatening reply, shot back, "I don't want to scare you, but you really don't have a lot of options."

Pete left it alone at that, and quickly regained his perspective and decided that Leslie had more than enough 'reality' to digest for the time being. He briefly entertained the option of throwing everything back into the car, securing her somewhere within it and hitting the open road. The other choice, the one he would eventually embrace, seemed to be more potentially productive. He would spend some therapeutic or constructive time with Leslie, while they both went about pondering their individual and collective situations.

Fortunately, while planning this adventure, Pete had the foresight to bring along a few choice items that might prove to be just what was needed for their predicament. As he grabbed the bag containing the games, Monopoly, Yahtzee, and a book of word search puzzles, he invited Leslie to join him on the bed for a little cerebral exercise.

Leslie didn't respond right away or initiate any movement, prompting Pete to do a little exploring. He needed to get some sense of what could be going on. He asked if she was feeling OK, and she answered directly, "My head is hurting." Pete told her to stay right there, as he went about fetching two Tylenol that she was able to ingest with some water.

The "game playing' would have to be put on hold. She needed rest and some time to let nature hopefully work its wonders. After getting her an ice-filled wash cloth to apply to her forehead, Pete encouraged Leslie to relax and leave everything to him.

Pete had no choice but to now accept that his most fruitful approach would lie in gaining whatever trust and confidence Leslie might be inclined to allow. In so doing, he would suggest and even invite her input, as he tried to formulate a workable agenda for them that would outline tentative plans on a daily, and if necessary, hourly basis. He was convinced it would be the only barometer of insight available to him that kept him abreast of any progressive or regressive clues to her recovery, or lack thereof.

For the time being, Pete was content to lay quietly on his side next to her and make certain her ice wrap was fresh and positioned properly, and that the room was peaceful. Not knowing if she was awake and could hear, Pete instinctively began thinking out loud and said softly, "If you're up to it later on, we can take a nice drive through some of the nearby Adirondack Mountains." He almost fell off the bed when Leslie quickly and concisely replied, "Fine!"

Pete was understandably content for the moment in this tranquil setting with Leslie peacefully at his side. That didn't prevent some of his thought processes from jumping ahead to a time, perhaps very soon, when things could be very different. He was in no hurry whatsoever to trade in the current state of affair for one that was virtually guaranteed to be significantly more adversarial and fraught with mistrust. That scenario would, however, exemplify in most respects what he had originally bargained for.

Pete could only hope that Leslie could not, at least for a while, dredge up any recollection of the brute force he utilized to gain control of both her body and mind. He was 99% sure she was also incapable of evoking any images related to the gun he had concealed, at least for now. Pete was not looking forward to the inevitable circumstance or crisis that would require that he brandish it again. He would very much prefer a less threatening alternative; however, if one existed that could prove to be quite that intimidating, it escaped him.

These were not the kinds of ruminations Pete enjoyed entertaining as he drifts off to sleep. They were unsettling and disturbing to his subconscious, and invariably resulted in a distressful and taxing slumber.

When he awoke a couple of hours later, for a second or two, he was panic stricken. Not only had Leslie vanished from his side, she was at the foot of the bed apparently rummaging through the clothing still in the suitcase. Before the cobwebs had a chance to diminish even a little, she had a bra still in its package, and while waving it back and forth asked, "Is this supposed to be for me?" Pete still groggy and stunned, replied encouragingly, "Oh, yeah. I hope it's alright; we can always pick up whatever else you feel you need anytime you want."

Leslie's intonation and curt reply, "This is not how I dress," succeeded in putting Pete on full alert. Very quickly, he needed to sort out and assess what might be happening. He reached two fairly obvious conclusions. At least for the moment, Leslie is feeling capable and confident enough to take charge of her physical appearance and knew what steps to initiate in this regard. The question now became, will she feel a similar inclination toward the more threatening considerations of her overall predicament?

The suspense would not linger, for after five minutes in the bathroom, Leslie emerged and while obviously no longer braless, she pulled up a chair at the dinette table. With surprising purpose and clarity she began with, "This is not where I should be. There are more important things I need to be attending to."

Pete, content with absorbing whatever she was offering voluntarily, attempted to probe just a little deeper, "Where do you feel you should be, and what specifically needs your attention?"

Leslie seemed to be struggling to identify and coordinate her thought processes, until eventually offering somewhat meekly, "I don't know. I just feel very strongly that someone, somewhere is waiting for me." Pete was somewhat relieved, and to a degree, satisfied that only "splinters" of Leslie's past were churning, probably non-stop at this point, within the deepest recesses of her subconscious. Apparently, grasping them and making any kind of congruent connection was still a major problem for her.

Pete was still convinced that his most effective strategy in this regard would be consistent and pragmatic verbal stimulation, limited to the 'here' and 'now.' Pete was fully aware that his efforts to invigorate Leslie could very well result in the sharpening of a 'double-edged instrument. Leslie could once again assume her spunk and vitality and present a daunting challenge, which was fine; however, her capacity to also become an unyielding adversary would hardly be a reality anticipated by Pete with any degree of enthusiasm.

Nonetheless, Pete was wholeheartedly committed to the effort, and in that vein, approached Leslie with, "If you're feeling a little better, why don't we take a nice drive up through those splendid mountains? I'll bet the views are awesome once we're up 5,000 or 10,000 feet."

Leslie's eyes, unable to disguise her befuddled expression, didn't keep her from offering, "I still have a slight headache, but I do want to get out of this room." With that affirmation, Pete quickly dug through the suitcase for the new Nike socks and sneakers he had bought for her just for a moment like this. A few minutes later, except for her flat affect, Leslie was on her feet looking pretty damn good.

It was late afternoon in the foothills of the Adirondacks when Pete finished helping Leslie secure her seatbelt, pulled out of the motel parking lot, and aimed the Merc towards Route 30, heading north. It was a windy, uphill climb all the way, and definitely a gas-guzzling drain on the car; however, the scenery and fresh air were wonderful. Leslie seemed to be far away and lost in her own bewilderment, as evidenced by one cognitive observation she offered about half-way up the mountain, "This landscape doesn't look anything like what I'm familiar with, and where I need to be." Pete tried reassuring her with, "I promise you that you will be back there soon enough, and perhaps you might try taking advantage of being 'here', now."

Leslie, a little later on as Pete was turning the car around to head back, for the first time addressed Pete by his name. "Pete, how long have you and I known each other?" He paused for an instant, then answered truthfully, "Almost three years." Instead of then following up with what Pete was expecting, she threw him a curve. "Why do I feel so strongly that I shouldn't be close to you?" Again, Pete stayed close to the facts, without volunteering more than she might be ready for. "Perhaps because you are a mental health doctor and have to be cautious at times, until you feel it's safe to trust someone."

If that rationalization seemed confusing to Leslie, it was at least in part intended. The puzzled expression on her face suggested to Pete that he had succeeded. He could only imagine the scope of what Leslie must be dealing with at this juncture. He couldn't help thinking how much we all take for granted, when it comes to this manner of 'functioning'. Always knowing who and where we are, where we've been and what we are trying to accomplish at any given time. To lose one of these faculties would be daunting enough. To have them all 'jumbled' simultaneously was virtually unfathomable.

Pete did a lot of ruminating as he cautiously guided the Merc down the twisting two-lane blacktop back to Amsterdam.

It was almost dark when they hit route 5 and by then, Pete was feeling hunger pangs. Leslie had dozed most of the way down the mountain, and he didn't see any reason to wake her as he first spotted, then headed for the drive-thru window of a Kentucky Fried Chicken establishment.

As he paid for his order and put the bags of chicken, Cole slaw and mashed potatoes on her lap, she awoke and once again, appeared puzzled as to where she was now, which even under the best of circumstances would be easily understandable. Pete delicately tried to penetrate her fogginess with, "I hope you like fried chicken, Leslie." As she gathered herself and sat up, she answered, I'm not really sure, but it does smell good enough to try."

On the way back to the motel, Pete decided to fill the gas tank of the Merc so it would be ready to roll in the morning.

He couldn't help wondering if by then, Leslie would be a willing traveler, especially if she improved enough to realize that heading in a westerly direction would only take her further away from where she felt she belonged. She seemed a bit more focused once they were back in the room and feasting on their KFC, thus prompting Pete to "test the waters" a little with, "Tomorrow morning we'll be heading in the general direction of Chicago". "Why do we need to go there?", Leslie shot back.

"Because heading that way is part of our adventure," Pete matter of factly, replied. "Adventure", Leslie exclaimed, and then after mulling the inherent implications of such a statement for a few seconds, added, "That is not at all what I need to be a part of right now. "Where are the people that I know and the places I am familiar with?"

Pete, convinced that he could not waiver, even the slightest, reminded Leslie that HE was the architect of this journey and would make all the decisions for now related to where and when they might go. He also added, "Leslie, you would not have come with me under any conventional conditions, so I had to remove you from all the people and routines you are accustomed to for the time being."

Leslie at this point had eaten all she wanted and had definitely had enough of Pete's 'power trip'. As she got up from the table, she kicked off her sneakers and yelled, "You bastard, you had no right to take me anywhere." She then threw herself onto the bed and buried her head in a pillow. She appeared to sob and whimper for a bit, which came as no surprise to Pete. He felt it would serve no purpose to overreact. After all, this was part and parcel of what he had expected from the very beginning. It was time to be composed and patient.

CHAPTER SIXTEEN

While waiting for Leslie to settle down some, Pete felt it best if he distanced himself from the emotional upheaval and did so by sliding a chair over in front of the door that she would have to pass through to exit the room. Hopefully, this might convey to Leslie in some indirect manner that it would be futile for her to think in terms of leaving abruptly.

Pete also felt it imperative that he acknowledge and attempt to 'buffer' her perceived plight by employing some heartfelt and soothing diplomatic dialogue. "You are absolutely justified in believing it is selfish, inconsiderate and unkind to do any of this to you, but I honestly didn't feel I had any choice. In time, I hope I am capable of helping you understand, at least somewhat, how I came to feel so desperate", Pete softly added.

If Leslie was receptive or inclined to relate to any of this, she gave no such indication. She did turn over placing her back toward Pete, and after a half-hour hadn't uttered a word. This entire development caused Pete to start thinking in terms of precautions and perhaps some security considerations. How aggressive he would have to be would be solely determined by how uncooperative and contentious she might be. Time would tell.

Pete's foremost agenda for the immediate future was when tomorrow morning comes, Leslie was in the car and fit to travel.

From now on, he anticipated being engaged or challenged by her in some manner of 'mind games', probably more so than any physical battles. He was even willing to concede that she might very well win her share; however, he hardly considered himself a novice in this regard, and welcomed the opportunity to go head-to-head with her.

What did seem to be relevant and critical at this juncture were the residual symptoms of her concussion. She was still drowsy, nodding off and would probably sleep for extended periods of time. If that was indeed the case, and it was temporary. Pete could utilize her lethargy as an ally. In this vein, he seized upon the opportunity presented with her current slumber to unplug and hide the phone and to pack a few things for tomorrow.

After finishing, and turning on the TV, he couldn't resist the urge to call out her name and 'jostle' her enough to bring her around. He had to get a sense of what scenario might lie immediately ahead, and that couldn't be achieved by watching her sleep. She responded half-heartedly with, "What do you want?" Pete answered, "I need to know what kind of companion you're going to be for the next day or two." Leslie, now lying on her side and facing him with her legs pulled up in a 'fetal' like position, replied quizzically, "Why do you want to know that?" Because I have to be prepared to see this through, one way or another, and I would prefer that we might work out some manner of understanding that won't require that I have force you to be cooperative," Pete answered, "What kinds of cooperation are you specifically referring to?" Leslie stoically asked of Pete.

"What I'm referring to is the two of us eating, sleeping and moving about without you screaming, trying to escape at every turn, or attempting to disable me while I'm preoccupied and in the process of trusting you." Leslie couldn't resist raising her voice and exclaiming, "You trusting me! I think you've got this seriously perverted." Pete smiled for a second, then responded, "There are a couple of factors you need to be aware of. I have a gun, some rope and duct tape, none of which I really want to subject you to; however, if necessary, I am prepared to do so in a heartbeat. Secondly, I have made a vow not to sexually assault or rape you. That I fully intend to abide by, so please examine the overall picture before you make any critical decisions."

Leslie, now sitting up and appearing remarkably alert, seemed to weigh her words carefully, as she offered, "I am not going to fight you, and I really don't know at this point what you feel you're going to accomplish, or what it is that you want from me. How can I believe anything you say in light of what you have already done?"

Pete, needing desperately to secure at least some marginal acquiescence from Leslie, tried in vain to hold her hands in his, and said, "I will release you at some point, unharmed; I promise you that on the lives of my children and grandchildren. Her curt response was far from assenting.

"Yeah, and just when might that take place?" Pete wasn't about to employ any manner of deception in this regard. She was in for the duration, and the sooner she accepted it, the better. "I have no pre-planned time frame. More than a week, and probably less than two, is as honest and accurate as I can be right now."

Leslie threw herself back down on the bed, rolling onto her side and lay there silently. Pete checked the alarm clock on the nightstand, it was 10:45, and his feeling was that they both needed rest before embarking on a five-hundred-mile journey tomorrow morning. He wasn't comfortable yet with their state of affairs, so he approached her again by gently lying down next to her and with one arm pulled her close. She was rigid and remained silent, as Pete, now with tears welling, appealed, "I know this seems all wrong, especially for you, but it doesn't have to be a tragedy. You'll have a long rewarding life after this is over." Leslie too, had been weeping silently and managed plea of her own. "It is more than all wrong, it's despicable. You have children and grandchildren. How can you think anything of them, and still throw your life away like this?"

Pete glared at Leslie for a second or two before making it crystal clear. "I have considered very carefully every conceivable risk, consequence and, yes, loss that could be associated with this deed. I feel in my gut that spending significant, concentrated and uninterrupted time with you is a desirable tradeoff. It's that simple."

Leslie broke away from Pete's grasp and sat at the edge of the bed for a moment, before offering, "I'm still not able to remember much of anything about my past, never mind yours; so how can I be expected to feel safe, and believe your motives are what you say they are?" Pete reflected for a second, then, "The last thing I wanted to happen, did. I didn't want you to be hurt or incapacitated in any manner, so that you would indeed be yourself in every way, shape and form. My feelings for you were born and nurtured over a span of three years, and apparently until you are capable of remembering some of that, and what your sense of me might be, you're just going to have to trust me.

Looking more and more exasperated, Leslie said, "You want me to agree to something, when in reality there are no other choices. I find that hard to accept. My instincts are telling me I need to employ any and all measures necessary to survive.

I can' believe you are incapable of appreciating the fear and terror you have perpetrated on me, the very same individual that you profess to care for so much."

Pete, becoming increasingly frustrated, raised his voice a decibel or two." Unfortunately, there didn't seem any way around that; however, be that as it may, you can't convince me you prefer having a gun to your head or being bound and gagged for hours at a time. Either way, the result is going to be the same whether you choose to accept the present reality or choose to resist. Please take some time to think this through. I'm going to get some tea with lemon, do you want some?"

Five minutes later, Pete returned with a cup for each of them, and since Leslie had yet to respond, added, "Why don't you sleep on it while I try to rest in the chair over there."

In between sips of tea, Pete took some long and hard drags on one of his Winston's. It wasn't long before Leslie, who had hardly touched her tea, had pulled the spread up over her shoulders, turned over and seemingly drifted off to sleep. A little later, after convincing himself that their prior exchange of sentiments had gone well enough, given the circumstances, he decided to slide in next to her, trusting his inclination to be a light sleeper, especially under conditions such as these.

Initially, he had plans to set the alarm for a 6:00 a.m. rise, but decided not to on the hunch that Leslie would probably benefit from a more casual wake-up experience. A couple of hours later in getting on the road were hardly going to alter the overall scenario. They just wouldn't arrive at the next stop as early.

Pete experienced a very restless night, tossing and turning and feeling like he had done repetitive time check s at least two or three times an hour. When 7:15 a.m. finally did roll around, he had 'rested' enough and groggily forced himself to his feet. Leslie, seemingly unaffected by his unsettled night, had hardly moved at all and was still fast asleep.

His plan now would be to shower quickly and slip over to the motel office and help himself to some continental breakfast before she came to and noticed he was gone. Just in case, he'd leave the cold-water shower running and close the bathroom door.

Luckily, she was just coming around as Pete with his heart pounding at double time turned the key and reentered the room. He had enough breakfast to get the both of them started. However, the folly of leaving her alone for ten minutes still weighed on him. It was an inexcusable tactical error that could have been disastrous. Anyway, she was still there, and obviously quite groggy as he put the cardboard tray on the table and meekly said, "Good morning little lady." By now she was on her feet and trying to feel her way toward the bathroom.

Pete was sure he heard a faint but distinct response of "Oh, hi," as he rushed to help her and subsequently to also turn the shower off.

As he was setting out the bagel, Danish, juice and coffee, Leslie reemerged, and Pete invited her to sit down at the table, which after a little hesitation, she did. Pete had decided at some point during his restless night to try letting Leslie voice her thoughts before he would inform her of his plans and conditional itinerary for the day.

There was an 'eerie' silence for a few moments, while they both nibbled at their pastry and swallowed some coffee, until Leslie broke the stillness with, "What kind of plans do you have for me when we arrive at the next destination of your agenda?" Pete had gone over in his mind for weeks, how he might respond to dialogue of this nature, and he felt no need to deceive or embellish his response even the slightest. "I don't have any plans FOR you, or to do anything TO you. I want us to spend time in the company of each other, so we can come to appreciate each other in a very special and unique manner." Leslie, sounding more like a 'probing' psychiatrist, didn't beat around the bush. "When you use terms like 'special' and 'unique,' are you expecting a sexual experience to be included?"

Pete didn't hesitate to answer, although he hadn't figured on dealing with this specific issue quite so soon. "As much as I would treasure an open, honest and shared sexual participation with you, I do not have any predisposition that dictates I make sure that is realized, solely for my own satisfaction. I have done that in my life and found that in the end, the value of the experience was greatly diminished. That is no longer a concept I can embrace and aspire to repeat."

Leslie, apparently disinclined at this point to pursue this particular line of Q&A, made one last ditch effort to deflate Pete's fantasy, and dissuade him from any further efforts. "How can you really expect to share quality time and experiences with someone who doesn't want to be with you, and wants desperately to be somewhere else?" Again, Pete's answer had been virtually rehearsed and thus on the tip of his tongue. "My dear, and sweet little shrink that is what is the essence of what this is all about? For three years now, you have seen fit to limit yourself to this incomplete and very business-like perception of what you think I am, probably in large part, formulated from your 'Diagnostics and Statistical Manual'. This encounter will be my only opportunity to enhance and broaden your insight significantly, and perhaps require that you see me as a 'whole' person."

Leslie's reluctance to take this exchange any further became obvious as she shook her head from side to side while throwing her hands up in frustration. However, she did cautiously and matter-of-factly offer some perspective for Pete to take under advisement. "I have already made it clear that I will not fight you on a physical level, but that doesn't mean I won't try to demean and deprecate most of what you seem to think is so inherently principled and decent about this whole 'contemptible' picture." Pete could only offer, "I understand and accept your position completely, at least for now."

With that off her chest, Leslie got up from the table and while asking Pete, "What else have you got in here that I can wear?", went over to the suitcase and started rummaging through its contents. Pete came over to join her, halting her foraging for a second as he said, "There is another outfit in there, but I can hardly see the need to put it on, unless you're planning to join me up front as a peaceable companion." Leslie, obviously perturbed, shot back, "I'll be damned if I'll let you 'hogtie' me; I'll go with you, but you better be on your guard every step of the way."

Pete's response, though silent, conveyed a powerful message all its own, as he retrieved his pistol from a bureau drawer where he had hidden it. He held it out in a deliberate conspicuous gesture, removing the clip, reinserting it, and then pulling the slide back to allow a bullet to enter the chamber. Leslie's heart began to beat a little faster; she had never been that close to a loaded gun. The sight and implication of its potential horror, sickened her.

That done, Pete quickly added, "I guess we're almost ready to travel. Leslie could only retreat to the bathroom, slip into her outfit, and surprisingly, when done sprucing up, gather all the toiletries and return them to the suitcase. Before leaving, Pete helped himself to some ice from the freezer, finished his coffee, and with Leslie's help put everything back in the car.

CHAPTER SEVENTEEN

As Pete guided the Merc back onto I-90 heading west, he was experiencing an uneasy calm as he asked himself, "Just what could Leslie be implying with that 'alert' she had red flagged to him back in the room. And, would he be able to maintain some kind of barometer of her intentions by simply observing as best he could. It didn't take long, maybe fifty miles or forty minutes into the day's journey, when his curiosity compelled him to put out a feeler.

"How would you feel about driving, say every other hundred miles?" Leslie turned toward him and snickered, "Ask me in a hundred miles." Pete nodded silently, then settled back as he tried to take in the comforting landscape of the medium sized farms, meadows and tiny towns that are sprinkled aesthetically throughout upper New York State.

In less than an hour and a half, the odometer had turned over 100 miles. Pete still felt relatively relaxed and didn't bother to mention any switching, as Leslie appeared content to remain silent, chew gum, and work somewhat feverishly on n her nails. This silence presented a troubling concern for Pete to somehow mitigate. It was the one ingredient of his 'design that he felt he would have little or no control over. He couldn't envision enduring ten to fourteen days of Leslie just 'biding' her time and refusing to interact at any conceivable level, except when she perceived it as absolutely necessary. Even more disturbing was if indeed this would be her coping strategy, what resources did he possess that might neutralize or offset it.

It wasn't long before he would have to adjust his focus to a more immediate concern: how and where to relieve themselves. His unease also extended to lunch. However, that could be dealt with later. They had been on the road for 2 1/2 hours, and Pete needed to stretch and take a leak.

At this point he was adamant about not trusting Leslie to vanish into one of the gargantuan restrooms on the turnpike. Eating would be a minor detour, since they still had a variety of things self-contained to snack and hydrate with.

In an attempt to get a feel for Leslie's notions in this regard, Pete threw out, "It would be nice if you could drive a little, and I need to pee, but we can't stop at any of these commercial rest areas." She responded quickly, "Then what are you expecting us to do?" Pete answered, "There are a couple of options available to me. That's not the problem. My concern is whether you choose to drive or not. I can't have you disappearing into any ladies' room on this interstate." Leslie, indignantly retorted, "Oh that's nice, what did you have in mind for me?"

Pete answered, "I guess you have three choices: there's a urinal in the back seat, the woods, or we can detour and seek out a small gas station or restaurant somewhere." It didn't take her long to choose. "The last one is the only one acceptable to me, and I will get behind the wheel for a while after that."

Pete had major reservations about letting her out of his sight for any reason but would hold off on describing in rigid terms the conditions under which he would concede just enough to allow her only this fundamental dignity. A few minutes later, he spotted an exit in Auburn, about twenty miles past Syracuse, that displayed icons indicating the accessibility of some appropriate facilities.

The last thing Pete wanted to do was put any ideas in Leslie's head; however, he did feel it necessary to clarify' any doubts she might harbor of what might take place should she bolt or enlist the aid of strangers. "Do you know what will happen if you try something really stupid?" Leslie's curiosity seemed provoked. "Tell me", she answered. Pete with fire in his eyes and a menacing voice, said, "I will run you down and fucking shoot you in the back if I have to, and the same goes for anyone who might be near you, OK, so you better think long and hard before you drag any innocent bystanders into this."

Leslie, appearing startled, paused briefly then said, "I'm not going to give you any sick excuse to fire that gun, and also, don't expect me to put any faith in anything you say, either."

Pete willingly acknowledged Leslie's heartfelt declaration, which compelled to him to respond, "I realize what I just said, and how it came across; and if it seems extremely threatening and intimidating, it should." I have made up my mind not to fail here and cannot allow you to leave one minute sooner than I feel is necessary to consummate our experience together. If that is difficult for you to accept or understand, that's the dynamic we will live with."

With that, Pete exited the thruway in search of accommodations that might fit his criteria. It wasn't long before he spotted a regular size Shell service station, and as luck would have it, slid into a parking lane only fifteen feet from the restrooms. As he turned off the ignition key, he reached over with his right hand to gently caress her left, and said softly, "Please try to meet me half-way on some of this, and nobody has to get hurt, OK?" Leslie didn't pull her hand away, and while peering straight into Pete's eyes, replied, "You are asking of me more than any reasonable person can be expected to give in this situation. I don't want to see anyone hurt or killed, not even you, so I will do whatever is necessary to keep that from happening. Any more than that, I can't promise."

Pete took that as satisfactory assurance and promptly opened his door, went around to hers and extended his hand once again, which she cautiously accepted. The men's room door was locked, the ladies' was not, so Pete quickly let her go, then hurriedly almost in a panic, made his way to the office front of the service station. As he returned to the side of the building, passing the ladies' room door, he felt a burst of anxiety, while struggling to muster enough blind faith that Leslie would still be inside and had not disappeared into the nearby woods.

Pete hurried through his business and was greatly relieved to come upon Leslie, exiting from hers at virtually the same time. As he passed her on his way to returning the key, he smiled and inquired, "Do you still want to drive, and how about something to snack on or drink?" She didn't return the smile but did answer as she made her way around the car to the appropriate side. "I'll try driving for a while, and if there's any iced tea or lemonade that's cold, that would be good."

Pete assisted her in adjusting the seat and the steering wheel, handed the iced tea to her, and in a few minutes, they were back on I-90, still heading west. Pete's initial hope was that if she felt up to it, she could stay behind the wheel until they approached a bypass close to Buffalo. As he instructed her on how to set the cruise control at 75 mph, it appeared to him that her ability to concentrate and judge distances had not been discernibly impaired. That established, he still could hardly expect to close his eyes and passively relax. At this juncture, and perhaps at any future interval in this odyssey, that would be expecting way too much.

To see Leslie behind the wheel definitely had an encouraging aura to it, Pete concluded. To him, they were literally and figuratively heading in the right direction. With her condition seemingly improving by the hour, he couldn't help believing that just maybe all the predetermined goals he had aspired to for so long were still alive and possible.

In that vein, he felt compelled to seize the opportunity presented to him while she was awake, alert and couldn't move to chip away at some of her guarded, clinical armor and peck away at the impassive facade she up till now, had proven so adept at maintaining. He felt the most productive results might arise from his sincere attempt at enlightening her to some of the history and details of their prior three years. After all, if her memory was still seriously impaired, she would have little choice other than to at least hear him out and accept his account as first-hand information, if nothing else.

The more he thought about it, Pete began to cultivate the idea of relating to her a complete, and on her part, willingly complicit fabrication of what had transpired between them. How could she with any degree of certainty believe any different? Given that scenario, how would she then avoid feeling at least some sense of responsibility or culpability for the current state of affairs between them? It was all very tempting, in fact so much so, that he cautiously determined and then convinced himself that a little circumstantial invention had the potential of being a very useful and persuasive implement, one that was right there at his disposal and much too valuable to dismiss out of some impeding and delayed sense of conscience or moral judgement.

Pete reluctantly decided to allow Leslie a period of grace, on the faint hope that she might adapt voluntarily to her circumstances and forgo the need for him to deceive her. As they moved steadily toward their next destination, he felt just for a brief moment like the "cat who just swallowed the canary." How long he dares to postpone his incursion into

Leslie's consciousness became a concern, for the partial or total recovery of her memory could occur at any time, rendering all his diabolical efforts virtually useless.

She had settled in nicely to her present task. The Merc was chewing up miles rapidly. In the absence of any meaningful dialogue from her, Pete found himself unable to resist for long the chance to get some kind of fix on just how her recall capabilities might be functioning, "Leslie, I feel a a very strong need to bridge this awareness gap that obviously y exists between us." Turning toward Pete, she quizzically offered, "Exactly what void are you referring to?" Pete, struggling to find the right words answered, "I mean, do you have any sense at all of just how all of this might have evolved, maybe from my perspective, or even yours, for that matter?"

Leslie hesitated for a few seconds and then, "I'm not sure how important that is at this point; it's this abhorrent criminal act that you ultimately executed that I am most concerned with." Pete was now getting revved up a little, continued, "Yes, I understand that, but you must agree that something like this just doesn't blossom out of thin air." He had to be careful now; he couldn't have it both ways. He needed to adhere to broader, more abstract statements that would not sabotage his ploy of embellishing the actual truth. Pete did, however, have one more salvo to fire. "I can assure you that you are not a random victim, and this deed of mine should not have come as a total surprise to you."

Leslie's blank expression, and sad, inquisitive brown eyes, suggested very strongly to Pete that she was unable or unwilling to relate to any of what may have taken place during the period in question. Instead, she chose to focus on his transgressions and even got somewhat adamant. "I can't believe that anything I may have innocently done or been remiss about played much of a part in inspiring or fostering these heinous choices you have made of your own free will." Pete reacted perhaps more quickly and aggressively than he wanted. "How can you possibly fucking know that; you of all people have got to be aware that we all project some kind of dynamic or communication while inter acting with people, and it just doesn't evaporate into some vacuum. Opinions are voiced, feelings are expressed, and then there is this sense of our own uniquely appealing look that we hope others might notice.

So please, do not off handedly dismiss what is, and isn't possible. You're much too shrewd for that."

The expression on Leslie's face left little doubt that she was not in agreement with Pete's 'take' on her unwitting contribution to her own fate. In fact, her irritation level seemed to be rising considerably, as evidenced by the manner she was now pushing the Merc to dangerous extremes. She had disengaged the cruise control and was leaning on the accelerator until the needle was bouncing at 90 mph, while she weaved from lane to lane avoiding slower traffic.

Pete in shock for a few seconds, managed to yell at her to "slow down", which she initially ignored, until he pulled the pistol from his waistband, stuck it in her ribs, and put his other hand on the ignition key. He was ready to boil over him self, as he emphatically imparted to her, "I don't know what you're trying to prove or pull, but it's not going to work.

If your idea is to attract law enforcement, the only thing you're going to accomplish is getting someone shot, and it just might be you, so pull over to the first lane and stay there until I tell where and when to stop."

Leslie, looking precariously close to a meltdown, finally complied and after easing down to 60 mph, blurted out, "I can't go along with this madness, you bastard: it's cruel and mercilessly unfair of you to take advantage of me like this. "Why are you so determined to destroy me; what satisfaction can you possibly derive from possessing someone who barely knows her own name?"

Pete couldn't help being affected by Leslie's outpouring of pain, vulnerability, and frustration. It was so out of character and spontaneous, he felt paralyzed for the moment.

Instinctively, he wanted to take her in his arms and comfort her and try his damndest to convince her everything would be OK. He couldn't do that because right now her prospects were anything but OK, and he was unable to make any promises that might convey a possible way out for her.

By now, the Merc was off the road, on the shoulder, and with her little hands still clutching the wheel, Leslie was sobbing. Pete didn't say a word, instead opting to shut off the engine and remove the keys from the ignition. There was a travel size package of Kleenex in the console, which he opened and placed on her lap. The hazard lights needed activating, so he did that too, then slumped back in his seat for a breather.

He had to think this through; his emotions were not as raw as hers, but they were chafed and sending him all manner of mixed, conflicted signals. They had to be sorted out before he could address this situation, and then perhaps, he could formulate a strategy for their immediate future.

CHAPTER EIGHTEEN

Pete was concerned that his sense of purpose was in danger of being compromised, and that his instinctive need to be compassionate toward Leslie could prove to be his Achilles Heel. He was also keenly aware of what that might cost in the long run. He would, in effect, be elevating her needs above his and he was not sure that was a road he could afford to go down. This journey was predicated on the empowerment he achieved and ultimately utilized, not the other way around. She had already had her opportunity as the advantaged, and to some extent that was what led them to where they are.

Right now, his intuition dictated that they shouldn't be sitting on the side of this road any longer, so as he slid up the center armrest, he said softly, "Look, Leslie, we can't stay here. It's too conspicuous and dangerous; slide over here, so I can drive. I promise I will try to talk this out with you, whenever you are ready." She didn't move or respond right away, her mind seemingly a thousand miles away, so Pete felt it necessary to slide one arm under her thighs and the other around her back, lifting her over to the passenger side. It was an awkward, strenuous undertaking, and his back let him know it, as a sharp, burning twinge of searing pain radiated through its entire sensory pathway.

Pete managed to negotiate his way around the perimeter of the Merc in halting baby steps and gingerly slide himself in behind the wheel. Once there he muttered, "What the fuck else can go wrong here?" as he started the engine and goosed the vehicle up to highway speed and into the traffic flow.

He wasn't about to sit there very long in silent agony, so an attempt at extending an olive branch to Leslie quickly followed. I don't know how far ahead you're thinking, or just how terrible you feel this experience will ultimately be, but I'm fairly certain you may be getting way ahead of yourself. None of this is written in stone, and I am willing to try and help you with your memory; besides, being a mental health professional, your skills are probably best utilized when you at least try to negotiate or mitigate some manner of conciliatory resolution! That should strike a familiar chord with you, since it's a proffer I have heard from you verbatim, on many an occasion."

Leslie may have been listening, but wasn't talking, not yet anyway, so Pete continued," I can fill you in on some of the details of your practice, at least at one location." "The other, all I can tell you is that it exists, where you maintain an office, and that it is flourishing. "Do you have any sense at all of what I'm referring to?"

Leslie appearing drowsier than stimulated by any of this virtually put an end to any further exchanges, by offering, I need more than bits and pieces of information from you. How about some medical attention, and some familiar faces and surroundings, if you really want to help me." Pete chewed on these suggestions for a few seconds, realizing fully that the consequences of what she was implying were not acceptable, and as graciously as he could, acknowledged her requests with, "It's highly probable that your injury related symptoms will resolve themselves, if you will just allow them some time. You are not alone here, and the other scenarios you feel are so necessary will also come to pass, in due time."

Leslie, seemingly more resigned to these elusive truths than frustrated at this juncture could only reply, "With circumstances as they are, I can only hope now, can't I?" and turned away. Pete had to guard against becoming increasingly doubtful and uncomfortable with some reservations that were beginning to take shape in his fragile perspective. He was more than a little concerned that his well-intentioned goals might be in danger of realistically being unattainable and that specific outcomes were no longer feasible. He hadn't even for one second, in any of his preplanned scenarios, anticipated reckoning with a Leslie, who was only a hollow resemblance of the spirited, feisty, and cerebral little dynamo that he had come to know, desire and ultimately decided to trade the rest of his life for. It was a sobering, numbing prospect, one that he now had to keep telling himself he could be premature in giving too much credence to quite so soon. As he slowed to pay the $10.50 toll at the end of the New York State Thruway, he checked his watch, providing a good reminder that this in fact was only day #3 of his all or nothing odyssey and much too early to be entertaining anything but encouraging, reassuring thoughts.

It was late Sunday afternoon when they left the Empire State in the rear-view mirror, and Pete's focus would now switch to zeroing in on a small town in Ohio (Elyria), where he had once spent a night when he passed through here on a much different kind of journey back in 1991. It was maybe fifty miles west of Cleveland, and he remembered it primarily because of its easy access, food and fuel availability, and clean, convenient lodging. His calculations, he felt, should put them there no later than 7:30.

Leslie, no doubt still experiencing some post-concussion symptoms, and perhaps some residual effects from her emotional discharge, seemed comfortable enough, dozing with her head leaning half against the backrest and half on the interior of her door. Pete could only wonder what version of this complex, confused little lady would wake up this time.

While she lay there, Pete couldn't help appreciating how appealing and even enticing a picture she conjured up. Her helplessness evoked a desire in him that suggested he should make an effort to pamper her in every conceivable fashion.

What Pete needed to balance these impulses with was the understanding and acceptance of whatever her mood or state might be when she woke up. Chances were there would be a series of radical adjustments all along the way: a test of wills with whatever guile each of them could muster.

Pete asked himself if maybe suggesting that they indulge in a little shopping, might appeal to Leslie. It might prove to be somewhat cathartic in that it was an activity a preponderance of women seems to indulge in in order to find relief from stress, boredom, frustration and who knows what else. He had complete faith in believing that she wouldn't attempt anything potentially disastrous as long he was armed and close by. The only provision would have to be no dressing or fitting room excursions.

Leslie woke up as they were approaching Cleveland and the stunning shores of Lake Erie. Her disposition seemingly some what improved, she asked Pete in a distinctly civil tone, "How much further are we going?" "About another fifty miles or forty minutes; I know a place there that I've stayed in before," Pete answered. "Oh", Leslie quipped and then, "I'm really hungry. Can we get some decent food once we get there?" Pete was so pleasantly surprised, he didn't give it a second thought. "Sure, I'd be glad to accompany you to a respectable restaurant, if you feel you're up to it. What kind of cuisine do you ordinarily favor, or is that still a mystery also?"

Leslie thought for a moment before, "I really don't know. Maybe I can look at a menu and something will tempt me." Pete said, "Fine, we can check out some places before we check in; you look OK, maybe you can just brush your hair a little."

Pete was hungry too and delighted at the prospect of sharing a sit-down meal and perhaps even a small amount of meaningful conversation. He had no idea what may have prompted the changes in her disposition, and other than being naturally curious, he didn't really care. It did, however, provoke some wonder how long it might last.

After managing to find the right exit for Elyria, Pete again checked with Leslie to confirm that she would prefer dining before they checked into the "Great Lakes Motor Inn" that was only two minutes removed from the Ohio Turnpike on state Route 2.

Leslie answered quite emphatically, "I'm hungry now; maybe we can find a family type restaurant without too much trouble, I would think." Pete in a totally agreeable tone, "Ok, if that's what you want, that's what we'll do," and proceeded to follow the arrow on a familiar directional icon, picturing a dinner plate with its accompanying knife and fork. Within minutes they were approaching a quaint, medium-sized wooden structure, whose sign at the roadway's edge spelled out, "The Crow's Nest, Elegant Family Dining." As he pulled in to look for an appropriate place to park the Merc, another bit of posted information alluded to their specialties and variations of steak, seafood, chicken and pasta dishes. As Leslie opened her door, she voiced her approval. "I should be able to find something appetizing enough here."

Pete couldn't help being a little surprised and even seduced by the invigorating spring in Leslie's step, as she walked in front of him and made her way to the entrance. It reminded him of the occasions at The Center when without fail, she would come out to waiting room to greet him for an appointment, and then move so briskly toward her office, sixty feet down a hall, that he couldn't help feeling that his customary, plodding gait was impeding her normal pace and causing her some concern. He had always felt intimidated by that dynamic. Right now, though, it was a welcome sight: first a healthy appetite, along with some rediscovered energy, and then perhaps a bit of pertinent and focused dialogue. "What can be next?", he asked himself.

At 7:45 on a summer Sunday night, the restaurant was barely half-full, and after a reactionary frown from Leslie, they were seated in the virtually unoccupied smoking section. Pete had noticed the full bar situated smack in the middle of the establishment when they entered but hadn't given it a second thought until a waitress approached them at their table. Leslie offered the customary 'ladies first' deference, wasted no time in ordering some white wine, or Zinfandel, and by doing so, unwittingly introduced a whole new element to their equation.

Pete for the last eight plus years had by necessity adapted himself to this manner of scenario, by quickly inquiring of the waitress the availability of a fruit juice selection, and it had served him well so far.

On this particular occasion though, for some patently irrational reason, he allowed himself to get caught up in the spur of the moment, and chose to ignore his undeniable aversion and tortuous history with alcohol. Instead, he matter-of-factly ordered a Johnny Walker Black Label on the rocks, which after the waitress left, precipitated a knot in his stomach, as he tried desperately to engage the depth of Leslie's bereft, brown eyes. Pete couldn't distinguish the exactness of what he longed for at that precise moment; however, there would be no redress: if she needed a drink, so did he. They were, after all, in this together.

Leslie, with all her faculties functioning at her normal standards, would have been keenly aware of Pete's history of chronic, acute alcoholism, and likewise his subsequent and considerable length of sobriety. However, this was not the rendering of the clinical and astute young doctor who was sitting across from him right now.

Pete didn't imbibe at all until she had already sampled her wine a couple of times, but when he did, and that first swallow hit bottom, the effect on his senses felt instantaneous. It was as if he had swallowed some kind magical potion or elixir.

Pete felt a 'tingling' sensation in every fiber of his body, and a warm glow. It was as if a long-lost love affair, had been miraculously 'rekindled'. The only question now being, would he still be as vulnerable as he had always been to this insidious, deceptive 'seductress'.

After ordering their meals, while nursing their respective drinks, the dialogue was limited to some rather terse observations related to the immediate surroundings. Pete tried in vain to lighten the mood with some wispy banter, however Leslie was all but irretrievably distracted in her own thoughts.

Thankfully, the food wasn't delayed long, and his spaghetti and meatballs and her scrod with baked potato were by then, eagerly anticipated. They proved to be excellent choices, and based on the manner in which she attacked it, Leslie apparently was every bit as famished as she had declared. Pete found it satisfying to see her enjoy this innate, simple pleasure.

His hunger also had been satiated, but his back although not quite as bad as before the scotch, still ached. Almost predictably, this would proffer and lend credence to the 'notion' that the proper amount of eighty-six proof Johnny Walker, just might eliminate his discomfort altogether. Pete gave this equation some serious consideration, and ultimately concluded that the only circumstances under which he would subscribe to such a reckless undertaking, would have to be with her also agreeing that having a bottle in the room, was a desirable option.

The six ounces of wine didn't seem to effect Leslie in any obviously discernible fashion and as she was about to finish, Pete said, "You seemed to enjoy that; do you feel a little better now?" "I guess there's a part of me that does," was her curt reply. Pete then made another suggestion. "Why don't we order some dessert to bring back to the room, along with a bottle of wine?" He got a decidedly mixed response. "The dessert sounds like it might hit the spot, if they've got anything rich and chocolaty; the wine I can do without."

Pete accepted Leslie's 50/50 proposition, and while summoning the waitress for a dessert menu, a sobering realization crept into his consciousness that helped finalize the deal. On a Sunday night, liquor stores are most likely closed, and he wasn't in the mood for beer, probably the only option available. At least for tonight, he would honor her wishes to the letter.

She settled on a humongous piece of German Chocolate cake, layered with strawberries, and he ordered a wedge of lemon meringue pie. Pete couldn't help thinking, Where is this petite and obviously calorie disciplined little lady going to put that? As Pete paid the tab, he checked his watch, it was 9:30.

Within a half-hour, they were checked into room #136 of the "Midwestern Motor Inn". Leslie had accompanied him into the motel office and conducted herself appropriately. In fact, she even picked up a copy of The Cleveland Plain Dealer, the local newspaper.

This room did not have kitchen facilities, which didn't matter a whole lot, since they would be leaving early Monday morning.

As Pete went about arranging the luggage and cooler in their proper holding areas of the room, he felt content in allowing Leslie to do her thing for now, whether it be silence, distance or whatever. Quite fittingly, this room had two queen sized beds, which afforded her an opportunity to choose whichever she preferred, get comfortable, and not have her space intruded upon, at least not right at the moment.

CHAPTER NINETEEN

Pete, while thinking in terms of overnight security, initially felt that he could let her go to sleep first, and then after blocking the door as an extra precaution, he would then slide into bed next to her. After some deliberation in this regard, he decided it would be better if she were made aware of his intentions beforehand. "You, of course, realize that I have to sleep next to you, so I can be sure where you are during the night; I trust that won't be a major hassle." Leslie, per using the newspaper while propped up on pillows against the headboard, didn't look at Pete, but managed to answer, stoically, "What do you want me to say, NO, you make my skin crawl, or how about, you don't have to take such extreme precautions, I won't try to escape; in either case, it's not going to matter is it?"

Pete felt a 'jolt' to his sensibilities upon hearing the first part of her offering, but didn't flinch one bit in his resolve. "Leslie, I have tried very hard to make this incursion into your life somehow tolerable. I have vowed to treat you with as much respect and dignity as is possible here; however, there are certain essential safeguards I must adhere to in order to protect my investment, so to speak. And that's you!"

Pete, once he got going, felt this was a fitting occasion to perhaps remind Leslie of a truth that apparently, she had failed to carefully consider or acknowledge. "If you really feel that allowing me to lie down next to you is that repulsive, you might try envisioning for a moment what your fate would be if I had no regard whatsoever for your dignity or honor, and instead forced you to submit to a variety of repeatedly disgusting experiences. I don't think I have to paint a picture."

Leslie pondered for a few seconds while seeming to sense that perhaps she had hit Pete below the belt, then said, "I apologize for being unnecessarily callous and insensitive; it's just that given the detrimental nature of this situation, and my limited options, I feel justified in somehow lashing out and trying to hurt you." Pete readily understood and let her know that he did, resulting in his feeling not quite so wounded, and eager to shift to something infinitely more pleasurable: their mouthwatering desserts. As he handed Leslie her cake, he smiled broadly and said, "Here, something sumptuous for a sweet little lady." She gently embraced it and answered, "Yeah, sure!"

The mood certainly wasn't jovial, but it had become far less contentious as they both indulged in their sinfully rich' pastries. Some iced tea from the cooler followed, and for Pete, it was time for a much-needed cigarette, which Leslie suddenly found so annoying and threatening. He playfully allowed her to both chastise and exile him to a far corner of the room. Considering that she did include 'please' in her admonition, Pete did her one better by standing in the open doorway and blowing all the secondhand smoke into the cool, clear night.

That done, he began to feel quite drowsy and virtually could have slept standing up; however, evidently, she wasn't and clicked on the TV. Apparently, she had been indulging in some serious cogitating while superficially holding the paper and came up with something 'out of the blue' that had all the earmarks of a "Let's Make A Deal" scenario. In short order, she felt it potentially worthy of presenting to him.

With a 'wily' smile she summoned Pete onto her bed for "something important", that required his undivided attention. His curiosity was 'piqued' as he sat down next to, and facing her, and with his hand holding her thigh just above the knee, said, "What can I do for you?"

She began with, "I remember you saying something about 'consummating this experience' before you could let me go, and that you felt it could take up to two weeks to accomplish whatever that might be. You also stated that the time frame was not etched in stone, am I correct so far?" Pete's attention was riveted to her sweet and 'pouty' little lips, as she tried so hard to articulate what was beginning to sound more and more like a proposition intent on placing him in a significantly less dominant, and substantially more compromising position.

Pete answered softly and unequivocally, while surrounding Leslie's hands with his, "Yes, that's exactly what I did state and still maintain. Are you finding that difficult to accept? That's our structured reality for the time being."

Leslie seemed to be reaching very deep within her for a few seconds, perhaps for what she felt might be her best trump card, then offered, "Well, there has to be some progression or sequence of events between us that will culminate in some manner of fulfillment; I mean, there has to be a beginning, middle and end, even to this, doesn't there?"

Pete still transfixed to where this dialogue might be heading, answered, "Yes, I suppose in theory there has to be; and in application, there will be, hopefully. "What is it, exactly, that you're trying to get at?"

Leslie now was desperately groping for the precise verbiage to put forth her, by now, extremely impassioned plea, one that would significantly alter whatever ominous agenda Pete apparently had plotted for her. There could not have been any prior such similar occasion in her relatively young life when she wanted and needed something quite so desperately, and it showed.

She began with," I don't believe what you are longing to realize with this escapade is within the realm of human relationship possibility, at least not from my perspective.

I don't think I am being dismissive, shortsighted or premature in concluding this. You obviously feel very strongly, otherwise."

Pete continued listening intently, as Leslie went on. "Now, be that as it may, it doesn't seem prudent to me that we must continue this charade for an undetermined or infinite period of time, when there just might be an alternative, we can both agree on, that will also afford both parties some measure of finality."

Pete is both amazed and intrigued by Leslie's sudden ability to consider and construct this critique of how she perceived everything to be, and also how she felt so capable of tentatively orchestrating its final resolution. This rendering was sounding more like the instinctively cerebral antagonist that he has prepared himself to encounter from the beginning. The only element he couldn't have envisioned and now painfully evident were the extremes of tension and strain, plainly visible in her body language, and the despairing passion in her voice.

Undoubtedly, this had to represent the highest stakes imaginable for this desperately vulnerable young psychiatrist.

Pete, at this juncture, felt totally compelled to assert in no uncertain terms, "With all due respect Dr. Greer, you have very little if anything to bargain with right now; it's way too early in this drama for that. But please, let me hear what you feel might possibly be an acceptable alternative. It doesn't hurt to listen and afford due consideration to anything."

The next few minutes were very difficult and painful. In all of his preplanned scenarios, Pete couldn't have prepared for what followed.

With tears cascading down her little cheeks, and her tiny body trembling, Leslie agonizingly managed to put forth, "I will do anything you want me to do, willingly and without reservations, for a period of twenty-four hours, if you will then promise to release me. This is extremely difficult for me to put into words, and even harder for me to accept as a viable option. I am desperate, and need my life back; the prospect of going another five-hundred miles in the wrong direction tomorrow, just for the sake of prolonging a fantasy that cannot possibly materialize, is sheer insanity. I'm very sorry, but that is the honest truth, and I think deep down you know that, too."

Pete maintained his silence and composure for a moment so he could organize his thoughts and allow Leslie ample time to calm herself. It was very distressing to see her in such a depleted emotional state. He couldn't help, however, reflecting for an instant during this 'time-out' how once again she was unable to justify devoting any parcels of her life to, in this case him, or probably anybody else, unless it was built into some pre-scheduled allotment of rigid, tiny time capsules.

Pete concluded that he now had little choice, other than impressing on Leslie a few inexorable and uncompromising realities. "You probably won't believe this, but there IS a part of me that would like nothing better than to put you on some plane, train or bus back to Providence, and make all your perceived agony disappear. Ideally, I guess going back to last year, we both might have addressed certain dynamics that developed in a far more thoughtful and considerate fashion.

Had we done that, perhaps we wouldn't be here now; we did not! I am firmly convinced that many opportunities existed where you might have afforded me the simplest, subtle acknowledgement, and by doing so, assuaged my feelings considerably. What ultimately became a desperate obsession didn't have to. Where am I going with this? We each played either an active or a passive role in what brings us here."

Pete paused for a few seconds before declaring the 'crux' of his conviction. "Now, certain imperatives have been thrust into motion that cannot be reversed. Unlike you, I no longer have the luxury of a viable life to return to; that is of paramount importance to me. If I let you walk away early, then I will be condemning myself to a nothing' life out here too."

They were at a hopeless impasse. Each had a lot more to convey to the other, undoubtedly in every conceivable form and with as much pathos as is humanly fathomable. Right now, though, it was painfully apparent that their fate would remain hanging, dangerously unresolved. Leslie, mournfully immersed in silence and loathsome resignation, had to recover and reload. Pete on the other hand, had somewhat of an advantage, resistance from Leslie. He also knew the clock was ticking away invaluable time.

With the time element becoming an increasingly omnipresent concern, Pete felt compelled to risk completely purging himself of whatever feelings he had left; his timing could not have worse. "You know Leslie, we are only coming up on our 4th day together, and for most of the first two, you were unfortunately disabled. That in itself made it very hard for me to accept that you can be so adamantly convinced based on such relatively short exposure, that there can be nothing enriching or worthwhile derived from any prolonged experiences we might share. "How can you be so goddamn sure?"

"Also, I am shocked that you are so willing to offer the kinds of concessions you are apparently suggesting, as possible barter or compensation for your so-called freedom. As much as the prospect of us actually confirming such a pact, is indeed titillating, it doesn't become you, and besides, it's much too early for such considerations."

Leslie, apparently still simmering beneath what appeared to be a calm exterior, had taken all she could. With one svelte aggressive move, she lunged at Pete with both hands, ferociously lashing into his face and neck; scratching and gouging, until they both tumbled hard to the floor between the beds. Before they hit, she screamed, "You son-of-a-bitching-psychopath, you're not going to get the best of me." Pete at 6 to 8 inches taller and 60lbs heavier than Leslie quickly subdued her for the most part, and was able to assume the upper hand by straddling her midsection and pinning her right hand down. With the other he muffled as best he could her incoherent wails while she continued punching with her left hand, until she completely exhausted all her energy.

Pete's neck and cheek on one side especially, were burning, and although he couldn't touch or see it, he knew she had succeeded in drawing blood. That, however, couldn't be his immediate concern: Leslie had to be totally neutralized, and then secured. He didn't have think very long, as he looked her square in the eyes and said, "I hope you're satisfied. I ought to knock you the fuck out; the only thing stopping me is that I want you conscious, and I'm not going to risk hurting you any more than you already are." With that, he dragged her over to the suitcase and felt around inside until he located the roll of duct tape. It was now necessary to force her down, face first while he again straddled her back, and ripped off a six-inch strip for her mouth, and a much longer piece for her wrists.

Before lifting her and placing her back on the bed, he retrieved his pistol to reinforce his persuasive efforts. Then, in dire need of some respite, he suspended all his faculties until he could eventually catch his breath.

CHAPTER TWENTY

As Pete sat there hoping and waiting for his deflated lungs to gradually expand, compounded by the fear that sooner or later they just might not ever again, he sensed an all the too familiar crisis of conviction looming. Usually when this occurred, he invariably felt compelled to shift immediately into a proactive mode. "You know, you're going to sleep like that, and probably travel restrained tomorrow as well, all for what? I'm not some Neanderthal that you have to wound or at any cost. Why is it so hard just to give me half a chance? All I want is to love and care for you." Leslie's eyes hardly revealed any semblance of a reaction, one way or the other, as Pete struggled to his feet and made his way to the bathroom, intent on further assessing the trauma to his face and neck.

Once in front of the mirror, he warily had to construe the not-so-minor scratches as extremely distressing, and not only because of their obvious medical concerns. He knew he could clean them, apply an antiseptic healing agent and time would do the rest; however, he wouldn't be shaving for a while. What also disturbed him was the prospect of these tell-tale wounds perhaps inviting some unwanted attention and scrutiny come tomorrow. He concluded that in the absence of a good-sized ill-mannered feline, how else does one sustain these abrasions?

Pete returned to the main room to get the first-aid kit without saying a word and barely glancing at Leslie, who remained pretty much in a fetal-like position. As he surveyed the whole ominous picture, he couldn't help instantaneously sizing up the entire situation as one well on its way to becoming a hellish nightmare.

He had an aching back that made it difficult for him to just manage for himself. His face and neck were lined with two-and-three-inch searing welts, and worst of all, the one object of all his hopes, desires and affections was lying there, bound and gagged. It had been a long time since Pete felt such an intense need for a bottle that he could just pop the cork and climb into for a spell.

After gently cleaning his wounds and dabbing on some Bactine ointment, he returned to the living room, falling into what had to pass for a parlor chair, and spewed, "Get this straight, you pig-headed cunt; we are definitely going to Minnesota tomorrow if I have to lock you in the trunk. I'll tell you something else too; if you don't smarten up pretty quick, I can guarantee you will end up a fucked-up mess in every conceivable way, a pathetic basket case long before you ever set foot back in that city where you're so sure all your needs are.

With that said, Pete went about searching out the alarm clock, and then sat on the adjoining bed facing Leslie to ask, "Do you need to use the bathroom? Nod your head one way or the other, because in two minutes it's going to be 'light out' in here." She nodded affirmatively, so Pete helped her off the bed, cut the tape binding her hands, adding tersely, "Leave the bathroom door open and don't fuck with that tape on your mouth; if you need to drink, I'll help you, but be warned, removing it could smart a little."

She was only gone a few minutes before returning, declining the offer of water and extending her hands behind her so he could reapply new tape. As he was finishing, he turned her around so their eyes could meet, and said, "Having to do this hurts me more than you will ever know, and in the morning, I'm counting on you trying to convince me it doesn't have to be this way.

Now, do you want to sleep on top of the covers, or under some of them? I'll show you and you can nod." She opted to sleep just under the spread, and as Pete was just about to tuck her in that way, he felt a pang of compassion and discovered he couldn't accept the sight or prospect of her trying to sleep with her mobility that restricted and experiencing increasing discomfort as the night wore on.

Pete again went to the suitcase, sought out some rope, and cut a piece about seven feet long, and said, "You'll be more comfortable with your hands in front of you; I just can't allow you to reach your mouth, so let me help you again." After utilizing the rope and tape, Leslie had much more range of motion. She was secure, and as ready for the night as Pete could cautiously feel comfortable with. Before leaving her side, he planted a soft kiss on her forehead, not because he wanted some approving reaction, but because it spontaneously felt like a feeling that he needed to express.

Pete now was literally and figuratively exhausted. Once his head hit the pillow, his thoughts shifted quickly to Monday morning and all its potential challenges and possibilities. It wouldn't have taken much for him to break down and cry, scream or whatever, just to reduce some of the accumulated tensions.

He was starting to seriously entertain thoughts of drastically altering his approach to dealing with Dr. Greer. Why not aggressively take the audacious step of trying to fuck or make love to her, forcibly or otherwise, just to remove that particular thorny subliminal element from this protracted dilemma and for all. It's a reality she had got to be 90-95% sure was going to take place at some point, anyway. An hour ago, she was in effect offering it as a viable option.

The other alternative would have to entail a diametrically opposing approach to such an egregious undertaking. And then again, maybe not. Pete always liked to plan in terms of allowing for at least a little wiggle room in every maneuver he attempted to conceptualize. What if he were to shamelessly appeal to her intrinsic need to be healing, caring and compassionate? How much might that kind of scenario impact the overall prevailing dynamics between them? How desperately needy might his perceived despair have to be, to awaken the 'first do no harm' and healing characteristics that Leslie so far had succeeded in repressing, in favor of obvious survival and personal safety concerns?

Could she actually up and abandon someone who appeared genuinely despondent and distraught, and while informing her that should she leave, his suicide will be imminent? As Pete drifted off to sleep, his head was full of complex ruminations, and very few if any answers. He did, however, take solace in knowing that tomorrow would afford him additional opportunities to decide what course might be most prudent to embrace.

It felt at 7:00 am as though the night had indeed passed very quickly, usually indicating that he had probably slept relatively well, a surprising development considering all the unresolved factors swirling all around him. Outside, as much as he could initially discern through the narrow spaces of the drawn drapes, the sky was a depressing gray, and the sounds of wind and rain pelting against the picture window, were unmistakable. Cleveland is a city often susceptible to squalls and storms that blow in from Lake Erie; for the natives it's an irrepressive element of the landscape here.

Leslie, as expected, had barely moved during the night, and as he opened the drapes a bit, his eyes met hers as he said, "Good morning, I'll be there to help you in one minute; it's raining pretty hard out there. Can you hear it?"

Pete was doggedly determined to start this day in an up beat mode and try desperately to get some of his zest and vitality to perhaps rub off on Leslie. As he approached her to remove the tape and rope, he paused for a moment to say, "Now, listen to me, and think before you answer. I want very much for you to feel free enough to move about, eat, drink and converse while you join me up front today. We are heading for Hudson, Minnesota, and after that I really haven't decided.

I've been doing a lot of thinking, and as of now I'm not sure which way I'm leaning. For now, you can shower if you wish, while I pack up, and then we can get a decent breakfast at a nearby Waffle House. We will also need to fuel up."

Pete then went about gently removing her hand restraints, and before tackling the tape covering her mouth added, "If you can somehow find the will to accept all of this strictly, on a day-to-day basis, I promise to approach each day with a similar mindset."

With Pete's half-truth proposition duly conveyed, he tried in vain to painlessly dislodge the duct tape from Leslie's tiny face before suggesting she wait while he fetched a warm, damp wash cloth that might help facilitate a less distressing procedure. After a few trips back and forth for hot soaks, her mouth was, except for a tiny amount of fiber glass residue, once again fully functional. The first words she spoke were encouraging. "I feel badly about inflicting those stinging wounds to your face; I've never done anything like that." Pete tried hard to ease what seemed genuine concern. "I understand totally, and accept a lot of the responsibility. They aren't that painful and should heal pretty quickly. Have you had a chance to consider my 'one day at a time' proposal?" Leslie's reply conveyed a sense of urgency. "I need to use the bathroom now; can we talk about that later?" "Sure, we're going to be together for at least the next twenty-four hours, anyway," Pete uttered. Leslie, halfheartedly, but distinctly quipped, "I guess so!"

In her absence, Pete hurriedly gathered all their travelling amenities in preparation for their transfer to the Merc, including the gun which he slid into his waistband, just in case.

Outside, the rain was still falling in windy torrents, indicating to Pete that he should wait for her, so they might perhaps coordinate a tandem dash through the raindrops.

She apparently decided to forgo a shower, and five minutes later returned to the main room clutching the travel bag containing all the toiletries. Before departing, Pete felt it important to solicit Leslie's input for a breakfast preference. She eagerly concurred that waffles might be a good choice, and then haltingly addressed what to her represented a significantly more burdensome issue. In an uncharacteristically deliberate and soft voice, "I don't know how much more of this I can take but I will make every effort to get through one more day, IF you will give me your solemn word, on the lives of your precious grandchildren that you are not trying to deceive me."

Pete answered Leslie with as much honesty and conviction as was accessible to him. "You have my word that this ordeal will indeed come to an end, much sooner than I might have wanted; and when it does, you will be able to walk away with your head held high." Leslie, after listening attentively, paused for a few seconds, then mustered, "I guess I have little choice, other than to trust you, and I have to believe on faith alone, that if you care for me as much as you have repeatedly stated you do, you will also consider at great length what is required maintain my well-being."

Pete found himself at a loss for any proper or suitable response. Leslie had thoroughly succeeded in capturing the absolute essence of his disheartening and unyielding predicament. He DID care and could never stop caring, and it was in direct conflict with whatever he might have expected to extract from this desperate experience. To him, this was the paradox of all paradoxes: "two truths that are mutually exclusive and can't exist together." If he really cared, he can't be perpetrating on this lady what he had already set in motion.

Pete had to switch his focus, and concluded that this was neither the time nor place for an all-out struggle with this irrepressible contradiction. He would tentatively be driving, sharing and listening to Leslie for the next 8-10 hours, and something positive had a chance of developing, he had to believe. "Are you ready to roll, and as hungry as I am"? Pete barked.

Leslie for the moment got slightly caught up in all the energy and spontaneity surrounding her, reflexively sharing the immediate task at hand. In no time flat the car was loaded, and the Waffle House sign beckoned.

Once inside Leslie's vitality quickly subsided, keeping her from sharing whatever it was she might have been pondering, and Pete similarly couldn't help being preoccupied with his own plethora of uncertainties. The one-inch-thick Belgian waffles topped with strawberries after their orange juice followed by some excellent coffee provided them a hearty, superlative breakfast.

The rain had almost stopped as Pete was topping off the fuel tank of the Gran Marquis, while at the same time keeping one eye on Leslie, who continued to appear listless and detached.

Pete felt it wasn't too difficult to extrapolate why: it had to be virtually impossible for her 'reconcile' with the reality of being taken further and further away from where her roots and familiarity were entrenched, and where she so desperately wanted to be. It was an understandable, reasonable apprehension.

In many ways, it conjured up the approximate plight of the death-row-inmate who is mistakenly informed that his sentence has been commuted; yet in short order, he is removed from his cell and escorted to the barber salon where they forcibly shave his head, and subsequently place him in a holding cell, adjacent to the execution chamber.

In essence, what was actually taking place was incompatible with what Leslie so desperately wanted to believe had been conveyed to her. Truth is, yes, she was being physically transported to parts unknown; however, neither Pete nor she, at this juncture, could draw any rock-solid conclusions related to what her ultimate fate may yet be.

Pete was in a mood to drive, and drive some more; if it had to be in detached silence for a spell, that's all right too. In direct contrast to Leslie, the greater the distance he could establish between their last stop and the next, the better he liked it. This issue was probably going to be an unbridgeable chasm for her, and nothing he could say or do, short of extending her instant freedom, was going to mitigate it. Pete felt as certain of that as he could be as he glanced into the rear-view mirror and acknowledged the undeniable reality of those revealing, hostile impressions on his face.

CHAPTER TWENTY ONE

This figures to be a long day on the road; the town of Hudson is located right on the border where Wisconsin and Minnesota meet and has to be a good 600 miles west/northwest of where they were embarking from in central Ohio. They would have to traverse the entire northern edge of Indiana, which would afford an extra hour as they cross into central time. After that, skirting Chicago in northeastern Illinois on I-294 would connect with I-94 in Wisconsin, which then must be crossed in virtually its entirety. The worst of the traffic would be on the 294 bypass, a 30-40 mile stretch that went around Chicago all right but is nonetheless congested at any given hour. Pete remembered it well, having negotiated it on a midafternoon weekday. It was a white-knuckle experience as cars and trucks allowed for very little spacing, zipping along 60-65 mph.

Pete always enjoyed taking in the sights and sounds on America's landscape, even on these superhighways that all seem to resemble one another. He felt a little sad that Leslie hardly was in a desirable position share in this pleasurable diversion. It took a good two hours before her melancholy mood would moderate a bit. When it did, she started sounding more like the psychiatrist, engaging Pete in some probing discourse.

Was it her intent to perhaps weaken Pete's resolve? Were her motivations rooted in her own selfish purposes, or did she actually have the capacity for unqualified concern in spite of these extremely trying personal conditions?

Whatever its genesis or intent for that matter, he knew it would be futile for him to try and resist any appearance of kindness or interest that Leslie might extemporaneously extend to him. Any gesture or dialogue that had some potential of nurturing warmth or closeness he was ready to receive with open arms.

Her choice of subject matter cut right to the heart of what she astutely perceived as Pete's repressed and undeniable anguish. "There must be some special people that you care a great deal for and are leaving behind, that will miss you and also have a difficult time understanding much of this." Pete was willing to be candid and forthright with regard to the important people in his life up until now but preferred to not be led into a protracted discussion that would primarily focus on the pain and loss of all concerned because of his less than conspicuous disappearance, or flight to freedom.

With that in mind, Pete's answer was concise and unequivocal. "Yeah. I'm sure they will for a while, but those so-called relationships alone were hardly enough to sustain me emotionally or translate into my feeling 'whole' as a human being. It's nobody's fault. I just needed a lot more than most people in today's world are inclined to offer. I don't know what that says about ME. It's just a deeply rooted emptiness that a majority of the time tormented me unmercifully."

Leslie processed that for a moment, then, "I'm not sure I understand your logic or purpose for that matter; if these relationships you have apparently cultivated for a lifetime are a substantially enriching element of your life, and by your own admission, all you have, why would you abandon or scuttle them? When you consider what your ultimate fate is likely to be here, you will undoubtedly end up with nothing."

Pete paused to carefully consider his answer before imparting in absolute terms. "There were a lot of complex and difficult factors that I painstakingly had to weigh and come to terms with before I decided on this odyssey as a worthwhile, justifiable pursuit, and I don't mean in any moral or legal sense. I ultimately concluded that an extended, compressed and occasionally intensive encounter with you would be worth more to me than I could ever reasonably expect to accrue or realize had my life remained pretty much unchanged. I even went so far as envisioning what my future prospects might entail, affording due consideration to the realistic capabilities I have now, or may ever hope to acquire in the future. It painted a pretty pathetic picture as far as I was concerned. Does that perhaps shed any light on what you find puzzling or troublesome?"

Leslie, somewhat perplexed and understandably threatened by the implied confirmation of Pete's entire dispatch asked, "Are you really that satisfied with what has taken place so for, or isn't there part of you that regrets initiating such a radical and life-altering course?"

Pete had to be careful now, his expectations were not even close to reaching fruition; however, at this juncture, the last dynamic he wanted to needlessly exacerbate was her current levels of fear, apprehension and defensiveness, so he chose his words carefully. "I do not, nor do I anticipate, ever feeling any pangs of self-reproach; that would hardly serve any worthwhile purpose at this point. As for my ultimate aspirations, they are elusive and challenging but by no means categorically unattainable. In fact, I consider this conversation we're sharing an encouraging step toward that inevitability."

Leslie's heart sank a little deeper; however, she didn't have a plethora of options available to her. She was a hostage in a car moving at 70 mph, somewhere in the vast landscape of a strange Midwestern state, and none of this was going to change any time soon. She felt compelled to explore further this disturbed individual's rationale and tendencies. "You can't tell me that the unnatural or counterfeit nature of what is taking place here, or the force you invoked to perpetrate your perceive reality is not somehow a compromising or tarnishing factor in your overall scheme?"

Pete's answer to that inexorable assertion was one that he had considered very carefully and come to acceptable terms with a long time ago. It pretty much summed all the motivating and evolving elements contained in this surreal encounter, at least from his perspective.

Any intended deference to Leslie's fragility and sensibilities would have to wait as he rambled on. "You're right. My perception is indeed my reality. In a fairytale world, anything you can imagine is possible; however, you and I are from much different places, and neither of them allows for 'storybook' endings. I wanted desperately to be with you; conventional reality dictated that my desire should be looked upon as misguided and even absurd. In my reality, you are here right now and that's how I prefer it. I literally ached for the chance to be even some small part of your everyday life and was slighted at virtually every turn. Here today, MY REALITY IS ALSO YOURS; and I must say, you can ill-afford to ignore me for very long.

In my heart of hearts, I foolishly allowed myself to hope that you could come to love me, as I love you; however, that I guess is beyond the realm of reasonable expectation. I have little choice other than to painfully acknowledge that; however, that realization in itself will hardly 'quench' my innate need to keep trying to for you see: in my reality, as of this very moment, that opportunity still very much exists."

Pete's rambling rationales with their inherent implications disturbed Leslie. She had wanted desperately to hear something congruent that would inspire hope that this ordeal was a lot closer to being interrupted. Instead, the obvious conclusion had to be one implicit with work-in-progress ramifications.

He hadn't given her anything at all, promising or reassuring to hang on to; and Leslie, despite her stated willingness to try and tough out another day, was having a difficult time lingering without any sense of control over her now, extremely precarious destiny.

Her fears were rapidly taking on a new dimension, seemingly multiplying by the minute. She had never felt so threatened and debilitated in her entire life and could only shudder when trying to imagine what kind of shape she might be in after another week or ten days of this. Compounding all of these frightening prospects was the over-riding horror that in a worst-case scenario, she might not make it out alive.

Dr. Leslie Greer's very nature would not allow her to passively submit to the irrational, dangerous and interminable designs of an unstable madman! Up until now, he'd been 'too good to be true', and eventually would demand a lot more of her. There was little doubt in Leslie's mind that at some point in these kinds of circumstances, all propriety and rational considerations fall by the wayside, and the situation deteriorates rapidly and then can easily culminate in horrific violence.

The time might just be at hand to conclude that she would have to prepare herself to present some substantive obstacles to ongoing, menacing fantasy. The more she analyzed and evaluated her situation, the more apparent the need for hatching her own devious scheme became. Her sanity and perhaps even her life could depend on it.

Her options are not what might be considered appealing or abundant for that matter. She could take her chances in a public setting by bolting and screaming for help in perhaps a half filled restaurant; however, that would endanger who knows how many innocent bystanders, as Pete was certain be close by and armed with a loaded gun. For now, that particular scenario was totally unacceptable. For someone else to die while she might survive, conjured up some extremely negative vibes.

That shelved for the time being seemed to suggest that she was perhaps limited to somehow nurturing, gaining and expanding Pete's trust to such an extent that he might very well become careless or cozy, and hopefully let his guard down, appreciably.

This was not a role Leslie could feel comfortable perpetrating for any extended period, thus requiring some thoughtful preparation. It needed to be accomplished in the most expedient fashion available to her.

What she did feel she had as an ally was some latitude, when the opportunities present themselves, to orchestrating times, places, and even the conditions, under which she would operate.

Pete thus far had shown an inclination to want to involve Leslie in planning their stops, meals and perhaps a side trip. This dynamic could eventually prove to be a critical plus from now on. It could aid her immeasurably in manipulating events and circumstances to her advantage and could prove invaluable toward her goal of somehow gaining the upper hand in this misguided odysscy.

That god-damned gun had to be at the very top of any list of Leslie's concerns. She, prior to this experience, had never even been close to one, engendering serious doubts as to her capacity to actually aim and fire one at another human being, regardless of the prevailing circumstances. All this considered seemed to undeniably indicate that gaining possession of Pete's weapon, in itself, just might not be as empowering and liberating as initially it might appear to be.

Another potentially malignant cause for grave concern and intimately related to the firearm was the ostensibly fatalistic mindset she felt Pete was capable of adopting once this nightmare began to unceremoniously unravel. This prospect was extremely frightening to Leslie, as she was keenly aware of the statistics that confirm the all too frequent occurrences of murder/suicide under the heading of 'crimes of passion'. It was not a fate she intended to fall victim to; and from this moment on would do everything in her power to avert.

It is a well-known and classic paradigm within the annals of the mental health community that individuals deemed a substantial risk of doing lethal harm to themselves are quite capable of also snuffing out the lives of those they once held dearest. The bottom line seems to indicate that someone whose appreciation and value for their own life has deteriorated to essentially nothing will more than likely find it hard to attach much significance and future tense to anyone else's life, either. There's probably a 'misery loves company' component somehow in play also.

The difficulty in predicting who might or might not b cap able of committing such a heinous act stems from, in most cases, complete lack of viable precipitating information; the dead can't reveal their motives and abhorrent conclusions to therapists to consider and evaluate. Statistically, more than 30,000 will die every year by their own hand in the U.S. Females make more attempts; however, more males actually complete the act. Just mention suicide and/or homicide in a mental health session and see the degree of attention or intervention it will expedite.

These undeniable and frightening prospects were casting a dark and ominous cloud over the entire spectrum of possible strategies and maneuvers Leslie might consider and subsequently initiate. She was still totally convinced that her primary focus would have to be getting her hands securely on the gun, if for no other reason than to dispose of it, removing it once and for all from the 'status' quo' and any future equation. It had to be eliminated.

Leslie, as she settled down and closed her eyes, pondered some of the possibilities and potential obstacles associated with what her next move would be. They were approaching a toll booth that would put Indiana in their rear-view mirror, and simultaneously open the road to Illinois. The traffic was heavier as late afternoon signaled the end of another workday and flooded I-294 with commuters, hell bent on getting home.

Pete was also immersed in tactical machinations when he wasn't of necessity totally focused on the task at hand: making sure they arrived safely at their next destination. The zaniness all around him conjured up his usual assessment of the situation: "What a fucking rat race!"

He was still having considerable difficulty deciding which approach or tack would potentially serve him best as he attempted to disarm Leslie's formidable defenses. If his instincts were on target, there would be layer upon layer of resistance. She was a highly trained professional in her mid-thirties, who had probably listened to a lot of horror stories detailing every conceivable form of physical and emotional abuse. How that translated to a little lady with only few and far between actual relationship encounters was hard to fathom. Pete could only hope to crack her shell somewhat, and maybe infiltrate himself close enough to capture just a little piece of her heart.

CHAPTER TWENTY TWO

These considerations posed an extremely critical dilemma for Pete, with the time element rapidly becoming a compounding adversarial factor. Waiting for the appropriate conditions to align themselves with some favorable dynamics could very well be an eventuality that would ultimately fail to present itself.

He was, with good reason, very reluctant to force the issue in a 'copulating' sense because other than its grossly diminished value and the demeaning effects on her, he feared the more debilitating repercussions he could experience. It had been a recurrent curse for most of his adult life, characterized by acute feelings of guilt, shame and remorse, and subsequently, disabling despair and ideas of suicide. Pete had experienced enough of these episodes to recognize what could precipitate one, and what can exacerbate its horror.

Their genesis he feels ran parallel to his years of black out drinking, when at one point he was diagnosed and treated for manic depression. Now that he had been sober for years, a plethora of other neuroses had surfaced, and the one with symptoms best describing his was classified in the Diagnostic and Statistical Manual, or DSM, as "anhedonia", or the "inability to experience normal and appropriate pleasure." It was an insidious affliction and could lead to any manner of avoidance and isolating patterns of defensive behaviors and had been perhaps Pete's most profound obstacle to the realization of any significantly intimate and rewarding experiences.

As it might relate to this situation with Leslie, he couldn't help but believe he would best be served by delaying any intensely pleasurable indulgences until all other options have been exhausted. His reasoning dictated that subsequent to the act itself, in his mind she would quickly metamorphose from an object of intense desire to a tortuous reminder of how pathetic this whole quest had been, from beginning to end, and his ultimate responsibility for its futility.

As these feelings invariably become more intense, he would conclude there were only two choices remaining: either release her to simply remove her from his sight or kill her. If the latter were to result; he would then feel even less justification than perhaps still faintly existed to tolerate his tortured existence any longer. A horrifying scenario, indeed.

The alternative was only slightly more promising. It would allow for spending more actual time with her; however, the quality of the shared experiences might very well be so hollow and unredeeming, and he would again be rendered deeply despondent from its unforgiving emptiness and abject pathos.

Leslie's life had been jolted, turned upside down and had, or would, before this was over, have been traumatized. If she survived, the chances were good, her 'viability' as a female adult human being could be painstakingly restored. For Pete there would be no future of any substance or value, should he somehow overcome the overwhelming odds that he might, also.

As the Merc sped its way toward the Great Plains of the upper Midwest, the stakes were about to escalate for both the doomed players, as each felt compelled to raise the ante in desperation-driven attempts to rescue what it was disparately, each one cherished most.

While carving their way across Wisconsin, with all its idyllic dairy farms, Leslie was immersed in trying to quantify what all her possible resources might be, and how and when the most feasible might be employed.

Pete had already stated that his master plan of predetermined destinations might be open to discussion, and Leslie was pondering if diverting him to uncharted territories might prove distracting to him and advantageous to her. As things stood now, they were heading unwaveringly toward one of the most barren and sparsely populated landscapes found anywhere in these United States. After leaving The Minneapolis/St. Paul region, there wouldn't be a city or town with 20,000 inhabitants for days, especially moving due west. Her initial attempts at short circuiting his machinations would have to begin soon.

Leslie could not allow Pete to 'shanghai' her unchallenged out to the 'middle of nowhere', For God only knows, what sinister purposes! What about some new clothing? Pete had already extended an open offer to outfit her as she might see fit. The clothes he brought along were pretty much all used up. An excursion to a mall could very well create some opportunities for her to feel her way around, and at the very least allow her to gain some measure of Pete's confidence.

With that in mind, she asked, "Does that offer to get me something fresh to wear still hold? These I've been wearing are comfortable, but I'm going to need a change, and I didn't see much left in the suitcase."

Pete as usual was delighted to hear Leslie initiate virtually, any kind of engaging or meaningful conversation, especially one that placed him in the position of perhaps accommodating one of her legitimate needs. So, he answered, "Absolutely. It's a good thing you spoke up now; there are some good-sized malls around the twin cities that can't be found for hundreds of miles after that. As luck will have it, we should be passing very close to that general area early tomorrow morning."

Leslie was, in a strangely remote sense, comforted by Pete's enthusiastic concession to her request and acknowledged his benevolence with, "That sounds good. I'll be fine until then."

In keeping with her new conviction that she must be more pro-active and aggressive, she added, "Isn't there someplace where we can stretch our legs, visit a rest room, and maybe get a drink?" Pete took a good minute to process in detail the three-pronged suggestion for his guidelines for maintaining rigid control of her movements, could not and would not be compromised for any reason, whatsoever.

As a possible alternative, he instead stoically enlisted her assistance, suggesting, "There is a Road Atlas on the floor behind my seat; if you can find an easily accessible somewhat parallel route near Eau Claire, we'll take a little detour and see what's there."

Leslie decided it would be in her interests to hone her map reading skills anyway, so she took full advantage of the opportunity. She would be needing some reference points to utilize if and when she felt a more significant diversion might be advantageous, and she was very quickly able to pinpoint a state route 53 that should afford them viable options for stopping without detouring them much at all.

Pete readily accepted her discovery and complimented her speedy resolution. He was trying not to show it, but his antennae were tuning in some unfamiliar signals. Leslie was suddenly a little too spirited' and obliging, and paradoxically. As much as he longed for some genuine sharing and warmth, under these circumstances, he also had to guard against being duped and manipulated. He might very well be in control of the situation in a strictly 'physical' sense; however, in the ever-shifting war of wits, she had at her disposal, a formidable arsenal of subtle weaponry. Leslie was exceptionally intelligent, cunningly shrewd and could no doubt turn on the charm and beguile him to a point where he wouldn't know which end was up. Compounding these resources was her highly developed sense of the frailties and sensibilities of basic human nature and perhaps especially those of her former patient, Pete Masters.

The more he brooded over these concerns, Pete found himself perplexed at how he could hope to triumph at virtually any stage of this extraordinary and seemingly 'futile' encounter. It's as though he must balance himself precariously on this razor thin line that separates trust from desire. Venturing a step too far in either direction could ultimately result in nothing less than complete disaster, and just another in a long list of pathetic failures.

As he slowed and gradually angled the Merc over the appropriate lane for exiting I-94, and then onto Wisconsin route 53, his vital 'priorities' were about to undergo another transformation. He was more and more convinced that attempting to suspend himself in some interminable holding mode, requiring time, patience and the inclinations of a saint, would not work for him. Especially given the likely assumption that Leslie would be subliminally engaging him any number of diverse, deceitful, and equivocating tactics, specifically designed to neutralize and ultimately defeat every one of his critical objectives.

There can be little doubt regardless of the immediate physical proximity they both occupied, and so tenuously shared, there is and would remain an unrelenting barrier to any semblance of consequential intimacy unless Pete either aggressively or reluctantly forced the issue.

His thinking in this regard seemed to dictate the precipitating need for an uncompromising increase in the fusion and unity factors of this void. That hopefully and ultimately would lead Leslie to a dynamic where she would in essence pick her own poison. It was not by any means what

Pete might consider a chivalrous undertaking; however, his vaporizing timeframe coupled with his steadfast conviction to somehow consummate this intensely personal dilemma left him little choice.

As they moved slowly along the parallel route Leslie had detected, Pete decided that refueling might also be conveniently prudent; so, a similar protocol to what had worked back in Ohio would be adhered to here as well. The only subliminal addition would be the increased attention and effort geared toward the possible connection quotient he planned to infuse into their every movement.

As luck would have it, there were numerous feasible options to take advantage of along this bucolic, quaint little slice of Mid-America. A not so contemporary Amoco service station that conveniently also had a "junk food" 7-eleven dispensary next to it should fit all their needs nicely, Pete determined.

As Pete pulled up adjacent to one of the gas pumps, Leslie readied herself to quickly exit the Merc and make her way toward one of these potentially liberating' opportunities.

With something very different in mind, Pete beat her to the punch, firmly grasping her left wrist, and making known, "I want you here with me; from now on we are going to be inseparable, as in 'joined at the hip', so keep that in mind, ok?!"

Leslie was incensed and barely able to contain her anger, as she stood there alongside the car "like some kind of idiot," she could be heard muttering. She detested any manner of physical coercion or intimidation, even if it is under these bizarre and revolting circumstances.

Her furor had subsided somewhat by the time Pete had finished filling the tank for her to 'sarcastically' request, "Is it all right if I accompany myself to the ladies' room now?" Pete was far from offended by the contemptuous nature of her remark; in fact, quite the opposite would be closer to the truth, as he somewhat blissful extended a hand while saying, "Come with me, babe. We're going to do this and everything else from now on in total togetherness."

Leslie, caught off-guard, and with her judgement tainted with self-doubt, reacted instinctively and completely out of character by slowly extending her left hand to Pete. In an Instant, the predator and his prey were tightly clasped together.

With one of her appendages reluctantly, but nonetheless securely interlocked with one belonging to her menacing adversary, Leslie felt compelled to ask of herself, "Why have I just allowed myself to seemingly convey this overt gesture of acceptance? What can be happening here?"

For Pete, it felt so warm and wonderful, he couldn't help longing for an extended opportunity, perhaps in the form of a leisurely two-mile walk, to immerse himself in and nurture the cherishing of the whole experience. For Leslie, there was burgeoning apprehension and misgivings; however, for the moment, neither was inclined to extemporaneously let go.

As they parted at the entrance to the respective restrooms, Leslie, while appreciating the protective and comforting solitude inherent there, couldn't help but be extremely wary and suspicious of what suddenly appeared as Pete's less than inhibited' sense of discretionary tact toward her. Compounding this concern was the stark realization that in doing so, he might very well have succeeded in trumping her ace by placing her once again in an acute defensive position, one that required that she be on constant alert for whatever it is Pete may have planned for her imminent future.

As she gathered herself and slowly emerged from the restroom, Pete was waiting and immediately wrapped one of his long arms around her slight waistline and pulled her close as they moved as one to the front of the establishment, returning the keys.

Leslie was feeling increasingly threatened by these unsolicited impositions to her space, and once again reacted instinctively by pushing Pete away from her. In an attempt to somehow buffer her angst and neutralize him she exclaimed, "We are not lovers; you are making me very uncomfortable forcing me to parade around in public in this manner. I'd like very much to walk through this 7-Eleven unattached, if I can."

Pete grabbed her arm and adamantly declared. "You are only half-right; I do believe I represent an equal component of this equation, and I feel very much like a lover, and furthermore, you are not calling the shots here." He was far from finished, but deferred for the moment to the less-than-ideal circumstances for making Leslie aware of a few unambiguous and unyielding realities.

"I will cut you some slack, under these particular conditions; however, I strongly suggest you find the means and soon to somehow mitigate your delicate sensibilities. If you don't, I'm afraid that given the implicit nature of your situation here, you can be assured that sooner or later, you're going to be categorically offended."

Leslie was startled to say the least. It is extremely unnerving and intimidating to actually hear Pete virtually spelling out his warped agenda for her. The only factor he failed to address was how, when and where these encroachments on her person would take place.

CHAPTER TWENTY THREE

Leslie's budding hopes of somehow eluding or circumventing some of the potentially 'detestable' eventualities inherent with this bizarre scenario were in danger of being dashed.

She had just briefly begun entertaining some prospective detours to her possible fate, and she needed some lag time to maneuver while whatever strategy she might have settled on, unfolded.

As Pete closely followed her through the familiar aisles of the standard-sized 7-Eleven, it was becoming crystal clear that he had not only compressed his so-called time frame significantly but also has apparently accelerated his perverse need for some manner of satisfaction or gratification.

As unequivocal evidence, she needed only to sensorily recognize the innumerable adolescent-like urges he shamelessly accommodated as they slowly made their way around the store.

Leslie had accurately construed how Pete had, indeed, indulged his impulses, and in the process had completely disregarded the protected space he had just promised her five minutes earlier.

To him, these innocent displays of unabashed affection including occasionally fondling her sweet little derriere, were pleasures he had been denying himself for much too long. He found it delightfully stimulating, especially given the tabooed nature of this entire state of affairs.

By now Leslie's built-in alarm was reverberating thru every constituent of her being. Her thought processes were being overtaxed as she tried to scan dozens of simultaneous messages, none of which she felt strongly enough about to embrace. She asked herself, "Should I take advantage of this opportunity and run, screaming toward the exit? There is a clerk and a woman with two small children in the next aisle, and who knows how many innocent by-standers on the other side of that door."

With Pete virtually glued to her every movement, she had to conclude that she wouldn't get very far, and chances were the gun would quickly become a factor she hardly felt assuming at least some responsibility for bringing to bear just yet. As she reached for a lemon-lime Gatorade from the cooler at the rear of the store, she managed to diffuse her fear and apprehension enough to determine that hopefully there would be other opportunities later that evening to make a move.

After paying for their snacks, and slowly making their way back to the car, Leslie could focus only on what might lie immediately ahead. There would be another restaurant, and if she was still unable to derail Pete's sinister agenda, following that, there would be another all-too disturbing sequester at some randomly selected 'Motor Inn". Her instincts were hard-pressed to favorably regard her chances of remaining intact longer, given what seemed to be evolving right before her eyes.

As they sped off toward I-94 and the final leg of today's arduous trek, the eighty miles or so that separated Eau Claire from Hudson, the tension in the Merc was mounting. Leslie could not stop herself from projecting ahead regardless of how hard she tried. Her only resource now seemed to be her incontrovertible wit, an asset that somehow could very well be frustratingly exhausted just trying to endure and survive the next 48 hours.

Pete, although he felt a strange and minimal sense of relief now that the accruing weight of his ambivalence had been lifted, found himself with an all too familiar sick emotional taste in his mouth The stark realization that even though a measure of forced and distasteful intimacy would be available, the heart-to-heart and soul-to-soul quality he so desperately longed for was now virtually inconceivable.

As he throttled up to turnpike speed and set the cruise control, he folded up the center armrest, and reached over gently placing his hand on Leslie's thigh and softly said, "How are we doing, Babe?" A cold star met Pete's eyes as she first lifted, then pushed his hand away, while blurting, "Don't touch me!" Pete already on the cusp of a partial meltdown had little left in his reserve of patience, understanding and compassion for himself or anyone else, as he venomously asserted, "You fucking bitch. You can't stomach being touched or even desired by the likes of me, can you? You think you're somehow above and insulated from all this; well, I've got a dose of reality for you.

"There's a drastically different order to things out here, one that you are obviously ignorant of and apparently inanely determined to resist. If I feel the need to casually impinge upon one of sacred body parts, then that's how it will be."

Leslie, close to being emotionally depleted and worn down by days of fear, uncertainty and apprehension, did her best to maintain at least some semblance of stature, "So, you're the big, powerful dictator now because you've got a gun that you used to take me by force, and now need to intimidate me with. You expect me to respect you and respond favorably to threats. I can't, and even if I did know how, I will not. If you had any courage at all, you'd take the same chances that everybody else has to take, upfront, on even terms, and then keep trying, until you finally might get it right."

Pete was now fuming and at a loss to communicate in any rational sense the pain associated with the surgical shattering of his fragile ego; however, that didn't stop him from rebutting in an outright bellow, "Yeah, you know so fucking much about interpersonal relationships. You hide and insulate yourself in that clinical shell, with all your aloof professionalism and label people from some fucking diagnostic manual. You couldn't even bring yourself to share some harmless tidbit from your background that just might help a sap like me to recognize that you also have some latent feelings, and are capable of perhaps appreciating some of the deficiencies so many of us try to overcome. Can it be all that threatening to allow those of us who bare their souls to you to feel some kind of humane connection with you?"

Leslie too, was just getting warmed up; she had worked hard and sacrificed tremendously to achieve her goals. And by doing so, had earned the right to selectively protect and insulate herself from potentially damaging incursions. This was definitely a 'black and white' issue as far as she was concerned. "I don't owe you anything; I tried my best and treated you, as I do with all my patients, with respect, empathy and concern. I didn't design or endorse the manner in which the mental health system has evolved. I just try to practice as efficiently as I can, within its framework and guidelines."

Pete wasn't in an accepting frame of mind for much of this politically correct rhetoric. "That is a piss-poor excuse for your personal failure to acknowledge, and give credence to a patently holistic concept – the feelings that any human being is capable of harboring and nurturing for another, regardless of who or what either of them might purport to represent themselves as. I'd wager right now that it will be a long time before you make that error in judgement again."

The dialogue and all its emotion had ebbed for the time being, as Pete's and then Leslie's attention, was commanded by a blur of brake lights being applied just ahead. After calming down somewhat from the unsettling tremors of what had virtually been a panic stop, it was apparent that as far ahead as they could see, nothing was moving. Whatever the reason, for all intents and purposes, I-94 heading west was shut down.

Pete was markedly distressed by this development, for a number of reasons. He unfailingly and instinctively begins to feel phobic symptoms when thrust into close-quartered situations that he could not readily extricate himself from. Compounding this one were the obvious complications inherent with having Leslie as a captive, who more than likely would make some effort to seize upon this opportunity to attract attention to her plight.

Being stopped dead in one of the interior lanes of a major east-west interstate, surrounded by strangers in vehicles of every shape and size, and presented a daunting dilemma for Pete.

One factor, perhaps in his favor though, was the rapidly setting sun, which would gradually be replaced by a welcome cloak of darkness that would shroud this bleak and seemingly endless landscape. That should make it difficult for any prying eyes to discern anything at all out of the ordinary.

Leslie so far wasn't giving away any discernible clues that she perceived this lull as an impromptu golden opportunity for her to try anything desperate. So, for about 30 minutes Pete was content to tilt his backrest and grudgingly bide his time. Some deep breathing, finger tapping, and a couple of addiction-fueled cigarettes were his only defenses for the time being.

The visual indicators ahead did not suggest they might be moving any time soon. Wisconsin state police vehicles had been whizzing' by in the breakdown lane at short intervals, with sirens blaring and in the distance what appears to be some kind of Medivac helicopter was readying itself to land.

Leslie had been curiously silent and staring straight ahead. Perhaps the surreal irony of this entire bizarre episode now painfully apparent to Pete was becoming more and more evident to her as well. Pete could only wonder what she must be agonizingly processing at this point, given the entire scope of what was involved from her tortuous perspective. When this was over, and she has regained some semblance of a life, Pete couldn't help but feel a projected sense of compassion for her. She would undoubtedly have a huge mountain to climb.

For him, even the feeble term salvage when he pondered what viable, acceptable options might still exist seemed to raise the bar unrealistically. Sure, he could screw' Leslie up, down and sideways, if and when the time came, but what redeeming or lasting satisfaction would that inspire? If anything, it would only add up to a singular, degrading indulgence perpetrated by another form of 'low-life.' Nothing more. Pete had never aspired to be cast in such disgusting company, for any undertaking he might initiate.

Even sparing her that appalling violation and releasing her unconditionally this very minute, would hardly elevate to any acceptable standard of moral acceptance that he was prepared to try and live with, and that's not even throwing into the mix the undeniable consequences that would be brought to bear from the law, courts, and the rest of society.

Bottom line, there is no salvation for him; and thus, there would definitely not be any turning back! "So, what the fuck?", Pete exasperatingly muttered to himself. In truth, there was one other convoluted option, albeit a most unattractive one: he could give himself up, be remorseful and try to seek out religion and eventually forgiveness in some shithole of a penitentiary, like so many other losers. As of right now, right here, his answer was a resounding, "NO FUCKING WAY."

As Pete had always felt, Leslie would ultimately play a huge part in influencing and determining her eventual fate; and also just how and when this miserable undertaking would reach its loathsome conclusion. It was by no means a fair and scrupulous predicament for her to be burdened with; however, perhaps it was much too late to be assessing accountability in such unyielding terms. She was probably to a greater degree than Pete having endured five days in an unrelenting wringer on the brink of emotional exhaustion. Compounding this dilemma was the realization that if she was unable to muster the resolve and energy to take some major 'risks' soon, the worst of all her fears had probably even yet to materialize.

Finally breaking this poignant, soul-searching silence was for Pete the welcome sound of engines being started. The big rig diesels were unmistakable with their roar, and no doubt with their driver's advantageous view from above everyone else, this was most likely a precursor to some imminent movement for the grid-locked masses.

"Perhaps they've opened one lane or the shoulder so traffic can slowly crawl by the accident scene," Pete softly declared.

Sure enough, there was some forward movement with all those at the controls gingerly maneuvering their vehicles in angular fits and starts, creeping inch by inch to gain an advantage, only to play 'follow the leader' for a while.

Finally moving, even at this crawling pace, should have been reason enough for Pete to feel a little upbeat, and perhaps even attempt to share the moment with a forlorn Leslie; however, he remained at a loss to see much of anything in a positive light anymore. He felt defeated and a failure, no matter how he sized up his prospects of achieving something meaningful.

Impacting nauseatingly his already depleted spirits and no doubt Leslie's as well was the sight of the horrific accident scene. A truck tractor had apparently somehow hit and mangled what appeared to be a minivan, almost beyond recognition. It would have taken a miracle for anyone to survive the complete and thorough annihilation of that vehicle. As they slowly moved pass the 'carnage', Pete couldn't help from saying as he briefly glanced at Leslie, "Will you look at that: one minute you're alive, vital and nurturing hopes and plans for the future, and instant it's all snuffed out." She didn't verbally reply or even passively acknowledge Pete's observation; however, there was no mistaking the tears 'welling up' in her now, sad and desolate brown eyes. God knows she had more than a 'fleeting' cause to feel heartsick!

The sobering fragility of virtually anyone's dreams and existence being so instantly dashed had a profoundly nauseating effect on each of the woeful duo as they went through the motions of resuming their ruinous trek toward what now had all the elements in place for a decimating and uncompromising rendezvous with destiny.

Pete's focus and timetable were once again assuming some perverted sense of clarity and resolve. He would commit himself to another twenty-four hours of respectful and reasonable exchanges with Leslie; and then reevaluate what options realistically remained. Hopefully, something, anything would transpire that would enhance his diminishing chances in one form or another of an acceptable, climactic, and final resolution.

Leslie was not at this juncture resigned to any measure of 'defeat'; however, for the time being, she was far from feeling adequately resourceful or energetic, either. She realized that they were now less than an hour from Pete's preplanned stop over for this night, and that was extremely distressing for her.

CHAPTER TWENTY FOUR

Pete, as expected, continued to grapple with hopelessly conflicted feelings of compassion and contempt for his bereft sweetheart, as their long day's journey approached its precarious conclusion. He was tempted to offer her a one-time opportunity to phone any significant 'other' of her choosing, whether it be in Rhode Island or anywhere else. Undoubtedly, her choice could prove interesting; however, his better judgement dictated that any caller-ID or phone tap at the other end would result in flooding the Hudson area with law-enforcement in nothing flat.

In the same vein, perhaps she might benefit from writing someone. Not so, if he stuck to the compressed timeframe he has just committed to. She would be home before the damn letter reached its destination. Still, how could she possibly even consider the likelihood of that happening, based on what she knew? Unquestionably, there existed a desperate need for her to make some manner of connection with her other life.

Hudson is a small 'border' town with one major thoroughfare, flanked by lots of motels, restaurants, and gas stations, with a couple of 'strip malls' thrown in for economic and aesthetic balance. The latter reminded Pete of an important detail he had almost forgotten, while he was preoccupied plotting his ever changing prospects. Leslie needed clothes, if for no other reason than to travel home in. Pete still had over $1500 and couldn't think of even one rationale whereby he should concern himself with saving any. There was no conceivable use he would have for money very shortly.

Not surprisingly, his spirits were lifted slightly as he allowed himself to entertain the prospect of doing something he considered peripherally positive and generous for Leslie; however, it did little to assuage the visceral disappointment and heartache the unremitting emotional void that separated them.

He had little choice, but to cling precariously to any possible thread of acquiescence that he could either manufacture or fabricate, for time was running out. And until, in his warped judgement, it was totally depleted, he would at least try to conduct himself in a manner worthy of some modicum of 'self-respect.

When all possible alternatives had been exhausted and every continuance had been extended, then the situation in all likelihood would change drastically.

Leslie was understandably, hardly in the mood to be ingratiated by whatever means, especially by someone who was in the process of perpetrating on her the worst of all nightmares.

She wanted no part of any generosity, flattery or grossly misguided attempts at charming her. Pete, in all honesty, had no such expectations; this gesture was all about trying to appease a need that perhaps each of them might have trouble acknowledging.

For him, a bit of subtle, emotional maintenance; and for her, a more practical remedy.

As they approached the main thoroughfare of Wisconsin's westernmost town, Pete verbalized his offering, hoping it might serve in some fashion as an ice-breaker. "Hey, we need to get you some new clothes; there's a Sears up the road, if you'd care to pick out a few things." Leslie, as much as she wasn't in the mood, instinctively felt a compelling need to at least physically or superficially freshen up and getting into some new attire couldn't hurt, so she softly replied, "Yeah, that sounds OK, I guess."

It was almost 8:30 when Pete parked the Merc in front of the Sears entrance, and both Pete and Leslie were hungry and tired. This necessary diversion was not going to take long. Neither had much to say, once inside the store, with Pete following closely, changing direction, and stopping whenever she did. The only conveyance between them being when he reminded her not to worry about spending two or three-hundred dollars, and perhaps to think in terms of getting enough for a few days.

Leslie acknowledged his suggestions, with a singular, monotone. "Really!" as she continued methodically browsing through some tops hanging on a chrome rack.

A strange and 'eerie' calm unexpectedly seemed to permeate the atmosphere for the half-hour spent clothes shopping, almost as though some small degree of resignation had infiltrated each of their subconscious psyches. Leslie managed to acquire a seemly variety of under and outerwear, to the tune of $197.50, and although there would be no blissful repartee or handholding, for Pete at least, a meaningful deed had been accomplished. For Leslie, it had little value other than tending to a basic requirement of her day-to-day existence.

From Sears, their next move would be diagonally across the highway to the Great Plains Steak & Rib House restaurant and cocktail bar. Pete, after locking her purchases in the trunk of the Merc, grabbed Leslie's hand and led her across the six lanes of divided asphalt into the spacious but sparsely patronized eatery.

It wasn't long before they were seated, once again in a smoking section way off in a corner where this time he didn't hesitate and ordered a "Chivas Regal" with soda water, and a white wine for her whether she wanted it or not. The omnipresent and unyielding tension that had managed to saturate virtually every waking moment of their encounter thus far, was in Pete's judgement, in dire need of the un-inhibiting qualities of a little 'social lubricant'. He could not envision how their situation could in any way shape or form, be more negatively impacted by a couple of harmless drinks.

Strangely enough, he found himself to some degree now reconciled to functioning inside the vacuum that each of them, for their own complex reasons, had grudgingly decided they must co-exist within.

If the time factor was not the unrelenting source of pressure and duress that it is, things might very well have a chance to turn out much differently. However, it is, and unfortunately that pervasive element dictated that everything be somewhat recklessly accelerated. While unhurriedly nursing their drinks, Pete seized upon the opportunity to hopefully stimulate Leslie with a couple of pieces of choice' information. "Would you like some good news first, or some not so good?" Leslie's eyes opened a bit wider as she answered, "Does it really matter? I've got a sneaking suspicion, that bottom line, they're probably going cancel each other out anyway, aren't they?"

Pete couldn't help smiling at her reflexive, intuitive grasp of undoubtedly the overall picture, and the subliminal wit that somehow managed to find its way to the surface, in spite of her ominous predicament.

He had always believed in saving uplifting news for last, reasoning it had a better chance of retaining its energy enhancing effects when not immediately followed by the bummer factor. So, he continued. "We've got one more day of extensive travel to complete, and we should be able to accomplish that tomorrow. By then we will be smack in the middle of what is commonly referred to as "God's Country", or more precisely, a little town in eastern Montana by the name of Wibaux. That is as far west as either of us will be going."

Leslie's heart sunk, but not so that her curiosity and need to hear something reassuring could not overcome, as she asked, "And what happens after we arrive there?" Pete was not completely comfortable answering that far-reaching a question in any specific detail. He knew something unique and memorable is going to take place, and she didn't need to have it spelled out this far in advance; so, he revealed as delicately as he could, what he felt she wanted and needed to hear. "I want you to spend one definitively special night with me, and the following morning, we'll arrange the most expeditious means available for you to go home."

Leslie virtually speechless, needed time to process and assimilate some of the possible ramifications of what Pete had just made known to her. She couldn't stop most of her perceptive energy from focusing on the "definitively special" phrasing Pete had chosen. To her that implied something markedly different than the previous ones, and could only imply one reasonable conclusion for all intents and purposes: he was planning to rape her.

Be that as it may, she felt compelled to explore and probe this bizarre, imaginative scenario a little further. "Why does it have to be Wibaux, or whatever it's called, in eastern Montana? Why can't you apply the same anatomy of reason to tonight and tomorrow?" Pete, after swallowing the last gulp of his precious scotch and soda, put the glass down, and while meeting Leslie's eyes head-on, straight forwardly answered, "I just have a visceral feeling about where, when, and how, I want certain things to materialize."

In truth, Leslie wasn't unduly 'jolted' by what Pete had just imparted to her; she had been virtually 'expecting' something along these lines to rear its ugly head, at some point and time. In fact, she felt that in her position of being essentially "the hunted," there were certain advantages to being briefed of sensitive information by her adversary.

She now had a fairly definite time-frame to operate within, and a strategic road map to reference should she decide and commit herself to some manner of liberation endeavor. Unquestionably, she would have a lot more than her food to chew on in her immediate and subsequently uncertain future.

As was the case in Ohio, there would only be one go-round with the demon in the bottle. They both would need their respective perceptive and cognitive capabilities functioning at near peak efficiency for the extremely critical ensuing thirty-six hours. As their timely orders of fries, ribs and a salad for her; and baked potato, steak and a salad for him were delivered; Pete couldn't resist trying to elicit some manner of purposeful reaction. "I don't detect any sense at all of 'relief' in your demeanor; I know you desperately want this nightmare to end, and you've just been informed that it will happen within a relatively short period of time."

Leslie took her sweet time answering. She was quite obviously immersed in both her thoughts and the pleasurable rhythm of nibbling on what looked to be some delicious spareribs. She did, however, pause long enough to offer, "The prospect of this ordeal somehow coming to an end and soon does foster some glimmer of hope. However, a lot can happen in the next day-and-a-half, so I can't allow myself to feel all that free just yet." Pete could neither contest nor add anything to Leslie's well-conceived declaration, so he simply nodded and said deliberately, "Touché! I think I have at least some sense of what you must be feeling."

After their touchéing but sadly remote meeting of the Minds, they both attended exclusively to finishing their excellent but somewhat pricey dinners. Neither wanted nor had any room for dessert; so, Pete, after leaving four $20 bills on the table, again escorted Leslie across the highway to where the Merc was parked. Next on the agenda was settling on a nice place to spend their next-to-last night together.

Finding a motel didn't present a problem. Being only fifteen miles east of Minneapolis/St.Paul, there were oodles of appropriate accommodation up and down the thoroughfare, where they had just shopped and dined. Pete deferred to Leslie, asking her to pick one, and she quickly pointed in the general direction of a 'Comfort Inn' and a 'Best Western', virtually side by side, about 1/4 mile west of where they were parked. Pete, based on prior experiences with both chains, suggested the former might be a tad more suitable, as he steered the Merc toward that heading.

CHAPTER TWENTY FIVE

The $89 room at the Inn was more than adequate. Their appetites now fully satiated, as might be expected exacerbated the need for some uninterrupted sleep. Strangely enough, it now seemed that out of some unequivocal necessity, they had fallen into a shared survival mode of sorts, one that on the surface, at least, had evolved to where it took on its own degree of importance. Unfortunately, it would be all too brief.

Pete enjoined Leslie to perhaps ready herself for bed before he would, and promised her, he had absolutely no intention of encroaching on her space or attempting anything untoward while she is either wide awake or sound asleep. She didn't overtly convey her appreciation; however, it was obvious that she felt some sense of albeit a distinctly uneasy and precarious gratitude.

There were two queen-sized beds in the room, and while Leslie was in the bathroom, Pete collapsed into a parlor chair so that when she came out, she could unobtrusively choose her place of slumber and settle in for the night. She willingly complied with Pete's request and 'luxuriated' in the relaxing comfort of a temperate shower before re-appearing twenty minutes later in some new satin-like, two-piece pajamas.

She looked and smelled so tantalizingly enticing that Pete, as exhausted as he was, had all he could do to keep from shamelessly reneging' on the promises he had so gallantly pronounced less than a half-hour before and indulging his burgeoning desire, right there and then.

Pete deep-down knew he wouldn't be able to live with himself, if he were to betray the trust he had just pledge for this particular night; so, he cautiously kept his distance and put his faith in the diversionary power of television, which he immediately turned on. He needed to stay awake anyway until Leslie was sound asleep. So, he bid her a restful good-night, as she snuggled in under the covers. He really didn't care if he had to spend the entire night in that chair as long as the alarm clock was set, and nearby.

Somewhat amusingly, this was going to be one of more quiet and uneventful nights ever experienced in any motel by a couple who were genetically unrelated, relatively healthy, and in many respects, young-at-heart. Pete couldn't help thinking how the sedate, sterile atmosphere now present in that room reminded him of what metaphorically might be construed as 'the calm before the storm'. In a brief moment of reflection, he found it hard to relish in any part of it: he had embarked on a life-altering undertaking that he was adamant about not allowing any recriminations to sully or any impulse to retreat to take hold. Agonizingly now, in all likelihood, his endeavors were condemned to suffer an iniquitous conclusion.

As Pete gazed over at a weary, and no doubt foreboding Leslie, he found some measure of solace in having at least tried to convey a reasonable manner of respect for her dignity thus far.

He may, out of desperation, have been driven to conduct himself as a predator, but that fact alone didn't have to transcend or dictate that he must also assume the baser characteristics of some kind of rapacious animal.

Pete, after determining Leslie had indeed fallen asleep, moved around the room quietly and cautiously, first relieving himself in the bathroom, and then indulging in what he thought would be his last cigarette of the night. An uneasy feeling about climbing into the other extremely inviting bed and falling into a deep sleep precipitated the conclusion that he'd best relegate himself to relying on one of the reasonably comfortable chair for any rest he might be able to absorb. After arranging two chairs so he could elevate his legs and prop one with a pillow, he settled in as best he could.

Pete always left the bathroom light on and the door slightly open in motel rooms. He found it disorienting to wake up suddenly in a pitch-dark, strange environment. So, after turning the TV off, he removed the pistol from his waistband and placed it on the chair next to his right leg and closed his eyes. His little diode illuminated alarm clock let him know it was 12:10 am, and the beginning of a new and perhaps extraordinarily momentous twenty-four hour experience.

Leslie did not linger long before dozing off; however, with all the apprehension and uncertainty agitating her psyche, a deep, uninterrupted slumber was virtually impossible. She twisted and turned while napping intermittently until finally at 3:30 she found herself wide-awake and frustrated.

While lying on her side facing Pete's profile, she instinctively began to monitor his breathing and stillness to perhaps determine conclusively just how deeply he might be sleeping. At the same time, with butterflies fluttering in her stomach, she began to run down a checklist of "what if's" or possibilities that might relate to her chances of making a break for her freedom.

She asked herself, "Where can I run to, if I'm lucky enough to get out the door undetected? Banging on doors of adjoining rooms while screaming is not going to help; these people are all in bed sound asleep, and Pete would most likely be there in a matter of seconds, 'gun in hand'. There has to be somebody on duty in the office, but that's a good hundred yards away.

Maybe an all-out dash for the nearby woods, and then hide until daylight; however, it is cold, and there could be animals and insects to say nothing of possible water, and even perhaps the misfortune of breaking an ankle or something."

"First things first," she thought. Leslie had to get an accurate feel or read' of just how unconscious Pete really might be. He had uncannily positioned the two chairs and himself at an angle that his eyes could not readily be observed. He definitely wasn't snoring or moving, and his chest is rhythmically rising and deflating as if in a deep sleep.

Leslie decided she had nothing to lose by slowly and quietly getting to her feet for an up-close assessment; however, before moving in the direction of the door, she would need to access the shopping bag from Sears on the unoccupied bed next to her for something she could throw on over her pajamas. So far, so good. As she probed as deliberately as humanly possible, until she found a pair of lightweight tan slacks that she had planned on wearing later anyway. As she slid into them, tags and all, and probing any further for a bra and top she deemed unwise. She had a warm-up jacket from her sweat suit that she felt would suffice. Her sneakers at the foot of the bed were also easily accessible.

While sitting on the bed as she was just finishing lacing them, Pete began to stir, first mumbling something incoherently, and then moving from one side of the chair to the other. Leslie stopped in mid-knot and didn't move a muscle, while breathing as shallowly and slowly as she could, for a good two minutes.

The clock read 4:05, when she felt enough time had passed, she cautiously rose to her feet and began tiptoeing toward her escape route. The closer she got to where Pete was, while also moving away from the meager light source coming from the bathroom, the more difficult it became for Leslie to identify distance and objects, and especially wherever he might have placed that gun. The tension and excitement were almost too extreme for her to endure as Leslie took another careful step toward where Pete was slumbering. The gun definitely wasn't in his waistband or on the floor anywhere close by, leaving really only one reasonable probability: somehow concealed on or close to his body.

As she got alongside Pete's chaise configuration and bent over slightly to focus, something shiny and appearing metallic caught her eye that appeared to be tightly wedged between his right leg and the side of the chair, tempting Leslie for the briefest of moments to strike somewhat as a coiled reptile might and quickly grab it.

All this instantaneous bravado, however, was quickly tempered by an equally trepidations impulse. She seriously doubted her ability once she might secure it to then take full advantage of its awesome, intimidating and destructive capability. Her indecision quickly found its resolve by determining that even if she held and pointed the gun at Pete, she in all probability would be hamstrung by not knowing how to chamber a round if necessary, or how to disengage the safety, if needed.

It virtually became a no brainer. "Screw the gun!" she said to herself "Why take the chance of waking him up to get my hands on a gun that I'm scared shit of and don't know the first thing about how it's actually supposed to be used?"

As Leslie finally reached the door and was applying her thumb and forefinger to flip the locking mechanism, Pete again began stirring, stopping her dead in her tracks. Drawing a few deep breaths, she watched intently as he groaned, mumbled and then moved his legs to side of the chair closest to her, a scant two feet from where she stood literally in a state of suspended animation.

She waited thirty seconds, then a minute and finally, after a good two minutes closed her eyes and clicked the bolt from a locked setting to an emancipating unlocked one. It seemed to her to be a resounding, resonating clack of meshing steel, as the cylinder moved from one side to the other.

Pete immediately began moving again; however, his eyelids never did lift and quickly he appeared to settle down once more allowing Leslie to turn the handle on the door and try to ease it open. It wasn't cooperating. "What can be keeping this goddamn door from opening?" she asked herself as she pulled a little harder, and then with all the strength she could muster without grunting and groaning. A piercing, searing 'RIP", and then another echoed through the room, and in a split-second Pete was on his feet and lunging for any part of her body he could latch onto.

He had vigorously applied two lengths of duct tape, one across the bottom of the door, and another from the frame to the door itself about six inches above the floor, where she couldn't see them.

Leslie had just expended all her energy tearing the tape away from its seal, and as Pete dragged her back into the room, kicking and struggling, all she could say was, "You son of bitch."

After picking Leslie up and literally dropping her onto the bed furthest from the door, Pete was still wobbly and trying to shake the cobwebs from his consciousness. His initial reaction was a terse. "Do I need to hogtie or gag you, or have you exhausted all your resources for now?" Leslie didn't answer and turned onto her side away from him.

Pete somewhat curiously concluded that he wasn't all that pissed off or frustrated by Leslie's futile escape attempt. It didn't take him long to perceive a scenario which would allow him to extract a potential benefit from being so abruptly and ungraciously roused from his slumber. He had decided that as far as either of them sleeping anymore this night, it wasn't going to be then or in that room.

That determined, he moved over to the bed and sat next to Leslie to inform her of his revised agenda. "Far be it from me to rub salt in your wound, now or eve, but you should have figured that I might employ extra safeguards to keep from losing you until I am completely prepared to. I don't blame you at all for trying, and now what is most important to me is how you plan to conduct yourself in the next twenty-four hours. Since we are both awake and dressed now, we might as well hit the road and rack up some miles before breakfast. We've got two good-sized states to cross, and we need to be in Montana by early evening."

Leslie was not only totally 'dispirited' by the 'booby trap' deterrent to her bid for freedom; she was also angry at herself for not 'disabling' Pete when she had the chance. She easily could have smashed his head while he slept with the heavy lamp that was conveniently nearby. It would have been a justifiable and appropriate choice, given her dire circumstances. Now, she could only tremble with the fear of what her uncompromising ideals of civility and refinement might ultimately cost.

Pete on the other hand, would just as soon dismiss what had just taken place. In the overall scheme of things, he hadn't lost her, and at this late stage with a potentially climactic vision on the horizon that was all that really mattered. He wasn't, however, by no means without understanding, compassion and sensitivity for her crushing disappointment and disheartened emotional state.

With that in mind, Pete tried as valiantly as he could despite his own depleted and desperate condition to assuage her wounds by dropping to his knees next to her bed and conveying softly, "Sometime tomorrow you will undoubtedly be on your way home.

I'm not going to lie to you and pretend that tonight is going to be just another night, because it won't. My feeling is you have already sensed as much; however, I will promise to treat you with the utmost respect and consideration and be as gentle with you as I can. I realize this is not what you wanted-or needed to hear, and that my propensity for being brutally honest can at times be misguided. I'm sorry, but you also need to know how much time and effort I have spent praying and hoping that somehow there might be a prospective and viable outcome that we could both find acceptable."

Leslie, with tears welling, sat up on the bed and replied, "Just like that, huh! You're going to take from me what you want when you feel like it. Oh, you are 'slick' at dressing it all up and making it sound almost trivial and painless, but the truth is, you are planning to rape me and by committing this appalling act you supposedly derive some perverted sense of satisfaction. Isn't that what this is all about?"

Pete, sensing this kind of provocative dialogue could only fan the flames of frustration for both of them gently took hold of both her wrists, while imploring, "Leslie, if that were truly my motivation, why would I have thus far chosen to pass on any number of golden opportunities to indulge myself? You mean a hell of a lot more to me than the sociopathic indulgences some shameless sexual gratification can engender. It may take years, but I firmly believe that somehow, in spite how you feel right now, you eventually will be capable of acknowledging that truth."

Leslie still sobbing a little and woefully sullen guardedly responded to Pete's gentle tug and rose to her feet. For now, she would accommodate his wishes to start packing so they could get moving and cover some ground before breakfast. If she had any more to say, it would have to be during the next 10-12 hours in the car, or once they were domiciled in Montana. Undoubtedly once there, there would be a compelling need to say or do something pretty drastic.

CHAPTER TWENTY SIX

Pete had already calibrated the distances they will be covering while waiting for Leslie to drift off earlier that night. From Hudson to Fargo, North Dakota - 260 miles; Fargo to Bismarck another 200; and finally, Bismarck on into Wibaux, Montana - about 160, for a grand total of 620 miles. He also figured on two stops for meals, and two for fuel. He also remembered that in this part of the country, normal traffic moves 75-85 miles per hour; in fact, in Montana there were no daytime speed limits, only designations for a reasonable and safe rate posted on the few signs there were.

Leslie passively acquiesced to pack the cosmetics, while Pete was readying everything else for transfer to the car.

By the time the keys were left, and the door closed behind them, dawn was just beginning to break at 5:15 a.m. As Pete started the engine and checked the gas gauge, he said, "We've got enough gas for at least two hours or 150 miles; then we'll stop for a hearty breakfast, OK?" Leslie, with her seat already reclined and bearing the look of someone being led to the slaughter, managed to acidly reply, "Don't insult me by insisting on fictitiously soliciting my approval when it has absolutely no value, or bearing on what you have already made up your mind to do."

Pete could easily understand Leslie's desperation and abject futility; however, he didn't feel she was being totally fair, so as he pulled onto I-294, he had to reply, "I guess it's just some wishful thinking, perhaps rooted in the hope that under some other circumstance we could both care and share equally in what our itinerary for the day might be. Obviously, we have two extremely opposing agendas here: you want more than anything else to be rid of me, and that happens to be the one accommodation I can't offer you." Leslie's final salvo for the moment cut right to the heart. "You are one seriously disturbed individual and should be locked up somewhere."

Pete was more than a little hurt by such a caustic and cruel condemnation, especially coming from Leslie; however, he respected her need to express it. One of his favorite and long held axioms, "that everything in life is relative", seemed to painfully apply here. He knew in his heart that his motives were honorable, and also that in a civilized society, his egregious breach of acceptable behavior, regardless of what may have precipitated it, could never be fully understood, condoned, or judged with any degree of compassion.

Everyone knows that what most uniquely distinguishes humans from all other life form is our innate ability to reason. Relatively speaking, Pete probably had an above average proficiency when it came to critical thinking, intellectually, that is. It's the other essential ingredients to rational, emotionally stable deduction or analysis, where he has major impediments. Maybe it was the interminable loneliness and isolation that could be debilitating! How about the incessant, gnawing emptiness that will wear on you! It didn't really matter at this point; however, Pete needed some kind of justification every now and then, for feeling so frustrated and unable to muster what it took to meet all of society's rigid standards. To him, these musings definitely warranted at least a fair amount of deliberate and compassionate examination.

He also couldn't help acknowledging, though quite sadly, how meaningless all the reflection, rationales, and heartfelt tete-a-tetes that had taken place with Leslie and within himself will soon be rendered.

The abduction and holding of her against her will were bad enough, but somehow, they seemed pale in comparison to what he was fervently committed to perpetrating in the next twenty-four hours. Pete neither wanted nor expected any quarter; however, it was important that he believe that someday, somehow Leslie would be able to find at least some understanding and acceptance of just how this perplexing and painful episode had come to pass.

As Pete settled in behind the wheel for the initial leg of the days' grueling trek across some badlands of the old west. He began to experience very subtle inklings of exactly what was going to be necessary, if he was to fulfill or realize his one remaining objective later that night.

He would be focusing all his efforts on achieving what would have to pass for an acceptable quality of physical intimacy with the little lady, who has been the elusive object of almost three years' worth of what seemed interminably repressed affection and desire.

In order to come to terms with this, he would have to start perceiving her in a different light, from a radically altered perspective. Pete knew all too well he could no longer exclusively behold her numerous charismatic attributes, and leave her way up on a pedestal as he had unwittingly been inclined to do for so long now. As unpalatable in many respects as that may be, he was convinced that in order for him to assimilate subjecting Leslie to the indignities of unwanted sexual intercourse, there was a prerequisite desensitizing process he must experience. He would have to bring her down to a level more characteristic of one representative of fair game.

Pete found most of this notably distasteful, for in effect, it would require the metamorphosing in his mind of what was now a uniquely holistic female human being into something comparable to a simplistic, pleasure-rendering sex object.

In a strange kind of equation for so long now, Leslie was in many respects the epitome of what an untouchable might be to Pete. There were lots of qualities she embodied that he was quite enamored with; but 'sexual intimacy' he had always felt could be relegated to the back burner, something that he felt might occur as part of a natural progression. That highly romanticized scenario, had now given way to something far less endearing, and unfortunately more servile in nature.

After about an hour and forty-five minutes on the road, Pete was starting to feel hunger pangs, and the fuel gauge in the Merc wasn't far behind. On this their final day on the road, these necessary interruptions were going to assume an increased amount of discriminating security considerations for a couple of reasons. First, he did not want Leslie out of the car and exposed to risks, any more than was absolutely necessary. The time for taking those kinds of chances in the interest hopefully ingratiating himself with Leslie had run its course and had failed to reap any significant rewards.

Secondly, once beyond St. Cloud, whose city limits were now conveniently upon them, there would only be a sprinkling of small prairie towns, except for Fargo and Bismarck, for the next 450 miles. Pete didn't want to be out and about in these little hamlets where ogling strangers could be the local's highlight of the day.

As for Leslie, if she wasn't sleeping, she had been doing a damn good job of faking it, Pete felt, as he exited I-94 and Scanned state route 23 for the most likely direction to lead him to not only a full-service gas station, but a drive-thru restaurant as well. Having amended his earlier impulsive declaration of a hearty breakfast, he was now opting for something quick, simple and virtually risk free, especially now that Leslie was asleep. Any place that offered juice, muffins of any kind, bagels, donuts or Danish, along with the requisite freshly brewed coffee, would suffice. If hers had to sit a while before she woke up, so be it!

His calculated excursionary choice proved to be satisfactory. Leslie slept through the refueling, but stirred and opened her eyes just as he stopped at the drive-thru window of a McDonald's.

He didn't consult with her regarding any preferences she might have, opting to keep the exercise brief and simple. "Two of everything," he barked, "orange juice, egg-McMuffins, hash browns, apple Danish, and regular coffee." By the time Leslie was alert enough to appreciate where they were and what was happening, their breakfast was in the car and on her lap.

With the dashboard clock indicating a still early 7:05, and 125 miles in the bank, Pete decided they could afford to park for 20 or 30 minutes and more or less enjoy an unhurried breakfast. The conversation understandably remained strained and measured, at least initially. She inquired as to their precise location, and Pete answered, "Just west of St. Cloud, Minnesota", and then offered a brief explanation for altering the breakfast plans. "I just didn't feel it was necessary, and that we wouldn't be comfortable in that atmosphere."

Leslie, as a reflex, could only say, "OH!", as she nodded a couple of times; however, after finishing all but her danish, and starting on her coffee, querulously continued, "In what regard has everything changed so dramatically and suddenly for that matter?" Pete, also saving his Danish for later, took a sip from his coffee, placed in a cup holder, and while starting the engine, answered cryptically, "I think you have a keen sense of what the answer might be to that question."

Leslie was far from satisfied with Pete's non-answer and instinctively felt the need to probe for more specifics. "I can't read your mind, and would appreciate being informed if there is a new dynamic or another dimension of an older one coming into play here; that's not asking for too much is it?" Pete had given more than enough thought and careful consideration to this most critical of issues, so he didn't require much of a pause before responding, "The new dynamic as you have fittingly described it, is the sad and desperate state-of-affairs we are so inescapably enmeshed in here, and how this latest reality has necessitated the appropriating of a more unambiguous and stringent definition to all of this."

Leslie had had a fairly good grasp of what Pete was directly and indirectly alluding to, but her analytical training and inquisitive nature compelled her to explore further. "What do you see as our 'new' reality, and what are you feeling is needed for a more exacting definition?" Pete found these 'poignant' inquiries, difficult and painful to address. They demanded if he were to be mercilessly forthright that he reveal his abhorrent rationales, which in essence reduced them both to not much more than a predator/ prey, captor/captive and most despicable of all, rapist and his victim. Even in his resolute, committed frame-of-mind, burgeoning fatalistic tendencies and all, this would be a deplorable admission to have to articulate, not only to Leslie, but to himself.

Pete had hatched, orchestrated and was close to finalizing what was left of this entire sickening incident. He was not about to start fudging any truths or acquiescing to cop some kind of plea; so, he did the best he could. "My dear little sweetheart shrink, it matters little at this point what events or circumstances have precipitated my crashing into your life, or what brings us to this particular place in our encounter. My motives are no longer a central issue or open to any manner of addressing or mitigation. It's much too late to be analyzing much of anything. I have obviously made two grievous errors here: one was falling hopelessly in love with you, and the other was embracing the absolute conviction, that if given enough time and opportunity, I could somehow compel you to need me as well. I have now painfully concluded that this is all an 'unattainable' fantasy, and hopelessly beyond my abilities to realize, no matter how hard I try. Unfortunately, however, for you, that's not going to be the end of it, for I cannot just allow that disheartening realization to translate into another failed and fruitless undertaking.

I have invested too much of myself and perpetrated any number of serious transgressions against a society that will want its pound of flesh. This is all on me and I don't see aborting and accepting defeat and humiliation as a viable option."

Leslie desperately interrupted in an effort to perhaps proffer and inject a last gas but unlikely solution, one that on the surface appeared to generate little optimism in light of the grievous and overall scope of this complex dilemma; however, also one that suggested there still existed a ray of spiritual light, if he would only open himself up, and let it in. She began with, "There is always another choice available, other than the one that seemingly offers the simplest immediate gratification. Often, these considerations are difficult to acknowledge, but nonetheless, they can more than likely be the moral or right one, and deep down, we usually know it."

Pete was barely able to contain his mounting frustration. Of course, she was right, and it hurt to hear the gut-wrenching truth, as he blurted out, "Please, Leslie, don't ask me to once again to carry the burden of being a pathetic failure here and end up crumbling into a poor excuse for a human being, right before your eyes." Pete's eyes were filling with tears, and his voice and body began to tremble, as he continued, "Even if you wanted to, and I doubt you will, there isn't a god-damn thing that can be done or said that will make all of this acceptable to you, me or anyone else. It's too late, period! You would end up spending the rest of your days hating me and everything I stand for, and I would be spending mine, locked up and hating myself."

Leslie, caught up in the middle of the most harrowing and threatening experience of her life, had little choice other than to keep pressing. Drawing on every morsel of her professional expertise, to say nothing of her instincts for survival, she offered, "Pete, my sense is that you are a spiritual and compassionate individual, and that the state of your soul is what is important and enriching to you. Down deep you are not anything like the monster you feel you are for having been victimized by some desperate error in judgement. You have a granddaughter and have shown the capacity to cherish her, and an elderly lady whom you have found reason to selflessly assist for an extended period now. That is the REAL you."

Pete, still shamelessly weeping, largely in response to the poignant reminders Leslie had dredged to the surface, needed to get it all out now, as he purged, "The real me has spent most of the last two years being tortured by visions and heartache for someone, and something, I could never realistically expect to experience. How can such an honest and wholesome hunger be so misguided and painful? I am extremely sorry, Leslie, but we are destined by fate alone to share at least extraordinarily memorable experience if it has to be last thing I ever do."

Leslie was beside herself, although frustrated more than anything else. What resources did she still possess that hadn't already been utilized to dissuade this sick bastard from his sole objective, methodical as it might be, of sexually assaulting her? She asked herself, "How do you reason with someone, or appeal to their sense of decency and justice, when they have apparently reached the point of no return?" That's exactly what this is all about He is planning on killing himself after satisfying some depraved, obsessive compulsion to be inside me.

Pete had said enough and struggled to regain his composure by lighting a cigarette and fiddling around in vain with the stereo. He hated country western music and it's maudlin, depressing themes, especially right now; in fact, there wasn't much of any style of music that could effectively soothe his despair.

He was beginning to feel more and more like a frustrated lowlife, complete with prisoner, victim and harmful intent. The only elements missing were the exact time and place, and they would soon be in order.

They each had approximately 12-15 hours to either reconcile with or alter their inevitable and disastrous fates, and Pete had a distinct advantage in both these determinations. He was the one who felt he has nothing to lose, and that alone put her in an extremely vulnerable and perilous place. Ultimately, she might be forced into choosing the lesser of two evils', and it was also becoming more and more apparent that the sooner she started preparing herself for just such a distressing eventuality, the better her chance of survival would be.

Pete, though grudgingly, has been priming himself in bits and pieces for any number of possible last resort and desperate conclusions, since the very inception of this odyssey. Now, one of them was a virtual certainty. Strangely, entertaining such probabilities in a fleeting fashion, he was discovering was not quite as disturbing as actually plotting their imminent and irreversible execution. It was beginning to weigh very heavily on Pete.

There had been very few instances in his life when Pete had been unable to extract something positive, or root out some silver lining from the most dismaying of circumstances. This scenario, however, seemed without any doubt to be the epitome of a dark, futile and unyielding state of affairs.

It brought to mind the age-old cliché: "A coward dies a thousand times; a hero dies but once." Pete didn't quite know where he might fit there, but he knew he had figuratively died often over the years and maybe this was his chance to go out with some conviction, purpose and pride for a change.

CHAPTER TWENTY SEVEN

Leslie was facing a daunting challenge; she had dealt with patients who were despondent and suicidal, but none of them had a loaded gun and a plan to rape her. This was a horse of a different color, one that was going to be of an extremely hazardous nature, with stakes nothing short of life and death.

She might now even be forced to compromise her idealized professional ethical principles somewhat in an all-out effort to impede the course of this insanity. In effect, she had to be willing to try anything, so she began, "Suppose, Peter, I insist to the authorities that I adamantly refuse to prefer charge and that you are in need of intensive and comprehensive psychiatric care in a hospital setting. I will make a solemn promise to you right here and now that I will do everything humanly possible to guarantee that your needs are appropriately met. Wouldn't that scenario at least be worth some consideration?"

Pete took his time processing Leslie's offer or plea. He had some significant difficulty dissecting its pragmatic value with respect to her motivation, sincerity and the ultimate feasibility of what she was proposing. His instincts were telling him she is getting her motivation from two intrinsically powerful forces; to survive and to heal, in that order. She was also most likely being as candid and truthful as her situation would allow; however, whether she realized it or not, her career and professional stature were going to take a major hit should she attempt to circumvent the legal machinations and ally herself in any way, shape or form on his behalf. Technically, Pete wasn't even her patient while this episode was playing itself out. Bottom line, Pete couldn't see any of this measuring up when subjected to the scrutiny of a plausibility test.

That said, he found himself at a loss to candidly respond to her offering.

He had already exhaustively considered all the relevant probabilities, and even if she were able to pull something like what she was suggesting off, he was tired of protracted and futile attempts at therapy, and looking into his soul for some deeper meaning. Besides, he also wasn't interested in discovering some miraculous passageway to whatever salvation might be. He had already come to terms with the abject reality, that this adventure had little or no chance of ending nicely for him.

For the time being, however, perhaps it wouldn't hurt to placate or accommodate Leslie's desperate efforts to somehow mediate their impending calamity; besides, he didn't have the heart to off-handedly dismiss her resourcefulness, and as a result, discourage her unnecessarily.

After a few minutes' interval, Pete tried hard to choose his words very carefully. "Leslie my dear, I am really touched that you would be willing to take that kind of a stand and commit yourself to all those extraordinary efforts on my behalf, but right now I don't feel that worthy or receptive. I am tired, I don't like myself or my life, and secondary to all of that, I don't want you linked negatively to me, like some kind of albatross that casts a dark shadow over you, long after this is over."

Leslie, intuitively adept at these kinds of exchanges, was quick to sort through and process Pete's dour assertion. "It must be difficult, even overwhelming, to have part of you desperately yearning to be in love, and another part nurturing some kind of death wish." Pete could immediately and viscerally relate, "Yeah, it's fucking near impossible, but it happens to be where I am right now. No wonder I'm desperate for some resolution to all of this."

Leslie could sense that engaging Pete in any type of fatalistic dialogue had the potential of unwittingly validating his desolate and morbid self-assessment, so she decided to make an adjustment in her approach. Pete, however, before she could continue, felt his own compelling need to just let things be. "Let's drop this for a while, OK! The 'die has been cast', and for once in my life, something is going to turn out, at least in some manner, the way I need it to."

By late morning, the condemned pair found themselves halfway between Fargo and Bismarck, North Dakota. In a moment of welcome distraction, Peter could only shudder as he imagined what it might be like up here in a January or February blizzard, with temps at minus 20 and 40 mph winds howling down from the Canadian Rockies across these plains. In a stalled car, and without a cell phone, one could easily freeze to death, and it wouldn't take long.

He couldn't help concluding, "People do die for all kinds of reasons, some for just being in the wrong place at a given time. Maybe it's not so terrible to end a shitty life on one's own terms and with a measure of satisfaction derived from consummating the ultimate, inconceivable experience."

When a finalized rendering of the awful truth was carefully dissected, the irony of all this is mind numbing. The much-anticipated pinnacle of Pete's impending carnal pleasure might very well only be eclipsed by the bottomless depth of Leslie's inexorable pain, an irreconcilable and disheartening prospect.

If Pete were to find any solace or consolation from any of this, it could be found in his unwavering belief that Leslie would not allow herself to be completely destroyed by this aggregate experience, or any particular inclusive incident. DEVASTATED, no doubt! PARALYZED for a while, probably! AFRAID TO BE ALONE, most likely! DIFFICULTY TRUSTING, chances are!

"SEX LIFE, GRIEVOUSLY AND PERMANENTLY SCARRED!" a good possibility. "DEPRESSION, ANXIETY, INSOMNIA." Pete began to feel sick, churning discomfort in his 'gut', when he sensed something was terribly wrong. Why am I going thru this litany of debilitating, residual torments Leslie will undoubtedly be left with as a direct result of his selfish and twisted needs? "Why is this 'shit' kicking in now?" he asked in anguish. "CONSCIENCE, EMPATHY AND COMPASSION are all major obstacles to SUBLIME GRATIFICATION!" A kidnapper and would-be rapist can hardly afford to acknowledge and perhaps yield to these incompatible and virtuous impulses. It just can't happen.

If Pete were not totally convinced that at this point, he was already on his way to hell, he might be more inclined to embrace somewhat these cajolers of restraint and decency. The truth was, however, when he took the giant leap of actually abducting Leslie, his morality and righteousness quotients suffered a crippling blow and could not function quite as scrupulously as they might have prior to that event.

Pete was able to suppress his brief but intense encounter with recrimination for the time being, and turned to the only source available for some much-needed diversion. It mattered little at this point, the manner or the quality of the engagement. If she had an agenda, be it overt or subliminal that was OK, too. Pete's focus was now fine-tuned exclusively in terms of real events and everything else must be relegated to incidental or secondary status. Not the outcome he had so fervently hoped for.

With that in mind, and in the interest of a wholesome and relevant exchange, he fast-forwarded to tomorrow, when Leslie's active role in this drama would have been un-majestically played out.

"What's it going to be like for you, as a celebrity of sorts, when you get back to civilization? Undoubtedly, you will be subjected to some ridiculous media curiosity to say nothing of the local, state and federal authorities who will probe you for detailed accounts of virtually every hour you were missing. There's got to be something positive, although I can't envision what, that you can extract from all of that. Have you given even a little thought to that whole scenario yet?"

Leslie appearing sad and dispirited was hardly inclined to share any speculation she may have privately engaged in along these lines, "Right now, I have other, more pressing and imminent concerns; and please do not insult my intelligence by trying to convince me how much you really care about any of it."

The doctor's conclusion, wasn't entirely accurate; however, Pete was not about to 'prevail upon her an argument that in essence had very little redeeming merit. Bismarck, the capital city of North Dakota, would be within view shortly, and he needed to concentrate on food and fuel accessibility. For the latter, this will be the last time that will be of any concern. "What might you feel like eating, Miss Greer? Maybe a pizza for a change?" Pete threw out as a feeler. Leslie didn't respond readily enough to satisfy him, so he persevered. "Come on, now, cheer up a little; it's a lot closer to being MY last meal than it is yours."

Not surprisingly, Leslie found it futile to even try associating any humor with Pete's 'macabre' analogy; however, she did realize it might be in her interest to take whatever steps were necessary to maintain her strength. She had yet to encounter what undoubtedly would be her most crucial battle, and felt her chances of successfully defending herself would be minimized if she were in a depleted physical state. "Yeah, pizza sounds like a reasonably nutritious and tasty choice", she finally and stoically declared.

Pete managed a wry smile, and said, "Great! Sounds to me like we have a plan; there's a "HUT" up there on the right, where we can go in together, order and then use their restrooms while waiting. I'm a cheese and pepperoni guy, so you can have them put whatever your little heart desires on the other half. There wasn't much for Leslie to respond to or add for that matter; he was calling all the shots, and as a not-so-subtle reminder, after parking the Merc, he pulled the gun from his waistband, slid the barrel back to cock it, and then re-concealed it again under his jacket.

The pizza was decent and as a bonus, they even had a beer and wine license, which Pete took advantage of, ordering and enjoying a Michelob, while Leslie opted for some iced tea with lemon. Eventually the conversation, primarily initiated by her, and of the exploratory nature, became purposeful, and would extend itself far beyond the forty minutes or so they would spend satisfying their basic vertebrate needs.

"So, abduction and rape are what you have chosen to be most remembered for. Seems kind of sad to me, after a relatively long life of conscientious effort and painful struggle to do the right thing the vast majority of the time, to end up with this as your epitaph."

Pete wasn't at all 'averse' to addressing Leslie's poignant assessment, feeling if anyone could grasp and appreciate the concept of abject futility in an aggregate form, she would have to qualify. Besides, she represented his final link to any hope of ever being understood or interpreted in a manner more conducive to an in-depth perspective.

"I have made a choice that I don't expect anyone to fully comprehend, with the possible exception of you. I know on the surface that sounds patently absurd, and perhaps even cruel, in light of what I will ultimately have put you through before this is over. Dying has no appeal to me whatsoever. It has all the enticing characteristics of an immense black hole that no one has ever come back from. It's living in the aching void of a seemingly endless vacuum, where nothing meaningful is ever realistically achievable, that I am no longer able to tolerate. That, and becoming increasingly frail, depressed and ultimately waiting to die alone!"

Leslie's attempts at weakening Pete's resolve were less rewarding than she had hoped. He was coming across in a very much, matter-of-fact fashion, and this troubled her. In her practice, and as a model throughout her extensive training, it is considered a red flag when at risk suicidal patients appear to uncharacteristically cross over to an apparent tranquil serenity that is often accompanied by the 'anomalous' dispensing of personal effects, and a total lack of future orientation. As far as she was concerned, Pete unquestionably fitted these criteria to a "T".

After finishing their sustenance and making their way back onto I-94, a strangely placid aura seemed to have transcended the space they occupied in the vehicle that would ultimately deliver Pete and Leslie to their final destination. He instinctively felt the need to at least try, to cultivate most upbeat atmosphere possible. "Please, Leslie, give me some clues to how I might lessen some of your fear and apprehension. You more than anyone should be able to appreciate the value and embrace the concept of 'verbalizing' all your dread and frustration. Far be it from me to even attempt counseling you; it's just I feel it extremely important that we explore every conceivable truth and consequence of what is really happening here. As compassionate human beings and perhaps for very different reasons, we both deserve at least that much."

Leslie was fast approaching the saturation level of an unyielding frustration. After well over a hundred hours of going back and forth with what she felt is nothing less than a deranged predator, she was virtually worn out. "What can possibly be left to analyze?", she blurted. "We both know the difference between right and wrong, force and consent and intimidation from willful sharing. If you're trying to elicit some kind of acquiescence or approval from me, you're never going to get it. As a matter of fact, why are you wasting all this time for the sake of some bizarre ritual, you have apparently conjured up in that sick mind of yours?"

Pete listened intently and then waited judiciously to be sure Leslie was through for the moment, then replied, "This entire scenario is as far as one can get from a right or wrong or black and white' matter. It has been conceived out of innocence and, yes, the love of one human being for another that just could not be suppressed or denied. I bared my soul to you, and opened up my heart, only to be discarded like yesterday's newspaper and left to bleed out. Do you have even the slightest clue what that might feel like, and ultimately can wreak on someone?

Pete bellowed on, "Have you ever run across anything like that in any of your theory-based training, or pray/tell something you might have experienced, first-hand? I have absolutely no desire or intention of raping you. What I will attempt is to make love to you in the most considerate, gentle manner possible. I dare say that even if you can't allow yourself to share in any of its pleasure, I don't believe you will disintegrate or feel the need to vomit because of the experience. I guess, however, that remains to be seen."

Pete also decided that perhaps the time was at hand to address some of the fear and uncertainty Leslie no doubt had swirling around her pretty little head with respect to some pertinent details. "DOC, I trust you will forgive my 'blunt' manner of speaking here, but there are a few vital particulars of this reality that need presenting. I don't have any clue as to what the quantity or quality of your sexual experience might be, prior to this, and for the most part it's a non-issue for me; that is, I would hope that this will not be your first; however, if that is the case, I must confess to some very mixed feelings in that regard. Something that special shouldn't be experienced in this manner, and under these conditions, but on the other hand, it's about time it is happening in some way, shape or form, is it not? The other obvious concern is the possibility of my impregnating you; I do have protection and intend to utilize it responsibly.

Pete finished up with, I know how crass this all must sound; it blows me away too, but we are not children and have consistently from both ends of the spectrum each embraced the necessity of addressing every issue openly."

There it was: it has all been spelled out for me, Leslie thought. Everything but the pain, anguish, and revulsion; he didn't mention any of that, at all. Probably because he couldn't care less, although it would be slightly more palatable to hope that he could, as strange as that may seem." She, too, wholeheartedly endorsed the theory that the majority of life's experiences can be interpreted in a relative sense. This scenario was indeed repugnant; however, there were more appalling offenses being committed somewhere, every hour of every day. Pete could just as easily have been one of those animals that beat and rape women repeatedly just for the sick 'macho' satisfaction they derive from doing it.

It was time for Leslie to hunker down if she intended to come out the other end' of this, as a viable survivor. She would have to embrace and utilize all the coping strategies she had so fervently advocated to every rape and incest victim she had ever counseled and felt empathy for since her early days of clinical training'.

The most difficult obstacle for her to overcome would no doubt center around the requirement she must at all costs adhere to: resisting the instinctive and self-defeating compulsion to treat herself.

CHAPTER TWENTY EIGHT

To Pete, not much of what had ultimately evolved here was a mystery, with the possible exception of how it was now apparently destined to reach its climactic termination. All the laudable and redeeming qualities of human nature had been exercised; however, their abject futility was every bit as evident as those undeniably more difficult to understand and accept.

In its most basic and purest form, it had been "cherchezla-femme", (man in pursuit of woman); for to Pete, Leslie was a bright, beautiful, sexy and accomplished young lady, a quite compelling combination, that when all is said and done, proved to be the intrinsic driving force, from the very beginning to this imminent culmination. Perhaps 99.9% of the male population would have checked their amorous impulses, and moved on to a more rational pursuit. Pete, however, not only could not, he was virtually powerless to even reason in those terms.

To him, it was the most natural of progressions, to want to share the most privately held and "intimate" emotions with this woman with whom he had become so hopelessly entranced. If it meant he had to cross some taboo delineation of moral turpitude, so be it, because that line had become increasingly obscure and un-inhibiting, the more he nurtured what had long since become an all-consuming passion.

Leslie lamentably finds herself at the diametrically opposite end of this irrational continuum. Soon she will be subjected to the most detestable form of personal encroachment, which she can only hope to cushion somewhat with as much nullifying emotion she could muster. Following that, she would then be challenged to deal with whatever potentially horrific events might follow.

Even given the best case scenario, with the deep psychological and physical scars and a life and career in total chaos and disarray would make her a prime candidate for some prolonged and comprehensive therapeutic support.

As they approached the North Dakota/Montana border, it was early evening and a glorious sunset hung over the vast western vista. It was awesome. Their personal horizons were precariously intertwined, with the only apparent uncertainty now being the precise manner and extent of the suffering before this fateful union was tragically 'ripped' to shreds.

Pete had impulsively decided to make one more logistical adjustment, as he pushed the Merc through and beyond the city limits of his original destination, Wibaux, Montana. A somewhat larger town, Glendive, was only another thirty miles north, and he was counting on finding a hotel/lodge big enough there to offer room service. If his memory served him right, they hosted regional rodeos annually, and should have more elaborate accommodations. He still had over $1100 and saw little reason to save any or take any unnecessary risks that eating in some dinky restaurant might present. Leslie had no comment or discernible reaction when Pete informed her of the change in plans.

His instincts were well-founded as they exited the turnpike and came upon a sign that would direct them to "The Big Sky Lodge and Restaurant". It was located on the southern end of town and unique in its log cabin style, and appeared to have 50 or 60 rooms. The vacancy sign was lit, and Pete breathe a small sigh of relief, as he pulled in and parked not far from the office. Leslie remained, incommunicado.

With her in tow, Pete quickly got them registered into a $180 a night suite and was able to obtain a menu that they would have until 10:00 to order from. It was now, 7:55.

Once inside the room, which was indeed spacious and nicely furnished in a rustic/western motif, with two king-sized beds, Pete threw the suitcase on one bed, and himself on the other. Leslie was content for the moment to just collapse into an antique stuffed wicker chair and get her bearings.

Since Pete was going to assume the role of initiator for most of this night, he felt it appropriate that he begin by outlining the preliminary elements of his agenda for her digestion, "I'm going to order a nice bottle of wine in a minute; once that's taken care of we can indulge in a soothing and relaxing 'soak' in the oversized tub that the clerk was so enthusiastically describing, and then order up some dinner. Think you can handle that?" Pete quipped. Leslie just stared silently at Pete for a moment, then replied glumly, "What choice do I have?" Pete smiled and then answered, "None, of course, but you know what: it's really not going to be all that terrible. In spite of how much you try to deny it, you also have some basic needs that need tending to once in a while".

Pete then opened the suitcase where he had stashed a small bottle of bath oil beads, just for this occasion. While grabbing the phone he flipped the aloe Vera to Leslie, and said, "Here, go in there and start filling the tub while I order the wine; this will relax every nerve and muscle in your tense little body, if you just let it."

She didn't say a word while slowly making her way to the bathroom and the closing the door behind her. Before calling down for what eventually turned out to be a $35 bottle of supposedly imported champagne, Pete waited and then smiled broadly as he actually heard the sound of water splashing into a soon to filled hot tub of potentially hedonistic euphoria.

After five or ten minutes of waiting for the bubbly to be delivered, he needed to check on Leslie's progress or the perhaps the deflating lack thereof, so he politely knocked on door and waited for a response. She didn't answer, but encouragingly, hadn't locked the door either, so he entered and found her sitting on the edge, swirling the blue water, and seemingly preoccupied with however her part in this dilemma was going to play itself out.

Pete, on the other hand, tried as best he could to ignore any and all dispiriting or impeding dynamics that might exist, and remain completely focused on his immediate agenda. "You can go ahead and get in whenever you're ready. I have to wait out there and pay whoever will be delivering our champagne." There wasn't much Leslie could say or do. She could sense just by looking at Pete that he wasn't going to be talked' out of any of this. This was going to be one element of what he had convinced himself would ultimately become his crowning achievement.

Pete left her there, as he heard what he thought was three loud knocks on the door, and he was right. There it was, complete with red ribbon, a bucket of ice, a corkscrew and two long-stem glasses. By the time he got the cork popped and sampled some, he could no longer hear the water running.

His heart skipped a beat or two with anticipation, as Pete purposefully reentered the bathroom and feasted upon the sight of Leslie naked in that tub. She looked so tranquil and positively tantalizing, with her head back and resting on a towel, her eyes meeting his with what Pete chose to interpret as an invitation to join her. As he eagerly moved closer to hand her a glass and place the other on the edge of the oversized rectangular tub, he whispered to himself, "Nice and easy now."

As a kind of moderating tactic, Pete figured he might try shaving around the still tender abrasions on his face and neck. So, as he stripped down to his boxer shorts and gently lathered up, he couldn't help quietly concluding, "This is as close to heaven on earth I'll ever get; fuck all the morals and complexities." Just anticipating indulging in this preliminary hedonistic pleasure had his heart on the verge of bursting.

"You know, Doc, it's been over twelve years since I've been fortunate enough to experience anything even resembling this. I've been in countless motel rooms all over this country during that time, and sadly, I was always alone. See how valuable you are, and how much joy you are capable of bringing into just one person's life."

Leslie, by now virtually submerged except for her tiny face, broke her silence with an acidic, "My value is in no way related to what is taking place here; and as for bringing you joy, you may be extracting a sick amusement or validation of sorts out of this, but I am not contributing anything but unmitigated contempt to this miserable situation."

Her sardonic expression didn't come anywhere near bursting Pete's bubble, but it may have pin-pricked it a bit. He no longer harbored the delusions he had so fervently entertained at one time, that would have 'romanticized' this encounter to a level approaching "Romeo and Juliet". It still hurt, though, to hear Leslie's put-down articulated so disdainfully.

After finishing his fragile attempt at navigating his razor around the unwounded portions of his face and neck, Pete slipped out of his shorts and nestled into the silky blue aqua, directly across from Leslie. There was little room for any conflicted emotion, only the sublime and precious moment seemed to matter. He had envisioned almost this exact setting dozens of times, and as his and Leslie's legs 'nuzzled' together under that water, it was nothing short of a dream come true.

She was keenly aware of how quickly the temperature was sure to rise, if she didn't effect some manner of distracting, moderating tactic, so in between sips of champagne, she sought to confirm their immediate agenda. "You did say this was going to be an opportunity to relax and absorb this emollient, did you not?" Pete was literally immersed in contentment, and blissfully expressed it. "We can stay right here, in this exact position, for as long as you like; when the water gets a little too cool for you, let me know and we'll order up some dinner."

Pete had conveniently brought the meal menu into the bathroom, and placed it on the floor closest to Leslie affording her a chance at initiating some choice and discretion, as his primary motivation.

As the warmth and stillness of this bizarre experience took precedence for the next ten or fifteen minutes, strangely, the apprehensive, foreboding sense of an uneasy and ominous reality seemed to subside.

As Pete was adding a little champagne to each of their glasses, Leslie continued with her diversionary strategies by going down the list of menu items. "Black Angus BBQ tender tips Augus, with sautéed onions; Chicken Cordon Bleu, Sauce Supreme; Honey Glazed Cornish Hen, with Wild Rice; Roast Tenderloin of Beef, Sauce Jardiniere," and on and on. Pete interrupted after a few minutes to offer, "In this part of the country, their specialty and what they've been raising for 150 years is beef, why don't we sample that first one, with the 'Augus' which I think is a gravy recipe, just to see how 'tender' and tasty, they can prepare it?" Leslie, just nodded with a faint "Ok."

After that was agreed upon, Pete still harbored a nagging curiosity or two that required some manner of satisfactory feedback. "What can be concluded from the reality that we have been together non-stop for almost a week, and I haven't tried to passionately kiss or touch you in any salacious manner? It's fucking weird, that's what it is. I mean there isn't any more natural instinct that human beings possess, is there, maybe self-preservation and hunger. I don't really expect you'll agree with me, and maybe you're right, it could be just some perverse, self-serving rationalization, but think about it: to go to these extremes to in effect just talk to you some more. Not even you, in your most honest, in-depth interpretation could find that motivation easy to comprehend."

Leslie, despite the outrageous immediate environment she found herself a part of felt a compelling need to try for perhaps the last time to invalidate or penetrate much of Pete's warped reasoning. "You are not a dim-witted individual, Pete. You articulate your needs at every level, quite efficiently, and grasp a pretty good sense of what human nature is capable of at both ends of the spectrum. Why you choose to ignore or disregard some of the most basic principles of human decency baffles me. The pleasure you feel you have somehow arbitrarily empowered yourself to indulge in at my expense is not only revolting, it's vile and unforgivable. My body and mind are the two most precious gifts I will ever have; and it should be for me to choose when and with who I might share any part or all of that essence."

Once Leslie got started, her venomous indictment of Pete's offenses kept rolling. "You have committed a major felonious assault by abducting me; but you don't want to take responsibility, or face the consequences. When people are victimized and often traumatized, they seek and are entitled to some manner of justice. Many also feel justified in also exacting some revenge or retribution.

If what is happening to me were perpetrated on your daughter or granddaughter, you would be ready to kill the offender, and who could really blame you?"

Pete was starting to cringe a little. The doctor had managed to hurt him in places he dared not even go himself.

Leslie had one more poison dart in her quiver. "If you really want to get right down to it, in many respects, there are those who would look upon your motives and actions as cowardly, and that's a term I rarely if ever perceive or apply judiciously to any specific act or event."

Pete was becoming more incensed than he could ever have imagined was possible, especially given his close proximity to Leslie, and under the prevailing resolute circumstances he had already forged. It shouldn't have mattered how or what she might desperately resort to, in an effort to weaken or diminish his resolve, but it did. "This water is getting too cold, and I'm hungry!" he exclaimed, as he stood up and wrapped a towel around his mid-section. That manner of escape, however, didn't stop his anger from intensifying, it only gave him pause enough to re-load.

"You really want to know something, Dr. Greer, the eminent, esteemed shrink," Pete shouted. "I couldn't give two-shits about the social mores or judicial predispositions of the times. I know fucking pain, isolation, depression and life sucking despair; and now you of all people believe I should renege on the one chance I'll ever have of realizing something extraordinary and acquiesce to 20 years in the slammer, instead. You better fucking well think again. It's really nothing personal after all is said and done; it's the luck of the drawer. "There were people in my life who were unwittingly instrumental in forging the burdens that I have to carry. Unfortunately for you, now, I'm going to perhaps not-so-innocently play that role in your life."

Still bellowing from the main room, Pete finished with, "I'm going to order the goddamn food before it's too late." Leslie didn't respond from inside the bathroom; she was busy sliding into some panties and slipping on a robe over her otherwise naked and trembling body. She couldn't help feeling that the last-ditch final volleys she had just rendered with respect to human decency and accountability had been an exercise in abject futility. They had little neutralizing or softening effect on Pete's steadfast conviction that he was all but obliged to violate her. Equally as troubling was the realization that the anger she had just helped facilitate bringing to the surface was more than likely to have exacerbated a bad situation, rather than help her cause in any mitigating sense.

As Pete sat on the edge of the bed waiting for the food, he now felt like a "cornered rat" or vermin the world at large and everyone in it wanted to eliminate, and it didn't matter to any of them how that was accomplished. Almost everything he had become so convinced he needed was in that room: his unrequited love and the power and opportunity to do anything with her his imagination could conjure up was at his fingertips. The irony, paradox, and disappointment of that alone not being satisfaction enough was sickening and almost too much to bear.

While trying to process this latest affront to his resolve, Pete's gut churned mercilessly. He needed help from Leslie to somehow, someway maintain his sick, but resolute perspective and conviction.

His train of thought, however, was soon interrupted by three loud knocks on the door, just as something resembling a deplorable, but nonetheless viable scheme began to take shape.

As he approached the dresser to grab three $20 bills, his eyes settled on what was now fated to play the major role in resolving his most profound and final dilemma: the .380 cal. semi-automatic weapon.

It didn't take long before he became totally convinced that utilized discriminately and purposefully this hunk of metal had the potential to be a lot more powerful and persuasive than anything either one of them could say or do.

CHAPTER TWENTY NINE

Leslie heard the exchange of food for money take place from inside the bathroom and decided that even if she wasn't as hungry as she should have been at this hour, she would try to eat. It would hardly serve any purpose to let her strength become slowly depleted, and it might help modulate somewhat her acute anxiety and apprehension.

As she approached the table where Pete had placed the two trays and what was left of the champagne, it was clear that there was little left to offer for discussion that might impact her ultimate and imminent fate. All the rationales, faux pas and arbitrary misrepresentations had been dissected and rehashed ad nauseum. As a trained, practicing psychiatrist, a major tenet of her therapeutic functioning revolved around recognizing and then directing patients toward a reality-based foundation before examining potential strategies and resolutions. She knew a tangible set of dire circumstances when they were right in front of her.

The beef was so exquisitely prepared and delectable, it melted in their mouths. In fact, if this had to be someone's proverbial last meal, it would have been a more suitable choice.

Pete having finished first, filled both their glasses with the last of the champagne, lit a cigarette, and then made his way over to where the gun was concealed, grabbed it and brought it over to the table. This ominous act and the accompanying scowl on his face immediately intensified the duress Leslie was already experiencing, as she attempted to finish and then hopefully begin digesting her meal.

As Pete placed the gun on the table closer to her than to him, he calmly exclaimed, "Here's the answer to all your fucking trepidations! You can in one split-second gain your freedom and safeguard whatever else you're so fearful of losing", he added as he re-gripped the gun, pulled the slide back and showed Leslie a shiny copper-jacketed .380 cal. bullet, as it was being injected into the chamber.

With a loaded gun now inches from her grasp and too stunned at this incredulous offer to respond right away, Pete proceeded to goad Leslie further. "The safety is off now; all you need do is aim and pull the trigger."

As she instinctively pulled her hands away and clasped them together on her lap, Leslie's body began to tremble as she was barely able to audibilize, "what is it you really expect me to do with this?" Pete didn't hesitate, almost as though drawing from some finely crafted script he was accessing just for this horrific spectacle. "I guess you'll do whatever it is you have to do once the pressure builds and you've had enough time for the only real option available to you to settle in. Very soon, I am going to walk or carry you over to that bed, and force you to either willingly or otherwise, be engaged in sexual intercourse for starters," Pete articulated very matter-of-factly. "The only way you're going to stop me, and save that sweet little ass of yours, is to use that gun. I'm too fucking selfish, cowardly or whatever to let you go without indulging in such gratification or contaminating you, so that puts the onus directly on you. Regrettably, things have gotten way too complicated for me, and the only way I know of dealing with them is to apply pressure until something or someone gives."

While her only chance of escaping this nightmare, with some semblance of 'wholeness' right at her fingertips, Leslie inexplicably wavered. She was completely bewildered and disoriented, and could only ponder, "Is this Pete's warped attempt at forcing me to indirectly choose and participate in my own undoing?" She was unfamiliar with and intimidated by such black and white ultimatums, and he had left her no 'wiggle' room at all.

He has set in motion a sequence of events that had the likely probability of provoking some terrifying consequences. She could all but see and touch the ugliness that was imminent in that room and felt virtually helpless.

Her choices were now crystal clear, and extremely daunting. Pete had emasculated her by offering her a deadly weapon that he felt certain she could never bring herself to use. And in the process, he had set the stage for her to ultimately acquiesce to her own rape.

Pete's audacious and self-assured demeanor strongly indicated to Leslie that he perceived her as all but powerless, given the frightening ultimatum he had just forcefully imposed on her fragile psyche. His assessment wasn't far from being totally justified.

Pete's adrenalin was starting to percolate uncontrollably. He didn't have Leslie in the ideal sense where he wanted her; however, she was now vulnerable in a manner he could reconcile with. She had been given an opportunity to end all of this on a platter, and instead of seizing it, found herself incapable of taking advantage. To Pete, this translated to them being soulmates at some significant level. Fear and indecision had plagued him his entire adult life; now, it was her turn to struggle futilely with these fallibilities and fragilities.

In its most basic design, and Pete always tried to interpret some of the more ironic and paradoxical dilemmas humans can face, in this context, this wasn't so hard to figure out. Every pertinent detail has been forthrightly introduced. He had made known what his intentions were, and she had to ultimately decide how vehemently she felt about her right and need to repel this pre-determined offense, and what means she was prepared to resort to in that regard. If that seemed a crude and debasing analysis, maybe it was; however, in the overall scheme and immediacy of this particular scenario, there wasn't a whole lot left for Leslie to waste time dissecting.

Leslie desperately needed some time and space, so once again she retreated to the solace and comfort of the bathroom. For the first time in her professional or personal life, she couldn't seem to summon the tenacity that might fuel some kind of viable solution to a sinister, threatening dilemma. This wasn't some unfortunate patient, giving an account of some perceived threat, past or present, that she could process, make sense of and ultimately provide counsel for; this was her sacred life and sanity in imminent danger of being invaded.

On top of everything else, feeling feeble and impotent only added considerable dread to an already overburdened soul. Right now, rape and homicide were realities too overwhelming to engage at any level. Perhaps she really has no choice but to 'capitulate' and hope to survive and fight another battle at some other time and place. Pete was as ready as he was ever going to be to initiate an exploration that held all the promise of being magnificently euphoric and also the danger of precipitating dire tragedy. He was and always had been a dyed-in-the-wool perfectionist, and very,

very few of his sexual encounters had ever risen to that demanding and unrealistic standard. When considering that these experiences were with partners he had invested time and nurturance before becoming physically intimate, the outcome here with Leslie under much more trying and bizarre conditions was more than likely in one form or another to be problematic.

Compounding oppressively the draconian consequences of this encounter was the irreversible leap Pete had taken six days ago. The daunting weight of that deed was now becoming unbearable, as his day of reckoning rapidly approached.

In an attempt to temper and distract himself from this unyielding incubus, Pete went over to the bed and pulled down the spread and covers on the selected bed, leaving only a sheet to contend with when Leslie decided to return. The gun also had to be moved from the dining area over to a nightstand where it would be easily accessible to either of them, depending on how this all played itself out. This was the desperate, resolute and impulsive frame-of-mind Pete now had embraced.

Soon, it occurred to Pete, that Leslie had been gone a good twenty minutes. Without the TV on, it had also become progressively and curiously too quiet, so he stealthily made his way over to the door and listened for a few seconds. Nothing! No sound or movement detected. Pete's adrenalin compelled him to call out to her, as he tried as forcefully as he could to turn the handle of a locked bathroom door.

"Leslie, what the fuck do you think you're pulling?", he bellowed. "If I have to force my way into that room, and the noise attracts any heroes whatsoever, I will kill the first cocksucker that comes through that front door, and you right after. Is that what you really want? I will give you two minutes and not one second more, while I wait in that bed for you. If you're not here next to me by then, it could get ugly really quick."

Pete was beside himself, pacing back and forth like a caged animal. When after about a minute and a half, Leslie sheepishly appeared and began taking baby-steps in his general direction, he was still fuming as she came within reaching distance, so Pete firmly took hold of both her forearms and stopped her in mid-step. "I am not about to nail you to a fucking cross here; I won't insult you by asking you to relax and enjoy it; however, it shouldn't be anything resembling torture, either."

Leslie apparently had been crying, with still the remnants of some painful tears evident. She couldn't or chose not to utter a single word, so Pete pulled her close and just held her tightly for what seemed like an eternity, but in fact was perhaps closer to 30 or 40 seconds.

The time had come to lift and place her gently on the bed, for as much as he might want one, there would never be a more fitting or suitable time, and it would be undeniably pointless and futile, to expect an ideal situation to ever materialize.

As she haltingly and delicately permitted her head to fall back onto the pillow, Pete whispered softly, I'll pull the sheet over you so you can remove your robe, or maybe just undoing the sash will be fine, OK?" Next, as was Pete's custom, the lighting in the room had to be adjusted down to a certain level, one he felt would enhance a climactic, quenching experience.

Chapter Thirty

Naked under the bedsheet and as close to Leslie as possible without initiating anything of an aggressive nature, Pete was content to just lie on his side head propped up in one hand and gaze quietly and unabashedly at this little lady and all that this moment had come to represent.

The silence and eerie sense of tranquility would be brief, however; as Leslie somehow mustered the will and conviction to put forth one final plea "Please don't do this, I beg of you!" Pete instinctively reached over with his left hand and gently ran his fingers through her tousled hair before also tenderly running his thumb across her cheeks to stem the welling tears as he whispered, "It will be all right. I could never hurt you. There is absolutely nothing for you to fear."

With that impetus, there remained little to prevent the inevitable, succumbing to the visceral, powerful biological forces that would become the pervasive dynamic element of this encounter.

Leslie still sobbing and filled with fear and apprehension, couldn't help from trembling, while at the same time, Pete's heart and adrenalin started pumping at an ever-increasing rate.

The white cotton shorty robe Leslie had put on before exiting the bathroom would only afford her a fleeting sense of safety or shelter as Pete untied the sash exposing Leslie's exquisitely contoured little torso.

As he leaned over to kiss her on the lips, Leslie instinct turned away, giving Pete pause for just a second or two. He had absolutely no intention of perhaps adding insult to injury by forcing her to reciprocate, especially with that fragile a facet of her being. He knew, as he gently but firmly wrapped a hand around one of her plump, sumptuous breasts, that it would be much harder for her to ignore or tune out some of the more caressing and sensation inducing explorations he had in mind.

As Pete now took the nipple of the other breast between his lips, Leslie groaned slightly as both quickly extended and became totally erect. By now, Pete was well on his way to full arousal, and the heat of Leslie's body was providing ample impetus to intensify his erection.

Her legs, initially pressed closely together, slowly parted in a gentle and accommodating manner as Pete's hand ventured down into the little satin panties and for a moment tenderly caressed the 'whole' of her supple vulva.

As her chest began to rise and sink more rapidly now, Pete while feverishly kissing as much of her as he could, stopped only long enough to rest his head on her chest, and to hear a little heart that was beating at a very brisk pace. The energy she subconsciously was discharging only heightened Pete's over all excitement.

Other than intense unadulterated desire, Pete had no reason whatsoever to accelerate any facet of this extraordinary, once in-a-lifetime encounter. In fact, there were compelling factors dictating that quite the opposite approach would much better serve his ominous fatalistic agenda.

However, none of these fleeting considerations would ultimately have any impact one way or the other. He was on fire, and way beyond indulging such frivolous concerns as he methodically went about removing Leslie's panties, and then lifting her firm little butt just enough to make room for a pillow.

Indescribable rapture soon followed as Pete gently nestled his head between Leslie's now uncoiled and silky thighs. As he delicately spread the vagina's lips and began making love to the exposed labia and clitoris, the intensity accompanying each kiss and lap of his burning tongue were almost too much to endure.

If only this experience could somehow be broadened to embody the whole essence of this dainty little lady. Unfortunately, her heart and mind were now and would always be beyond his ability to capture.

Leslie, too now, with all her defenses completely compromised had gradually succumbed to an un-obliging ecstasy as her back arched, her hips subtly began to undulate, and unconscious murmurs became more pronounced and frequent. Pete had no idea if or not orgasmic is this dignified, little professional had ever been before this, but his senses were telling him she might just be approaching a pretty good facsimile of one pretty soon.

For Pete a complete physical if not emotional satisfaction would only be attainable when regrettably the only tangible facet of his being was alive and vibrant deep inside her. It would ultimately the only part of him that he might be capable of forcing her to grudgingly accept. He desperately needed such a de facto union, as tainted as it would be, to somehow validate the love and desire he felt and had nurtured so fervently and futilely.

Leslie was deliciously wet and magnificently primed. Pete had promised her some basic protection, and he did have a condom close by; however, in his excitement and desire for undiluted realism, he felt he could safely at least enter her, dawdle a bit and absorb the tender euphoria for as long as he could sustain it.

Fortunately, Pete's erection was as potent as it was, for apparently no one before him had ever venture as far as he was about to. Although distracting, he failed to sense that she was experiencing any inordinate physical distress; however, perhaps in 'morbid' contrast, the ultimately painful, lingering psychic ramifications were impossible right now to gain any real sense of. Only Leslie and the arduous passage of time, perhaps, would mollify this consequence.

Now deep inside Leslie, and in no hurry to effect an inevitable, but tainted climax, Pete was already beginning to feel the sense of foreboding that always pre-cursed the ominous crash that lay in wait for him. Even in this moment of ecstasy, he would be unable to escape the haunting realism that this rapturous interlude was at best a transitory respite, and very soon he would be back where he started: failing miserably at waging combat within himself.

This time the prevailing scenario had a much darker fate in store. There would be no more tomorrows or next weeks that might allow for some artful dodging of his bleak reality and futile attempts at denying inescapable consequences. Right here and now, Pete was literally and figuratively "shooting-his-load," and as so often in the past, it was an ill-conceived, misguided and unavailing quest for some measure of fulfillment.

Meanwhile, he had no intention of falling victim to what would amount to the ultimate humiliation, losing what was left of this constrained, fleeting exhilaration and perhaps Leslie too because of a limp dick. So, suppressing any inklings of an impending doom became his primary focus.

As Pete picked up the pace of thrusting deep and then slowly

Withdrawing to the edge of Leslie's magnificent cunt, he simultaneously managed to tear open the foil of the condom package and held it ready, for ostensibly the quickest application humanly possible.

Seconds later, Pete would again fall victim to another of his long line of crushing faux pa experiences. After gently clutching and moving Leslie's thighs and derriere to a slightly different position, he exploded' deep inside her. He had felt it coming and stopped for an instant she then moved ever so delicately, and it was over!

Just like in so many instances before, failure! As he pulled out and collapsed not on her but alongside, so she could go tend to what had to be a repulsive mess, Pete could feel the life being sucked out of him. His vision of himself now very much conjured up images resembling the zombies of Night of the Living Dead; however, unlike them, he was still breathing and had a reservoir of guilt and shame to endure. He also knew he didn't have either the will or the strength to fight that battle for very much longer.

Once finished in the bathroom, the peremptory words out of mouth were scathing and delivered bitterly. "I hope you're satisfied now; I'm not going to waste any time and energy telling you what I think of you: I just want to get out of here, and qet as far away from you as I can."

Pete had absolutely no intention of attempting to mount any kind of futile defense, or engaging in any feeble plea for some degree of understanding; however, he wasn't about to just let her walk away either. Grotesquely, he would need her now more than ever!

Pete, "I know what kind of scum I am, and I probably harbor as much contempt for myself right as you also have every right to feel. I'm also aware of how desperately you want and need to get away from me; however, we are not quite finished here, just yet."

Leslie, while feverishly rummaging through the suitcase for something simple and quick to put on, stopped to take a few steps toward Pete while blistering," I knew you couldn't be trusted in any manner whatsoever. As soon as I'm dressed, I am walking out that door. What more can you possibly expect from me?"

"You will be leaving soon enough, but not right now!" Pete retorted, ·while still sitting on the bed in his shorts, and nervously fondling his semi-automatic handgun. Leslie, as she flung a sneaker that narrowly missed, blurted, "You son-of-a-bitching pathetic bastard."

Now, literally being swallowed up by his intensifying self-hatred, Pete was incapable of mincing words as he continued, "I can't allow the government to judge me, and subsequently order punishment as it sees fit. You are the one I have committed these ghastly crimes against and have hurt very deeply.

This will be the ultimate stroke of justice and perhaps the only measure of atonement available to me. Moreover, if I have to die, and I must, I want you near me when it happens. Please don't waste your energy imparting to me, how insane or abhorrent this proposal undoubtedly seems to you. That's not an issue. The hard facts are, it's much too late for other considerations." As Pete got up to approach Leslie to ensure there wouldn't be a desperate, impulsive dash for freedom, he held the gun by the barrel, extending her the grip while pleading, "Can you please do this for me, and perhaps for yourself too?"

Leslie was speechless; she could not believe that given what had just transpired moments ago, she might still be trapped in the throes of an unmitigated, bizarre level of madness. "Now he expects me to be a part of some manner of manslaughter/suicide incident, and he's probably concocted some feasible plot to ensure this heinous event materializes, something akin to the rape that was just orchestrated. How many ways can there be to force someone who is repulsed by the thought to fire a gun at someone else?" she pondered for a few fleeting seconds. She could not really envision any in the little time allotted her for even considering such a nightmarish scenario.

Meanwhile, Pete's unremitting guilt and anguish rapidly and mercilessly persisted in consuming him. Leslie had grudgingly already surrendered, by any rational standard of expectation all that she was capable of, to appease some of Pete's deranged needs, and now on the brink of absolute physical and emotional despair, she found herself once again trapped. The weapon that Pete had introduced and brandished so menacingly while abducting Leslie and sporadically since, was now destined to determine the ultimate, lamentable outcome of this desperate encounter.

Pete's latent but powerful instincts of compassion and empathy for this gentle little lady's predicament intermittently dictated he should seize upon this fleeting opportunity and just let her go right now!

However, his total disdain and disgust for being alone within his own skin at this point was an overwhelming and unyielding force that would not allow for any such altruistic, liberating capitulation.

Pete could sense by Leslie's demeanor and the horror in her eyes that she would never accept his plea to take possession of that weapon, so he grabbed her right hand by the thumb, twisting it exposing the palm, into which he forcefully jammed the gun's grip.

Before she could even blink her eyes, Pete lunged at Leslie grabbing her by the throat, so that she fell backwards onto the bed, with Pete virtually on top of her. With both hands around her neck now, Pete began viciously strangling Leslie while half screaming and crying, "Just remember that I did love you, and always will. Please forgive me!"

With her oxygen supply cut off, and in horrific fear of imminently losing consciousness or worse, Leslie instinctively summoned just enough strength to bring the gun up to where the barrel was inches from Pete's left side and pulled the trigger.

A deafening "POW" resonated through the room and sent Pete sprawling to the edge of the bed, and then face first to the floor.

Leslie, gasping for air, managed to roll off the bed to the far side and began screaming and sobbing. Shaking and still struggling to breathe, she dropped the gun and just stood there, trembling uncontrollably for what seemed like an eternity, but was perhaps 1-2 minutes.

Once under some modicum of control, Leslie's instinct and perhaps some measure of compassion, compelled her to haltingly make her way in the general direction of where Pete lay. Once there, the pool of blood thickening around him, sickened her. The one side of his face she was momentarily courageous enough to peek at revealed an eye that was partially open, but very still and lifeless. To Leslie, Pete definitely appeared more dead than alive. Her perception could hardly have been more factual.

The bullet had ripped through his liver and pancreas, and had exited after tearing a kidney on the other side. Blood was oozing from each of these wounds, and either could have been fatal without the other.

Leslie had seen more than enough. She felt sick to her stomach and fearful of imminently passing out when a loud, persistent banging on the door, accompanied by an authoritative voice, yelling, "We heard a gunshot. Open this door right now!" interrupted her terrifying paralysis.

Leslie, still acutely traumatized, was unable to verbally respond but was able to stagger over to the door and open it after fumbling with the lock. Crudely, she related to a man dressed in what looked like what a security guard at a mall would be wearing. "There's a man over there between the beds whom I've just shot. He abducted me in Providence, Rhode Island, sometime last week, and he was trying to kill me. My name is Dr. Leslie Greer, I'm a psychiatrist."

After assessing Pete's condition in a cursory manner, the man immediately went to the phone and dialed 911. Leslie, too panicked to pay much if any attention, could hear him relating to the dispatcher, "It looks like one male victim. Gunshot, and also a lady here, who says she is a doctor who was kidnapped and forced to fire the weapon in self-defense."

As a crowd gathered outside room #136, sirens could be heard close-by, and in the distance. Soon, the Montana State Police, local detectives, paramedics and ultimately the county coroner would be here, shuffling in-and-out, observing, and taking notes, while investigating what undoubtedly had become an unfortunate, regrettable incident. To them, it was nothing more or less than the scene of a major crime, and Leslie and Pete were a subject and the deceased.

Leslie, still trembling and wrapped in a bedspread, repeated her initial story over and over. She still was far from free, and wouldn't be going home for days. She was now a material witness to a homicide. Undoubtedly, this incident will eventually end up being classified as a justifiable homicide; however, more than likely she will have to endure a formal inquest at some point, where circumstances and pertinent details are sure to be questioned, reviewed and reconstructed from every conceivable perspective imaginable.

She had been reported missing, and her car and personal possessions recovered. They also/now were evidentiary property in the custody of police back in Rhode Island.

In short, Leslie will continue to face the arduous challenge of attempting to restore some semblance of order to her life out of total, unmitigated chaos. Unfortunately, this daunting process will represent only 'phase one' of the interminable impact Pete and this episode will have had on the rest of her life.

As for Pete, which of his children would receive the dreaded phone call first? There were some phone numbers in his wallet that at least for his daughter Susan (his eldest child) which were current, since she hadn't moved in 20 years. His body would be autopsied, and subsequently at some point released to his next of kin for transport back to Providence at someone's not so minor expense.

How will they go about trying to make sense of this tragedy? Surely, Dr. Greer won't be making herself available to them and she won't be at any funeral or memorial service. Perhaps they can peruse his medical records and some of the incomplete or un-mailed letters to her that are still gathering dust in his cluttered apartment. Those would speak volumes perhaps as to how, but offer precious little as to 'why' this all came to pass.

Pete's desperate quest to win the heart of his former caretaker, whom he felt embodied everything he desired in a soulmate had failed; however, all was not in vain. There were moments when he was able to render his tender care and comfort when she was in need; and also, a small but precious capsule in time when he was able to love her with all his being. In the final analysis, he chose to not continue living without her, and that wish he was undeniably successful in making come true.

-FINIS-

Printed in the United States
by Baker & Taylor Publisher Services